hate to haunt you

afterlife incorporated
book two

Alli Temple

This is an uncorrected copy distributed for review purposes. Small typographical errors may exist in the body of the manuscript that will be corrected prior to publication.

Copyright © 2025 by Alli Temple
Hate To Haunt You
All rights reserved.

ISBN 978-1-990719-16-5 (ebook)
ISBN 978-1-990719-19-6 (paperback)

No part of this book may be reproduced in any form or by any electronic or mechanical means, including information storage and retrieval systems, without written permission from the author, except for the use of brief quotations in a book review.

This is a work of fiction. Names, characters, places, and incidents are a product of the author's imagination or are used fictitiously. Any resemblance to actual events, places, or persons, living or dead, is entirely coincidental.

Cover design is for illustrative purposes only, and any person(s) featured is a model.

Cover Design: We Got You Covered Book Design
Developmental Editing: Kristi Yanta, Edits by Kristi
Copy Editing: Adam Mongaya, Tessera Editorial
Proofreading: Lori Parks

Created with Vellum

For my cats, because after 17 books I'm running out of people to dedicate these things to.
So far only one out of three cats I've had in my adult life could conceivably be a goddess hiding in a furry body and I take comfort in that.

join the a-list

For news on future releases, join the A-List, my monthly newsletter at AlliTemple.com/newsletter.

content warnings

This is a book about death. I tried to make it funny, but people are still going to die. For more details, visit the content warnings page.

chapter
one

DEAR SPARKS, how have you been? We haven't talked in a little while. Sorry, I kept meaning to reach out, but I've been busy, and time flows differently here at Afterlife Incorporated. I think it's been about a year since I died. Does that sound right to you?

Before I let you in on all the stuff I've been doing, I want to take a moment to do a simple visualization exercise. Close your eyes. Take a deep breath. In through your nose, out through your mouth. That's it. One more time. In your nose. Out your mouth. Got it?

Now imagine you don't need to do that anymore. Like ever. Because you're dead, and while you can breathe as a hobby, you don't actually need to do it for survival. One less thing to worry about. Sounds pretty cool, right?

Well, that's good, because currently I am worrying that I might have to kill an entire room of immortal reapers just to get this meeting to end.

In through your nose, out through your mouth. And again. Close your eyes if you have to.

"Okay," Bang says, checking something off her tablet. "Where are we on the ATT?"

The boardroom gets quiet. I hide my clenched fists beneath

the heavy wooden table so no one can see my frustration. We've just spent the last two hours—I assume it's been two hours, but it might have been two days, what with that whole wibbly wobbly time thing here at good old Afterlife HQ—debating the curriculum for wraith reading hour, even though it's unclear whether wraiths are even sentient enough to read anything. But no, rather than pausing the discussion to find out that crucial piece of information, Zach, Bang and Minerva went around in circles debating whether the best place to start would be *Shahnameh* from Ancient Persia—this was Zach's pick, which he says he read sometime in his wanderings after he died and got lost by Afterlife —or *Confessions of a Shopaholic*—a surprising pick from Minerva who only justified the choice by saying, "Richard said it was very relatable."

Two hours!

Someone clears their throat, and I realize they're all looking at me.

"You're next on the agenda," Minerva says, with an arch of her bright blue eyebrow. She taps her nails on the table, and sparks shoots from them, blackening the wood.

I sit up a little straighter, struggling to remember what was just said. The ATT. What the hell is that? I don't have anything to do with—

"You mean the Afterlife Transition Team?" I ask, dread already settling in the bottom of my stomach.

"Yes," Bang says with an eager nod. She shoots a nervous glance towards Minerva, then back to me, clearly trying to urge me into action before Minerva gets even more irritated.

"We've talked about this before," I say, still fighting for patience, "but acronyms can be really alienating, especially for people in unfamiliar territory. It creates a real us-and-them divide, which is exactly the opposite of what we're trying to achieve with the Afterlife Transition Team."

More silence. Minerva might actually be carving her name into the tabletop like she's a one-reaper wood-burning kit. Tiny tendrils of smoke spiral up from her fingertip. Zach's staring off into space while running a finger just beneath his chin in a motion that says he's trying to decide if the pimple there is ready to be popped yet. Only Bang is paying attention to me, though all she does is give me an apologetic smile.

"We've had pretty good uptake from the lost souls who came from the Other Side. They're keen to be of use"—I don't mention that their enthusiasm is motivated in part by the fact there's currently nowhere else for them to go, since Minerva and Bang haven't reopened the districts yet and no one has signed up for voluntary memory wiping—"but we're having trouble getting buy-in from reapers who are looking to be partnered up."

The silence is punctuated by an uncomfortable cough, though no one makes eye contact long enough to own up to the interjection. The Afterlife Transition Team has been my baby for the last few months. I tried to get involved with the district reopening, but Bang assigned me this task instead, and since she's in charge now, I decided to run with it. Prove myself, as it were. Which turned out to be easier said than done, unfortunately.

Since we're still waiting on the districts, the most recently dead have basically been put in holding in unused parts of Afterlife. Like an endless waiting room. With the Afterlife Transition Team I'm trying to create a partnership between experienced lost souls and reapers, so that when we're finally ready to move these new ghosts to the districts, it's quicker to get them acclimated. The lost souls function as a translator of sorts, since reapers can't be bothered to explain anything. Sort of like a post-mortem buddy system. But as much as they don't like to explain, reapers also don't like to show up, as it turns out. I've had a couple open houses—Bang wanted to call them AEA, "ask Ember anything," but I declined for the reasons regarding acronyms I've just stated above—to provide more information for my vision of the plan. But only a handful of reapers attended, and most admitted they were there because they'd heard I'd brought snacks. I had—what's a meeting without coffee and Timbits?—but tiny sugary donut holes should not be the motivator for trying to make things work better at Afterlife.

In short, in the year since I died, I've accomplished a big fat nothing, other than wasting hours and possibly days of my afterlife sitting around this meeting table while Bang talks about activity items and I remind her the term is action items, and then the three of them all laugh at me for being such a silly little lost soul in a room full of big bad reapers. Never mind that Zach isn't even a reaper, though honestly I don't know what he is. He's got powers like a reaper but still has his memories. And somehow, after trying to take over the place by sneaking in the backdoor, these days he's part of the inner circle, and I'm left handing out flyers and hoping people turn out for my grassroots endeavours, only to get sneered at when I try to make progress reports.

This is so not what I visualized when I thought about death.

The door to my right slams open, making Zach jump. Minerva and Bang both lean a little farther back in their chairs, like they're trying to make room for the presence that has just entered. Fortunately for me, I felt them coming long before they opened the door, just like I pretty much know where they are all the time as long as we're both either in Afterlife or at home in Toronto. Since Kelly got their powers back, their presence is like the soft ambient noise of a fridge running or the TV being on in another room. I'm aware of it all the time, but unless they get closer, I can mostly tune it out.

When they walk into the meeting, though, it's like magnets. I have to put a palm on the table because it feels like my chair is about to roll across the floor towards them, taking me on an involuntary trip. It's not Kelly, per se, that pulls at me. They're the same as they always are. Flat gaze, wide mouth. Their hair is braided along the top of their head, before being left to flow over their back and shoulders in a bleached blond cascade. Same old, same old. Infuriating and unearthly.

But what's inside them. The thing that makes them a reaper and not a lost soul like me is undeniable. Kelly's reaper power keeps me from losing my sense of self, but also it wants me to reach out and touch it whenever I'm close. Tap into it. Just a puff. We could slide from here to the house in Etobicoke in the space between two thoughts. I'm getting better at it. The last time Kelly let me try, we wound up at the end of our street, which was a vast improvement over the time before when we landed somewhere in the middle of Lake Ontario.

"You're late," Minerva says with a narrow glare.

"You told me to bring Ziggy," Kelly says to Bang, ignoring Minerva entirely.

Bang glances around, like the errant keeper of HELL might be hiding behind the doorframe, ready to pop out and play a hilarious practical joke.

"Where is he?" she asks.

Kelly slides into the chair beside me with a careless shrug.

"Couldn't find him. The reaper on duty at HELL said something about him being mad that no one wanted to hear his suggestion for wraith book club."

Minerva scoffs. "It's called wraith reading hour. Which Ziggy would know if he ever bothered to show up for these meetings."

I can only roll my eyes. Despite having been here for almost a year, I still have never met the infamous Ziggy. Somehow he's always away from the office when I pop down to HELL to introduce myself. In a place where allies are few and far between, I'm getting desperate, but I can never seem to pin him down long enough to say hi.

"If you couldn't find Ziggy, what are you doing here?" Zach asks Kelly with a sneer. Never mind that Kelly could almost certainly send Zach off into another plain with no more effort than it would take to flick an ant off a picnic table. Now that Zach's got Minerva at his back, he's getting bold. And super annoying. He always had that smooth tech/finance bro attitude, but now that he's been given a seat at the table, it comes with a sense of authority that makes me grind my teeth at the very sight of his salesman's smile.

"I came to get Ember," they say. "We have to go."

I blush like a teenager with a crush. Because when in doubt, at least Kelly's looking out for me . . . as much as anyone is. They're not super interested in bettering things here at Afterlife, but they're happy enough to carpool when they're not busy collecting souls in Toronto and making sure they don't slip through the cracks at intake. It's sad that even their tiny bit of caring is enough to make me sit up a little straighter. All they're really saying is they're bored and ready to go home, and it's up to me if I want to slide with them or take the subway. What with changing stations, the solo commute is over an hour, and by the time I get home, I'm usually pretty strung out and twitchy. Staying close to Kelly or sticking near Jupiter's runes once I'm back in Etobicoke are the only things that keep me from degrading into a predatory lost soul and feeding on new ghosts. I can manage the subway, but the timing is tight on a good day, and on a day like today when I'm already frustrated and fed up with the lack of progress at work—as much as I can call Afterlife a job, since they don't pay me or even seem to want me around most days—I'll be lucky if I don't eat someone on my way home.

"We need more reapers to volunteer for the ATT." I grimace as the acronym slips out from between my lips. "The Afterlife Transition Team. Bang, is there anything we can do to get more of them interested?"

She shakes her head. "We can barely keep the regular SRU fully staffed. When I suggest being partnered with lost souls, most are refusing."

"Refusing?" Kelly asks.

"More like they're threatening to walk off the job. They all want to go to the archives."

I slump in my chair. Of course they are. Since Richard's revelation that reapers are just humans with no memories of their past life, more and more have walked off the job to go search for the details of their lost identities. It's understandable. Finding out who they used to be is no different than an adopted person looking for their birth family or a child asking their grandparents for another story of what it was like growing up in the good old days. We all want to know who we are and where we come from, and the reapers quite literally had that taken from them without their consent. But every one of them who goes chasing their old identity is one less reaper to collect souls, which leaves us even fewer for things like new initiatives. Change is hard, and made harder given our work force is leaking like a sieve.

Also, there's the fact that so far no one's been able to find any information in the archives, even though the cavernous facility houses literally every record the reapers have ever kept. Apparently that paper trail doesn't stretch as far as the souls that were deemed strong enough to survive the conversion process to become a reaper. And, of course, Richard has no idea who he might have selected for the special privilege of ferrying souls off the living plain without realizing they had once been one of those very same souls. Richard's replies to questions along that line have been very "chill out, man" and "why would I bother remembering that when there are so many sunsets to remember?"

"It's been centuries," he said with a lazy wave of his hand when we pressed the issue. "I can't even remember if my favourite food when I was a cat was tuna or sardines. You think I remember the names of the souls who became reapers?"

But his thoughtlessness means that those who go searching for their identities will be off work for an indefinite amount of time. With no way of knowing where or how they will find the information they're looking for—or if that information even exists in the first place—their return to office date is unclear. So far, the number of reapers who have stepped back from their duties is still a minority, but every day a few more seem to decide knowing their full history is more important than a job they never signed up to do. And while I can't blame them, I'm allowed to be annoyed when that decision impacts my ability to accomplish the tasks I set out for myself. The Afterlife Transition Team program was my idea, and if the reapers are unwilling to participate, it's already dead in the water.

As I sulk silently, Kelly coughs a few times into the sleeve of their shirt. Each exhalation is punctuated by a small burst of power that buffets me. I raise a protective arm, mostly out of an old living reflex to ward off germs. Not that reapers get sick. And not that I get sick either. What would a virus want with me? I'm already dead.

"I'll talk to the reapers," Kelly says to Bang. "Organize a meeting next week with the ones most likely to come back to the project."

For all they didn't want to run things, Kelly still has a lot of pull at Afterlife. Minerva didn't do herself many favours with her centuries of "because I said so" leadership. Despite the fact they still spend a lot of their time back in Toronto blowing up stuff in video games, whenever Kelly pops into Afterlife, heads turn. If anyone can convince the reapers to reconsider, Kelly can.

Bang gives them a grateful smile. She's the right reaper for the job, but she appreciates their support. Reorganizing Afterlife in a way that treats human souls fairly without disrupting the day-to-day tasks of collecting ghosts before they turn into wraiths is not for the faint of heart. I'm frustrated with our slow progress. We have way too many chefs in the supernatural kitchen and ghostly fingers in the pot, but Bang is doing her absolute best to keep the wheels of death turning.

With a final nod, she taps on her tablet screen again. She opens her mouth, but Minerva speaks first.

"All right, that's everything for today. I'll have my assistant send out the hours and if you can get back to me on your assigned activity items by the end of the month, that would be great."

Neither Zach nor Kelly reacts to Minerva's declaration. Bang's brows pinch into a frown beneath her cat-eye glasses. Technically, Richard left her in charge, but it's not the first time Minerva's talked over her like that. I wait for her to say something to make it clear she'll be the one following up on action-activity items, but all she does is nod one more time before making a beeline for the door while she clutches her tablet.

"Kelly," Zach says with a mocking dip of his chin. "Pleasure as always."

Then he and Minerva exit the same way Bang did, and Kelly and I are left alone.

The ripple of power that fills the space makes me stand up straighter as I shiver. Whenever Kelly uses their abilities, I want to find out how far they can go, because part of me thinks I might be able to do the same someday.

"You don't have to keep coming to these things, you know," Kelly says, sounding casual. They always sound casual. I'd make a joke about how if they got any more relaxed, they'd be dead but . . . well . . . Ghost, meet reaper.

"Someone has to. Otherwise, the only action item after the meeting would be to have another meeting and they'd pat themselves on the back for achieving their targets." I sigh. Ghosts don't get tired, but I can still be over it. All of it. For now, anyway. Time to recharge a little. So Kelly's right. I hold out my arms. "Let's go. My turn to drive."

Strictly speaking, we don't need more than a handhold to do this anymore. Kelly says reapers can do it without any contact at all if the ghost is close enough and willing to slide. But Kelly is heavy, in a metaphysical sense. Carrying them through the dimensions takes concentration, like if I stopped paying attention, the power could consume me and we'd show up in Toronto as a jumble of arms and legs connected in the wrong places from one torso. Being close to them means I don't have to work so hard to control it.

They settle into my arms with a gentle grunt like I've stepped on their toe.

"Everything okay?" I ask, mentally rooting around for the link that lets me tap into their power. Sometimes I find it helps if I think of it as separate from them. Less invasive. Kelly knows what I'm doing, but even their consent doesn't keep me from feeling like I'm freeloading on something I'm not meant to touch.

"Fine," they say, oblivious to my moral quandaries. "Just thinking about next week. Convincing the reapers to leave the archives and get back to work is a pain in the asshole. This is the problem with giving them choices. They take them even when it's inconvenient."

"Have you been to the archives?" I ask. "You're not curious to find out more about who you used to be?"

Kelly's old. We all know this. After Minerva and Richard—though I'm still not sure Richard isn't a god instead of a reaper—Kelly is the oldest reaper here. They're old in the same way the pyramids are so old, even ancient Egyptians considered them to be even more ancient.

"Why would I be curious about that?" they ask.

"People want to know where they come from?"

They knit their brows together in an expression I've come to think of as *Ember is being unnecessarily sentimental.*

"Context is only important when everyone around you has it and you don't. None of the reapers know who they are, so it doesn't bother me that I don't either. What would I gain from learning that information? Everyone I ever knew in my life would have burned out thousands of years ago."

It's not really that I get overly sentimental, it's that Kelly never lets something as pedestrian as sentimentality enter their train of thought. Richard's belief that stripping lost souls of their memories builds a more efficient reaper has its poster child in Kelly. No sense letting feelings get in the way when there is always another ghost to cross over to Afterlife.

They cough again, sounding more uncomfortable than before. "Were you planning on going back to Toronto any time soon?"

We're still embracing in the boardroom. If anyone walked in on us, the scene would be embarrassingly intimate, when it's really just about transportation. Heat flushes over my cheeks, and I close my eyes, focusing on the energy that will take us home.

As the room fades away, Kelly lets out another gentle cough. My hold on them slips. It's like they've suddenly grown three sizes. That not-physical weight grows accordingly, and holding on to them is like trying to keep a concrete block from sinking to the bottom of the ocean. I gasp, concentrating on not letting them slip away, but suddenly I'm alone. The space around me is completely dark. I'm standing on solid ground, but when I look down, I can't see anything.

What the hell? Except not HELL. Afterlife's version of eternal damnation is endless hallways of paranormally reinforced cells. This is just . . . nothing? I could be in a cell myself or a space the size of an aircraft hangar. It's so dark, I'll never be able to tell.

"Kelly?" I don't know why I'm whispering.

"Ember?" Their voice is crystal clear, like they're standing right behind me, but when I turn, no one's there. I put a hand out, expecting to find their strong solid body in the darkness, maybe paired with a weary request to not grope them without their permission, but there's nothing.

"Kelly?" I ask again, louder this time. Fear prickles in my chest. What is going on?

"Are we going?" they ask.

"Yes. Yes. We were and then—" I don't know what happened. I'm not an expert at sliding yet, but I've been getting better. The hardest part is the landing. Taking off is pretty straightforward. All I have to do is turn my attention to the pressure of Kelly's arms around me, imagine we're two bright balls of light and—

The dark vanishes. We're still in the boardroom. Kelly's still in my arms.

"What just happened?" I gasp.

"Are we going or not?" they ask, ignoring my own question, because of course they do.

"We did. We are." I blink, trying to piece together how we went from here to nothing and back here again.

Kelly lets go of me, clearing their throat impatiently.

"I'm meeting some people online for a raid soon. Do you want me to do it?"

"No." I shake my head, more to wipe away questions than in denial. Kelly *would* be more worried about their games than making sure my sliding technique doesn't get us separated in an empty room. I take hold of their shirt, crushing the material in big fistfuls. "I've got it."

Baby steps. My sliding technique isn't perfect. It was probably just a glitch. Kelly doesn't seem to have noticed anything wrong. I press into them, mostly to make sure I won't drop them, but also maybe to make myself feel better. Being close to Kelly, as annoying as they can be, always makes me feel more confident. I can do this.

Time to go home.

chapter
two

I GET CLOSE. About halfway through, I feel a wobble, like we might get off course and wind up in Lake Ontario, but Kelly adjusts their touch on the small of my back, and next thing I know, we're standing in front of The Witchery.

"What are we doing here?" Kelly asks. "I told you I had to go home for a raid."

I gape, opening and closing my mouth a few times. That's all I get? No "thanks, Ember. That was a good try"? or "a few blocks from home is close enough for me"? Nope, all they can think of is their busy gaming schedule.

"Do you have your transit pass?" I ask, still feeling flustered about the blip back at the office. There's a bus idling at the intersection. Kelly could hop on if they hurry. But why aren't they saying anything about what happened? Did they go to the dark place too, or were they standing in the boardroom the whole time? And if so, didn't they notice when I vanished and reappeared?

But Kelly is not the best at noticing things out of the ordinary. Maybe they've seen so much weirdness in their time that nothing fazes them anymore. Like right now. They're completely oblivious to my discomposure.

"Never mind. The new manga delivery was today anyway.

There are a few I was waiting for." They sigh in annoyance and walk to the store's front door.

We bought The Witchery last fall. And by "we" I mean Kelly. We couldn't keep lighting runed candles at home. It had a nasty habit of luring lost souls to our porch, and even if the neighbours couldn't see them, things were getting weird in the neighbourhood. There were mornings where a dozen squirrels had all been hit by cars on our street overnight. The flowers that never seem to stop blooming by the porch were suddenly black and withered. And anyone out walking a dog suddenly found their furry best friend wouldn't get too close to the house. Most insisted on dragging their humans across the street to avoid the bad mojo.

It was fortunate that a film crew reached out to Kelly around the same time. The production company somehow managed to track down the owner of a particular crumbling castle in Scotland. They said they were filming a new big-budget time traveling saga and the castle was the perfect backdrop for what the director and location scouts had envisioned for the treasure hunting team's hidden base. The money they offered to rent the property for four months was too good to pass up. We used it for a down payment on a small strip mall not far from our Etobicoke bungalow and to fix up what had been a former pot dispensary in the corner unit. These days it's The Witchery, specializing in new age and spiritual products and services, where Jupiter greets customers from behind the counter and does readings with the families of the recently deceased when she can find the appropriate ghost before they cross over. She's gaining a bit of a name for herself in the GTA, and the shop's also popular with more local demographics like teenagers devouring manga with paranormal themes and women hoping the crystals in the front window will help them grab hold of their feminine power. It's all very human and most of the people who come into The Witchery have no idea it's staffed by two genuine mediums and regularly visited by a grim reaper and your friendly neighbourhood lost soul. At least it means the dogs walk past our house again and we've had no more than the usual number of squirrel deaths in the last few months.

And yes, I said two mediums. X is still here too. As Kelly and I walk into the shop, Jupiter's golden retriever boyfriend is speaking to someone behind the shimmering curtain that leads to the back room.

"He says he loves you, but he can't remember where the list of passwords is."

"He has to," an anguished woman says. "I wasn't logged into Netflix on any of my devices before he died. We always watched it on his laptop, but I don't have the password for that either, and now I can't get into our streaming accounts. What am I supposed to do?"

"Uh . . ." X sounds uncertain for a moment, but fortunately inspiration comes through when he needs it most. "I can give you my password?"

"No you can't," Jupiter calls. She's sitting up front by the cash register, trying to feed a fresh roll of receipt paper into the point-of-sale terminal. She gives us an irritated look as we pass. "Can you go help him before he adds them to the lease?"

"I'll do it," I say, and she gives me a grateful smile. Ever since Kelly got their power back and we first met Richard, Jupiter has been able to see me, which is nice. Those weeks right after I died were a whirlwind, but there was something strangely demoralizing about one of my closest allies never quite looking at me.

When I pass through the curtain into the reading room, X is sitting stiffly in a high-backed chair. The table in front of him is scattered with various tarot cards and dried flower petals. They're mostly for show. X doesn't need props to commune with the dead, but he and Jupiter found early on customers had a harder time believing them when they spoke on behalf of ghostly loved ones if they did it in an empty room. On the opposite side of the table, a middle-aged white woman with heavy eyeliner and bright purple lips is shredding a tissue while she cries softly.

"Just call the credit card company and cancel the account," another man is saying. He looks like he's twenty-five, though given that he's dead, his appearance doesn't really mean anything. His frown is equal parts worry and annoyance. "It's not like I planned to hide my passwords from you. I didn't plan any of this. How the fuck was I supposed to know the tumor would—"

"Excuse me," I say. The man and X both turn to me. The woman is still staring at the table. She can't hear me. "It's time for him to go."

"Go? Go where?" His frown deepens, resolving into suspicion. "Who are you?"

I try to look confident as I say, "My name is Ember. I'm here to take you to Afterlife. It's time for you to cross over."

He scoffs. "Screw that. I'm not going anywhere. I'm not supposed to be dead."

"I know it's hard to accept but—"

"I was forty-nine years old." His voice rises. "The doctor said the tumor was treatable. I didn't even get a chance—"

"Doctors can be wrong," X says.

"Wrong?" The tearful woman sniffles. "Wrong about what? Did they make a mistake? They told me that Ryan would—"

"It happens sometimes," I say, ignoring her as I move through the table toward the angry man. "Doctors are fallible and—"

"Fuck that." Ryan's eyes flash and his skin goes pale. "That's bullshit. I'm not old enough to be dead. What about my kids? My wife. She can't do anything by herself. She can't even remember our Netflix password, for god's sake." He rushes toward her, standing in front of her unseeing eyes. "Why are you so useless, Natalie?"

Okay. Time to leave. Here at The Witchery, we aim to give our customers closure and one more chance to speak with their dead loved ones. We do not permit abusive behaviour toward our staff or any kind of wife shaming.

The man lifts his arm like he's going to hit her. Not that she'd feel it as anything more than a shiver while his hand passes through her. It's still not okay. I grab hold of his wrist as his arm comes down. He's strong, even in death, but I'm stronger. As I grunt, the tendril of Kelly's power that always seems to trail after me bursts forth, knocking him off his feet. It's a pretty neat trick, if I do say so myself. The cards and flower petals on the table even ruffle on an undead breeze.

"Woah," X says softly, because he's nothing if not perpetually amazed by everything the supernatural world has to offer. I preen a little, because yeah. Woah, indeed. Who needs Minerva, Bang and Zach's meetings when I can be kicking ass down here?

"What was that?" The sniffling Natalie looks around her warily. Her husband is sprawled on the floor, groaning softly. The curtain separating the room from the rest of the store is pulled back as Jupiter and Kelly hurry in.

"Everything okay?" Jupiter asks, glancing around worriedly. Even Kelly is breathing hard, though their gaze goes from me to the man on the floor and their eyes widen.

"Wraith," they say.

"Already?" Jupiter asks. "She said he only died a few days ago."

The man on the floor sits up, glaring at all of us. A thin trickle of something black and oily dribbles down his chin.

"What the fuck was that?" he asks, spitting on the floor. "Did you hit me?"

"Like you were going to hit your wife?" I ask, though Kelly puts a hand on my shoulder to keep me from rushing at him.

"Should we call the quarantine team?" X asks. Jupiter curses under her breath. The quarantine team is less busy than they used to be, what with Zach no longer releasing lost souls back to the living world, but it hasn't helped their customer service skills in the slightest. They're not the most supportive of Jupiter and X's business venture, and any time we'd had to call them here, the tension is thick. You'd think they'd be more appreciative of the way Jupiter's runes call to wraiths and unstable lost souls. It makes the quarantine team's job a lot easier, since they already know where to find them. But maybe they were always in it for the love of the hunt. Either way, no one wants them here.

"I'll take him," Kelly says. "His decay isn't too bad, but I'm sure Ziggy has a fresh cell we can use."

There's a rush as the two of them disappear. The sudden distance between me and Kelly leaves me feeling shaky, and I moan as I grab the edge of the table to keep from collapsing. In other contexts, the sound might be embarrassingly suggestive. But right now it's more in response to a sensation like half of me has suddenly been turned off with a light switch. I'm very aware that my ability to come and go from the living world is due in large part to Kelly's presence. The runes help, but I'd be much less stable without them nearby. No one likes a clingy ghost, though, so I hold it together as best I can when they're somewhere else.

X helps the still-crying Natalie back out to the front of the shop, telling her she'll be fine, while Jupiter slowly picks up the scattered cards and flower petals.

"You okay?" she asks.

"Fine." I focus on taking deep breaths while I wait for my equilibrium to return.

She snorts. "Sure you are. I know what that noise means."

I laugh a little too loudly, trying to cover sudden discomfort. "I don't know what you're talking about."

She moans. If it's anything like the sound I just made, anyone who can hear us out front is definitely getting the wrong idea. It's soft, breathy, and the warming sensation in my belly and breasts confirms it is undoubtedly lusty.

"Like that," Jupiter says with a wicked grin. "Kelly and that asshole vanished and you were all . . ." She does it again.

"Stop." I can't help my laughter. "It's not like that. It's just a power thing."

She laughs too. "Uh huh. A power thing. Are you hot for

Kelly's power? Wanna touch it?" Jupiter runs her tongue over her bottom lip, exposing the stud.

My cheeks are on fire and I have no way to cool them. "I touch it all the time. What are you talking about?"

Her eyes widen and she cackles. "All the time? When? You guys don't even sleep. You don't—" She gasps. "Is that what you do while X and I are sleeping? You two are really quiet then. I never hear any—"

I lunge for her, growling playfully. She stumbles back, still laughing.

"Trust me. If Kelly and I were having sex, you wouldn't be able to sleep. I'm a screamer."

She squeals and runs away, darting back through the curtain. At least my embarrassment is gone.

"What's a screamer?" Kelly's cool voice comes from behind me.

Nope. Hello again, humiliation. Are you moving in permanently?

Funny that I didn't feel the moment they slid back into the shop. Now that I know Kelly has returned, their power inflates me like helium in a balloon. Too bad it won't let me float away entirely.

I turn around, eyes locked on my shoes. One of the small perks of being a lost soul with access to reaper power is I can change my clothes. I can't change my physical appearance the way Kelly does, but at least I can switch things up when it feels like a jeans and T-shirt day instead of a sweatpants day. Today I'm in a houndstooth dress and a pair of kitten heels that seemed like a smart professional choice when I went over to Afterlife but that I now regret because it's hard to do anything but a dainty jog in them when what I really want to do is sprint for the door.

When I glance up, Kelly is watching me with their usual flat expression. No judgement. Barely even any curiosity.

"That was a fast trip," I say weakly.

They cough once. Like at Afterlife, I waver a bit as their power washes over me again, but this time the pleasure I feel at the sensation just leaves me flushed and confused. Is Jupiter right? Am I getting off on this? Kelly and I are friends . . . sort of. Respected coworkers for sure. We're not likely to go out for dinner and we're definitely not dating. I don't think that's even something reapers do. All they ever seem to do is work, to be honest. Not once in all my trips to Afterlife have I heard about any kind of social activities. There's no reaper happy hour. No reaper families. They don't make reaper babies or have reaper weddings. I wonder if there's an untapped market for reaper dating apps . . .

"Sliding usually calms the most fractious ghosts. Ziggy said he'd take care of it. What were you and Jupiter talking about? Someone was screaming?"

I study them carefully, at first to see if they're joking. Reapers —Kelly in particular—don't have much of a sense of humour. If all they heard were my last words, I can deny a lot. Kelly's obsession with semantics means they're as likely to assume I was screaming out of fear than anything. Slowly, though, my study shifts, until I'm considering their face. They change their features less often these days. Their hair is still a revolving wheel of colours and styles, but their face has remained consistent more and more. Hawk-like nose. Wide-set eyes. Thin lips around a wide mouth. Utterly genderless. They may say gender is a useless human construct, but to the best of my knowledge, I've only ever been attracted to women, and Kelly is . . . not a woman. They're not a man either, or even some trans, nonbinary, fluid or other person on the ever-growing spectrum of gender identities. They're Kelly and they are one of a kind.

But am I attracted to them? Is that what I've been feeling? The very question shakes me like almost nothing has since I died. It's impossible. They're annoying. Superior. I value what they bring in terms of calling out bullshit at Afterlife, and how their power keeps me from turning into a monster with a taste for living souls.

And yeah, sometimes our relationship is a bit touchy feely because being close to Kelly's power is like—

Oh nooooo.

I stare at them, horrified. They blink once, owl-like. Is that attractive? Is Jupiter right? My fingers curl into my palms as I hold back the desire to press them to Kelly's chest and . . .

They shrug, clearly giving up on me answering the question I've already forgotten, and brush past me. The moment of contact sets a fire ablaze inside my chest. I gasp and tremble, imagining what it would be like to let all that power just take me. Let Kelly take me. Hold me down, cover me with their mouth and body and—

Like they can read my mind, Kelly gasps too, but before I can even speak, the gasp turns to a groan. Not a sexy one. They put a hand to their chest, exactly where I thought about touching just a moment earlier, but then their face twists in something like pain.

"Ember?" they say, and their voice is breathy and strangled. "I think—"

But whatever they're thinking doesn't matter. Our gazes meet for a split second before their expression goes vacant and their features go slack. Their eyes roll back in their head, and Kelly drops to the floor, unconscious.

"KELLY? KELLY?" I fall to my knees, shaking them. They went down hard, taking the table over with them and not even bothering to try and stop their fall.

"Holy shit, what just happened?" Jupiter and X rush in, skidding to the floor in an instant.

"Are they dead?" X asks. "Is that something reapers do?"

The very suggestion makes me go cold, but they can't be dead. The power between us pulses erratically, but it's still there. But Kelly is deathly pale, and slowly the colour fades from their hair too, until the braid over their scalp is paper white.

"Should we call an ambulance?" Jupiter asks, but that doesn't seem like the answer. Whatever this is, it's not a human issue. Not like we can blame a blood sugar drop or a wonky nervous system. Reapers don't have to worry about those things any more than I do.

Just as suddenly as they collapsed, Kelly's eyes fly open and they gasp, sucking in air like it's the first breath of their life. Even their power pulls away from me so sharply it slashes pain through my chest and I have to put a palm on the floor to steady myself until my vision clears.

"Are you okay?" X asks while my head spins. The candles

burning on a shelf nearby flicker and go out, leaving thin lines of smoke to rise up in the air. Kelly looks around, dazed. Their eyes are fully white. It's their most basic of default settings, probably the way all reapers look after they're first created before they choose a preferred form. I've only seen it a few times before, and always after something catastrophic, like when they got caught in the quarantine team's blue HELL beam.

They push up, teeth chattering like they just walked in from the freezing cold. It's a strangely vulnerable thing to see from Kelly. I put my hands to their face, and the skin beneath my palms is clammy.

"What was that?" I ask.

They take my wrists but don't pull me away. I hold their paint-white gaze and focus on breathing, imagining a loop between us. I push calm toward them and they seem to catch the idea. Neither of us actually needs to breathe, but it's as good an exercise for the undead as it is for any living person needing to focus and centre themself. Without meaning to, I close my eyes, hoping to hide how shaken I am. Most of the time, I think of them like a stray cat who has grudgingly decided to live in our house because we feed them twice a day. But there's no denying they're so much more than a pet. They might have been human once, but they've been so much more for a very long time. Reapers, even the newest least powerful ones, have an aura of invincibility. For someone as far up the hier-archy as Kelly to collapse like that is truly terrifying.

When I open my eyes again, their gaze is steady. Dark brown eyes watch me, with just the faintest lines of a frown pinching between their eyebrows. Their hair is still white, but they climb to their feet in a fast, fluid motion, bringing me with them.

"I'm fine," they say.

"It was like all your batteries stopped working at the same time," X says. "One second you were all upright and handsome, the next you were all . . . blah." He sticks his tongue out and tilts his head at a weird angle as he recreates Kelly's collapse.

"You think Kelly's handsome?" Jupiter asks, though the question holds no jealousy or teasing. It's simply a request for information.

"Like this he is," X says. He's picked up Jupiter's preference for the "pin the pronoun on the reaper" approach to referring to Kelly on a day-to-day basis, while I'm still defaulting to "they." Since Kelly has no thoughts on the matter, it all works.

Kelly grunts, clearly uncomfortable with the praise or possibly with X's attraction, such as it is. Jupiter and X are good together, but if Kelly is our stray cat, X is definitely our rescue dog. He offers infinite affection but not a lot of insight into the state of the world.

"I'm going home," Kelly says, glancing at me. "I'll see you all there."

I go to offer to come along. What if they collapse again? What if that's just the beginning of something? Reapers don't get the flu, but there has to be an equivalent. The process of becoming a reaper protects them from the decay and instability that wraiths and lost souls face, along with the slow burning out that brings ghosts to their final ending. But what if they're not completely infallible after all?

Yet their back is straight and their shoulders tight as they walk out the shop's front door. Everything about their posture says they want to be left alone.

"Call me if—" I say, but the door swings shut with a decisive bang, leaving the three of us to watch them walk out to the street and disappear around the corner.

Jupiter and X let out simultaneous breaths as soon as Kelly's out of sight.

"That was really scary," X says, though the smile on his face says he found the whole thing equally exhilarating.

"You think Kelly's okay?" Jupiter asks, gaze still on the front window.

"Sure," I say, hoping I sound confident for their sakes. They may be operating with more information than the average human, but the two of them are still very living and fragile. I don't want to shake their confidence. Not like how mine has been shaken. Because there was a split second as they fell where I couldn't feel Kelly at all. Every mote of power they wield vanished, until there was no trace of their existence, and in that moment I felt empty and very, very afraid. Because their absence was like a void inside me. A giant sucking thing that would eventually consume my lingering humanity, and I don't think any amount of carefully carved runes and deep breathing techniques would have stopped it.

I may not be in love with them, but they have been the closest thing to a constant presence and confidant in my afterlife, and they are the only reason I'm not sitting in a giant holding room at Afterlife along with everyone else who's died in the last year. Whatever that was better have been a blip. A quick reset after an update was installed. Because if something happens to Kelly, I'm not sure what I will do.

▭

Two days later, Kelly and I have been sent to Barrie, about an hour north of Toronto, where there are rumours of a lost soul causing problems. Or rather, Kelly's been sent, and I tagged along because I needed an excuse to get out and stretch my legs. It has nothing to do with the fact that I thought I heard Kelly sneeze this morning and even the idea of a reaper with allergies or a sinus infection was so unnerving I decided today was a good day to not let them out of my sight.

We're walking down the main commercial street in Barrie— usually they're called King Street in this part of Canada, but Kelly slid us into the middle of the block so I haven't seen any street signs—toward an old stone building with a wide patio out front.

"What are you doing here?" A reaper I don't know is standing on the street. They're from the quarantine team, if their tactical gear is anything to go by. The getup looks incredibly out of place on this average street in an average town where the dress code is mostly jeans, sweatpants and nylon jackets to keep out the brisk spring breeze that blows down the sidewalk.

"Lost soul," Kelly says. "You?"

The reaper swears. "Goran sent me. Said there was a wraith."

I wrinkle my nose. After everything, Goran has been the most stubborn reaper. Anything we suggest, he refuses. The head of the quarantine team is ready to die—again—on the hill of the status quo. Everything he and his team do is perfect, they have no issues with communication or resource management, and they don't need to look at how effective their operations are. Never mind that Goran had been carting lost souls off to HELL willy-nilly without even realizing it. He doesn't even believe lost souls are distinct from wraiths. They're all monsters who need containing and only his people are qualified enough to do it.

Case in point: the reaper examines me for a moment before their lip curls up in undisguised disgust.

"You must be the pet," they say. "I've heard about you. The tame wraith."

I open my mouth to protest, but Kelly surprises me by stepping between us.

"Ember is a valuable member of this team and my friend. Whereas you can't even tell the difference between a lost soul and wraith."

Yeah. So there. Maybe Kelly's got a heart after all. Or they just like sticking it to assholes as much as I do.

The reaper sneers, but whatever reply they might have made is interrupted by the way the ground beneath our feet suddenly shakes violently. Kelly and I have to grab hold of each other to keep from falling, and the other reaper staggers, attention suddenly back on the building in front of us. Looking at it head-on now, it feels like an old saloon, or maybe an old-timey hotel. Above the veranda, three stories of rectangular windows and painted brick stretch to the sky. Potted palm trees that must get taken in for the winter sway gently on the balcony that runs across the entire second floor, providing shade to people eating from small tables while they look over the street. None of them show even the slightest indication that they felt the tremor we just did. They bite into their burgers and sip their beer without so much as a look around them.

Something is going on.

The reaper takes a step back, looking nervous.

"You've got this covered, don't you? I have to report back to headquarters."

Before we can answer, they slide away, leaving us to face whatever is inside alone.

We walk through the front door. Inside is a dark entryway that splits in two on our left and right, with a staircase rising away from us in the back. On the right is an empty space that might be a night club once the sun is down. On the left is a restaurant and bar area where more people are chatting as servers move between the tables, delivering food and drinks.

"Which way?" I ask. I was expecting more with the zooming and the screeching. It's pretty much an unstable lost soul's bread and butter. Instead, as we head toward the bar, a live band is playing classic rock, and a group of people on the back patio cheer as they watch the game playing on one of the many TVs mounted around the area. It's all very normal. Very alive. Not much for us to do here unless Kelly feels like stopping for a pint.

"Eric? Eric? Eric, where the hell are you?" a woman calls behind me. She staggers in from the direction we came, weaving between tables. "I said I was only going to be a minute. You were supposed to wait for me." Her words are slurred and her make up is smeared around her eyes. A rat's nest of blond hair falls from her battered straw cowboy hat, and the cleavage that spills from her half-unbuttoned flannel shirt would be enough to make even the most uptight reaper blush. As she keeps calling for Eric, she bumps against a table, and the glasses on it wobble, splashing beer onto the wood. The people seated there catch their drinks before they topple entirely, and the woman doesn't apologize or acknowledge them at all.

She is roaringly drunk and also entirely dead. The living have this watercolour quality that means they always appear a little blurry around the edges, while the dead are crystal clear. This woman is vivid, from the way her cut-off shorts are a little longer on her right thigh than her left, to the revelation—as she gets closer —that it's not smeared make up around her eyes, but the black goo that is the signature of wraiths and lost souls. It runs over her cheeks as she cries, still calling out for Eric, whoever that is.

"Guess we're here for her," I say.

"Eric, I'm not joking right now." She veers toward the bar, passing through patrons like they're not even there. But as she floats through the wooden bar, the bartender shrieks when the soda gun she's holding suddenly explodes in her hand, drenching her and the customers closest to her. The woman floats on, unde-terred. "You asshole. You're with her, aren't you? You think you can fool me?"

"Who's Eric?" Kelly asks me in a comical stage whisper, even though the people here can't see or hear us.

"How should I know?" I ask, watching as the woman disap-pears through the next wall toward the ladies' washroom.

"You're human."

Not really. Not anymore.

I roll my eyes. "You're the one who's always pointing out how many of us there are. Asking me if I know Eric because we were both alive at one point is like asking me if I know Bill in Vancouver because we're both Canadian."

"Who's Bill?" Kelly asks in confusion. I have to swallow down my laughter and instead pat their chest.

"We'll talk about it later. Leave this one to me. I know how to handle a drunk girl at the bar."

I head to the restroom, shaking my head as I go while I pull ever so gently on Kelly's power. My hair, always up in its high ponytail, tumbles loose, and as I run my hands over my shirt, it changes from the oversized button-down I chose this morning to a flannel I tie tight at my waist and leave unbuttoned at the top. A quick click of my heels, and my sneakers turn to cowboy boots. I look every inch the girl who has just wrapped up camping at a long weekend country music festival. It's not quite the vibe of the bar, but if it's how our charge is dressing, it's how I'm going to go too. Meet people, living or otherwise, where they're at. That's what I would tell the Sparks in this situation.

She's at the end of the long row of sinks, spinning in tight circles as she mutters to herself about the things she's going to do to Eric when she finally finds him. Whoever he is, he's lucky she's dead, because her revenge plan is detailed and precise.

"He deserves it," I say, letting myself slump against the counter before pulling upright again. The trick to pretending you're drunk is to remember drunk people desperately want you to think they're sober. I give her a friendly smile, and wobble for a second before I clear my throat.

She stops her spinning long enough to glare at me.

"Who are you?" she asks.

"I'm looking for Eric too." Sisters in arms. That's what we need.

But she snarls and her teeth are blackened fangs as she glides over the floor at inhuman speed. I back up, only to collide with the wall.

"Who *are* you?" she asks again on a growl. "How do you know Eric?"

"He told me to meet him here. Said he had news to share. But he never showed up. Is that what he told you?"

She studies me, eyes darting back and forth. Her hand is raised like she might go for my throat. Hopefully Kelly is still within screaming distance. This woman is coherent enough to have a conversation for now, but lost souls outside Afterlife are unpredictable, and she could decide I'm better off mangled at any moment.

So I'm not at all prepared when her face crumples and big oily tears tumble over her eyelashes. Her mouth opens on a wordless noise for a moment, before she takes a big breath and a wailing sob escapes her. She slumps to the floor, crushing her already crushed hat between her hands.

"I knew it," she says, shuddering as she cries. "I knew he was cheating on me. I was coming here to drop his cheating ass when—"

I slide next to her, putting an arm over her shoulder. "He doesn't deserve you," I say sympathetically. "You're way too good for someone like him."

"No, I'm not." She moans like the world is ending. "He was the best. So funny. So sexy. He used to do this thing with his finger, where he'd—" She pokes her finger toward me like she wants to put it in my mouth. The skin around the nail is blackened and I clamp my lips tight. No way do I want a taste of that.

"Nooo," I say, pushing her away. "He's a jerk. You're better off without him." If there's one thing drunk girls in a bar bathroom can agree on, regardless of their sexuality, it's that men are the worst.

She sniffles. "I just don't like that I died without confronting him, you know? That he never found out I knew. I even came back from the afterlife to tell him. He probably thinks he won, when really—" She collapses into a heap of tears yet again. I pat her back. For a second there, I thought she might not know she was dead, which was going to make this conversation even more complicated.

"You came back?" I ask. Of course she did. Afterlife wouldn't have called Kelly to find a lost soul if she were an average wraith. But that means she's another person slipped through the cracks and is going to get screwed.

She nods, face still buried in her arms so she's unaware of my annoyance. When she lifts it to meet my gaze, her cheeks are a mess of black ooze, and I try to clean it away with my sleeve.

"You always haunt the ones you love, right?" she says with a rueful smile. "And I think, even after everything, I really did love him. I just needed him to know. But he's not here. I've been waiting for days. He used to come here every day after work for a drink. But he doesn't do that anymore. Is it because he didn't want to come home to me? Did he think I wasn't—" The question is lost in a fresh round of crying. Slowly, I help her to her feet. I wish we were solid enough I could wash her face before we took her to Afterlife. No one should go anywhere looking like a toner cartridge exploded on them. "You know, you're really pretty," she says, voice turning warm. She laughs to herself. "What's your name?"

"I'm Ember," I say, guiding her toward the door. All we have to do is get to Kelly and they can slide us to Afterlife so I can help get our new friend cleaned up.

"I'm Jessica," she says. "Are you dead too?"

We squeeze through the doorway. Kelly's waiting for us, leaning against the wall, head down and arms folded across their chest. To anyone passing by, they might look like they're asleep.

"Okay, let's go," I say, but they don't move. Today they're in a baby blue tank that shows off their arms nicely, and their hair is the blue-grey colour of a sky right before a thunderstorm. I nudge the toe of their black skate shoe with my cowboy boot. "Kelly."

Their head shoots up on a gasp. "What?"

"Who are you?" Jessica asks. She's stopped crying, but her words are still slurred.

"This is Kelly. They're going to take you back to Afterlife." I sound confident, but nerves tingle inside me as Kelly blinks slowly. It's not their usual blink, the one that says humans are beneath them and they're not going to dignify my irrelevant question or concern with an answer. More like I just woke them up from a very deep sleep and they're not sure what day it is or where we are. Only reapers don't sleep.

Jessica pouts. "I don't want to go back there. It was boring."

"You all right?" I ask Kelly, watching them closely. They swallow hard, glancing around, and even the delay in their reply only serves to make me worry more.

"Fine." They hold out a hand. "Let's go."

"But what about Eric?" Jessica asks. She's started crying again. "I have to tell him. I have to—"

I put my hand in Kelly's and close my eyes, waiting for the brief feeling like I've been staked onto the spinny end of an immersion blender as we zip through time and space to wind up at the intake area of Afterlife.

Only nothing happens. No falling feeling. No sensation like my insides are being spiralized and reassembled. If anything, the sound of the band playing in the bar gets louder. I open one eye, then the other. We're still in Barrie. Still standing by the washroom. A woman actually walks through me on her way inside, and I choke on the nausea of being so invaded. It doesn't happen very often anymore, since I can usually just slide myself a couple steps out of the way if I have to, so when it does it's extra unpleasant.

"Are we going?" I ask Kelly.

"Yes." Their lips are pressed together in concentration.

Jessica tugs on my hand, still whining. "Let me go. If Eric's not here, then he's probably at the brewery. It's right across the street. I can—"

Without any warning, the blender grabs hold of us, flinging me away. Jessica screams. The sound is terrified and directed straight into my ear, creating an instant headache. Or maybe that's the sensation of someone pulling on my hair.

"Ember!" Kelly sounds alarmed, but it fades almost before I can hear it. Jessica's scream is still too loud, taking hold of all my senses. So much so that when I open my eyes, everything is dark while my head rings.

"What's going on? Where are we? Take me back. Take me back. Please, let me go." Jessica is hysterical. She struggles and kicks, but when she twists my hand painfully and I try to get free, she won't let go of me either.

"For god's sake, Kelly," I mutter, trying to find a position where it doesn't feel like my arm is about to be corkscrewed off at the elbow, "if you're not going to keep both hands on the wheel, then what's the point of—"

The end of the question gets cut off as we're launched back through the ether. Jessica's cries spiral all around me. Then, just as suddenly, we land, hitting something solid.

The impact is jarring. I lose my grip on Jessica, skidding across a hard cool surface. I grunt as my cheek takes the brunt of the slide, until my face—and eventually the rest of me—comes to a halt.

We're in the atrium at the Afterlife office. Jessica is crumpled in a ball not far away. Her hat has been shredded to ragged pieces, and her flannel shirt has been torn open, revealing a lacey lavender bra beneath. A couple reapers have turned to see what the commotion of our arrival is. But none of them are Kelly.

In fact, Kelly's not here at all. The atrium is busy, but their landing can't have been any more graceful than ours, so a reaper sprawled across the floor should be easy enough to spot.

But somehow, in the space between one slide and the next, from the bar to Afterlife, Kelly has vanished.

chapter
four

"EMBER?"

"Kelly? Kelly?" They're not one to play coy. One second we were at the bar, the next I was here. When did they let go of my hand?

Only it's not Kelly who said my name. I whirl, and Bang has suddenly slid into the lobby. Her glasses slide down her nose as she frowns.

"I lost Kelly." I'm shaking, both from leftover adrenaline after our crash, and from a growing certainty that something very wrong has just happened. Why wouldn't they have come with me? "Is there something in the in-between when I'm sliding?" I didn't really have time to consider my surroundings when Jessica was screaming directly in my ear, but what if we were in that black space again? Is Kelly stuck there? Nightmare scenarios of trying to find them in an endless ether play through my mind.

"Something between sliding?" Bang sounds like the concept has never even crossed her mind. "What are you talking about?"

I can't explain it. Not more than I already have. But I also can't fight the wave of terror that something has gone off the rails. That Kelly might be hurt or trapped. Between their collapse the other day and their little cat nap just now, they aren't themself, and that's a problem given reapers are impervious to pretty much everything.

"Who's this?" Bang asks, motioning toward Jessica, who I've essentially forgotten about.

"Lost soul. Broken heart. One of Goran's goons was there and said she was a wraith. You need to bring the hammer down on quarantine or you're going to wind up with more lost souls in HELL again." I'm not really talking to her. More like letting the words trail behind me as I hurry towards the main doors. I have to get back. It's going to take such a long time. Take the subway from here back to Lower Bay. More subway to Etobicoke to find Jupiter and X. Then north to Barrie. I can't drive myself, so one of them will have to do it for me. Will I even be okay by then? Just the trip back to Toronto usually leaves me feeling shaky. It'll be more than two hours by the time I get to Barrie and if Kelly's not there, then —"Bang." I sound like Kelly when I say it. It's equal parts name and onomatopoeia.

"Ember?" She stops short beside me, still sounding confused.

"I need someone to slide me back to the bar we found Jessica in."

"The bar?"

Why is all of this so hard to follow? Something is wrong, doing all the legwork myself will not be good for my stability, and no one else is putting the pieces together.

I force myself to speak slowly. "Kelly and I got separated." My palms sweat and a panicky shiver runs up my spine. I have to find them. "I've brought you the lost soul you sent us for. All I want now is a ride back to where I came from."

Her worried look clears and she visibly relaxes. She signals to one of the reapers standing by, who hurries to join us. "Ember needs a lift. Take her wherever she needs to go."

"Barrie, Ontario," I say, taking the surprised reaper's hand and preparing for the slide. Except the contact doesn't go as planned. It should be simple. Think and you're there. But as we touch, the shiver inside me turns hot and something like lighting bursts forth, shooting the reaper and me apart. For the second time in as many minutes, I'm thrown across the marble floor, only this time when I finally skid to a halt against the security desk, the pain has me seeing stars and a distinct burning smell is coming from my clothes. I pat myself down, looking for smouldering parts, but everything appears fine, other than the way my ears are ringing from the second crash in as many minutes.

"I'm sorry." The reaper Bang assigned hurries toward me. Their hair sticks out from their head in clumps like they've also been electrocuted. "Are you okay?" Their eyes get big as they notice the scorch marks on my skin.

"I don't know," I say, stammering as I flex my fingers. The reaper reaches for me and I shrink back. No way I'm doing that again . . . whatever *that* was. It was like being shot backwards from a cannon. Nothing like the way it feels when I reach for Kelly. Their power is light. Springy. Like taking hold of a bungie cord and—

It's like someone grabbing me by the bra strap and yanking me through the void. One second I'm gathering myself in the Afterlife atrium, the next I'm back in the bathroom at the bar. If I could, I'd chip a tooth on the floor. Maybe give myself a concussion. At least I don't have to worry about getting a staph infection from whatever parasites live on the tile.

"What the fuck?" I can't help myself when I ask the question out loud. What the fuck is going on?

I push myself up, then have to squint as a bright light shines from the floor. No, not the floor. From me, then reflecting off the tile back at me. It's coming from the general direction of my chest, but when I go to touch it, it extinguishes like a flame, and everything in the bathroom becomes very normal.

At least I'm still invisible. A woman comes out of the stall closest to me and walks through my legs. I curse and pull myself up to my feet, steadying myself against the wall until I can take a few stumbling steps forward. Kelly. I have to find Kelly.

But I already know they're not here before I even get out of the washroom. Even though internally I feel like week-old tuna salad, I should still be able to sense Kelly's power before I can see them, and there's nothing there.

The spot outside the door is empty, and around me, the bar is the same as it was. Band. Servers. Patrons. No more Jessica knocking things over, but otherwise, completely unchanged and very much alive. No ghosts or reapers to be had . . . except for me, of course.

I stagger outside, hoping maybe Kelly went out for a bit of fresh air. If they're feeling off, they might have wanted to clear their head while they figured out their next move. But the street is just as mundane as the bar's interior was.

What if they really are stuck in the middle of that dark nothing? I don't even know how that's possible, but the idea fills me with dread. Afterlife is still a mess and whatever is going on with me, I can't even use the reapers for an Uber back to a place I've already been. If I have to go hunting for Kelly in a space that doesn't really exist, I'll be on my own and—

I have only a split second to prepare before I'm whipped off my feet again. The light comes once more, starting in my chest before shooting down my front and wrapping around my ankles, before pulling tight like a rope and jerking me into the dark. This time, at least, I can steer . . . sort of. Sliding always happens too fast for any real thought or decision-making. But it does take just long enough for there to be some intention to it, and I focus on the memory of Kelly and their power. The glowing whip around my ankles pulses in reply. Is that it? But where's Kelly? Yes, it feels familiar as it pulls me along, dragging me away from Barrie and back to—

I drop back into the living world in the dining room of our little house in Etobicoke. More specifically, I land on top of the small table where X and Jupiter eat their meals. I drop through the wood like a rock, and whatever the hell is happening, I gotta stop crashing like this. Even if I'm dead, this shit still hurts.

"Ember?" Jupiter calls from up the hallway. "Ember, is that you?"

I blink a few times to get my bearings, and as I finally do, I realize that she's not just asking because who else would be crash landing in her house unannounced? She sounds genuinely scared.

"I'm here." I stumble to my feet, nearly tripping over Lip Balm—that would be the new Russian Blue cat that X and Jupiter adopted last month; he hates me, but as far as we can tell he's a hundred percent cat and zero percent god, reaper or anything else preternatural—in my hurry to get to the hall. Lip Balm hisses. I'll apologize to him later. I miss Carrot Stick. As Richard, he's obnoxious and lazy and has done nothing to help things run more smoothly at Afterlife. Half the time the reapers still don't know where he is. But Carrot Stick was a lap cat who didn't mind that I was dead. Lip Balm is still reserving judgement.

But I'll worry about that later, because as I rush to Jupiter's bedroom, she appears in the doorway—of Kelly's room, not hers. She looks terrified.

"I don't know what's wrong," she says, voice cracking as she tries not to cry. "I don't know how to make it stop."

"Make what—"

But when I get through the door, the answer is obvious. Kelly is lying on their bed. I'm not a doctor, but it looks like they're having a seizure. They thrash on the covers, body and limbs shaking in a random pattern. X is sprawled on top of them, holding them down while Kelly moans.

"Kelly? Kelly?" I crawl toward them. Their power whips toward me, crackling through the air. That's not how it usually works. Normally it feels like it's looking for me. Seeking. And when it finds me, everything is calm again. Now, as it passes through me, new pain bursts through my body and I collapse to the mattress. Kelly arches up on the bed. X is a decent-sized guy, and he's having to use every pound of his weight to keep Kelly from bucking him off.

"What's happening?" Jupiter asks, her hands up around her mouth like she might have to muffle a scream. "They came back a few minutes ago without you. They said you went to Afterlife and they were going to crash until you got back, and then . . . This. Ember. I don't know what to do."

Neither do I. There's no way I'm chancing a slide back to Afterlife to get help, assuming the slide works at all. But Kelly's power is still flailing around the room. Trying to grab hold of it is like trying to grab a pissed-off shark by the tail. So instead, I take hold of what feels safest—their face.

"Kelly." I place my palms on either side of their head. Their body is rigid and their eyes are completely white. Their teeth are clamped shut, and they make little grunting sounds as they shake. "Kelly. Look at me. It's Ember. Look. I'm back. Come on."

This close, it's like being in the eye of the storm, instead of on the outside watching it consume everything in its path. Kelly's power rages like a fire, crackling and sizzling on fuel I can't see. I shift so I can put their head in my lap. They don't respond to my touch in any way. I keep one hand on their chest as I push my senses outward, looking for something familiar. Something I can touch. That third party in our working relationship that is Kelly's power. When I finally find it, it's bright as a bonfire and—if something insentient could have emotions—royally pissed off.

"Shh, shh," I whisper, like I'm talking to a fractious cat or a screaming baby. I can almost see it. I reach out a hand, bracing for the shock like when I touched the other reaper at Afterlife. But as the tail of it whips around, it lands in my palm like it's been waiting for me the entire time. There's still a jolt, but instead of blasting me backward, it's more like it's filling me. Like it's been waiting for me to open the drain this whole time. I gasp. It's bigger and faster than it's ever been before, but as I get swallowed by it, Kelly stills in my lap. Their thrashing stops and their hands, which have been clawing my arm, relax. Welts have formed on my skin, but even as I watch they begin to heal and fade. Kelly's chest rises slowly under my palm and their breathing becomes less frantic. The flood of power ebbs as we re-establish some balance. Kelly's eyes are closed and their brows pinch together in a frown for a moment before their whole face goes slack.

"Kelly?" I ask softly, giving them a gentle shake. They don't answer. Cool perspiration dots their skin. I've seen Kelly breathe before. Seen them eat, even though they don't need to for survival. I have never, ever, seen them sweat.

"What was that?" Jupiter asks. She's still wringing her hands, and X has a protective arm around her.

I study Kelly's features, running a finger over their brow. No fever, though I don't know why I thought there might be. Sometime since the bar, their hair has gone from stormy blue to mousey brown, with white at the roots and temples. Their skin has also turned mottled, a patchy soft gold-brown in some places and chalky white in others.

"Do we call a doctor?" X asks. "I really don't think that was supposed to happen."

"You think a doctor will know what to do?" I ask, protectively tightening my hold on Kelly's unmoving form. They're so vulnerable right now. I don't know why, but I'm certain I'm the only one who can help them. Me and the power that pulses inside me. It almost felt like it was the power that rocket launched me from Afterlife back to the bar and then to here. Disconnected, it reached out to me to make sure I found my way back here as fast as possible. To do what, though?

An inquisitive meow comes from the doorway. Lip Balm is watching us with yellow eyes. Now would be a good time for them to reveal they've secretly been a cat god this whole time. If anyone would know what to—

"Richard," I say, clearing my throat as the second syllable cracks in my throat. "We need Richard.

"Richard doesn't live here anymore," X says.

"Go get him then," I shout without meaning to, and they both take a step back when the room rumbles around us. Something seriously weird is going on. Kelly's head is still in my lap and I smooth away a loose strand of hair as I force myself to calm. "Sorry. Go to Afterlife. Tell them what happened and don't leave until they find him."

They glance at each other nervously. Jupiter and X have never gone to Afterlife without a reaper escort. But Kelly's in no shape for travel and I'm not going anywhere until they open their eyes.

Whatever my face looks like, it's enough to convince Jupiter and X that I'm not going to stand for negotiations or Plan B. Richard knows more about reapers than anyone. I'm not here to wait around for test results and a review of the research. I did that once and I died. We're not going down that path with Kelly.

"We'll be back soon," Jupiter says softly, though the reassurance only helps a little. They'll be gone for at least a couple hours. If anything happens to Kelly in that time, I'll be on my own. My fingers tighten in their shirt. We can do this. I'll make sure they're okay.

"Please hurry," I say. The longer Kelly is unconscious, the bigger the lump of dread in my stomach grows.

chapter
five

I THINK KELLY IS DREAMING. After Jupiter and X leave, I stay where I am, holding Kelly as I lean against the headboard for another half hour or so, waiting for them to wake up. But they don't, and eventually a kink in my hip makes me move because it's either that or my whole leg will go numb. I wheel Kelly's big white gaming chair to the side of the bed and take up my vigil there.

It's weird when you realize you've never seen someone sleep before. Weirder still when it's Kelly. Their face is still slack and their lips are parted. Their eyes move behind the lids, darting back and forth. They flex their fingers in the sheets, curling their hands into fists and releasing them.

"Kelly?" I ask, placing a palm on the bed, hoping they hear me. "Kelly, whatever is going on, I need you to wake up."

They twitch and make a small gasping sound. Then, just like nothing has happened at all, they open their eyes. I expect their default white, but instead I get a very normal grey-blue as they study me.

"Kelly?" My dead heart is in my throat.

They lick their lips a few times before asking, "Why are you in my room?"

The fear and anxiety wash out of me and I slump forward until my head hits the covers.

"Oh, thank god." Without sitting up, I grope around until I find their hand and tangle my fingers with theirs. They don't pull away, and their skin is cool and dry.

"What's wrong?" they ask. Their voice is hoarse. "What are we doing here? I thought we were going to Harry."

"Barrie," I say. "We did. You don't remember?"

When I look up, they're watching me. Their face is all one colour again—putty grey, unfortunately—and the rest of their hair has also faded to white. They look about a million years old. A tear falls down my cheek and I slap a palm over it. Now is not the time for theatrics. It's Kelly. They've lived for thousands of years. Whatever is happening to them, there's an answer and they'll live for thousands more. Kelly doesn't want my tears. They barely want me around half the time. Jupiter and I might joke about me falling in love, but that's all it is. A joke. Not that I don't care, but that's all we have. Basic human—or ghostly—caring.

Kelly goes to push up on their elbows, then grimaces and lies back down again.

"What happened to me? The last thing I remember, we were here and Bang called to say there was a lost soul in . . . Barrie?" They glance at me and I nod. "Then . . . I was here. I mean in bed. The last thing I remember I was in the living room. What time is it?"

I don't even know. From the time I slid away from them at the bar until I got back here was only a few minutes. And their seizure lasted a few minutes more, though in the moment it felt like a lifetime . . . or a death time, which in theory is even longer.

"Not much later," I say. "Don't get up. X and Jupiter went to get Richard."

Kelly snorts, but their eyes are closed. "What's he going to do?"

"More than we can," I say. "Kelly, you're sick."

"That's impossible. We're already dead. How could I get sick?" Kelly lets out a racking cough that has them rolling to one side and curling around themself. Each cough sends a little shock of power through me, like it did the other times they've coughed over the last few days. I can't believe I didn't realize something was up. I push the chair back to create a little space between us, but it doesn't help. Without leaving the house—possibly the entire city—I will not be able to get far away enough.

"Richard will know what to do," I say, more to myself than to Kelly.

When Kelly stops coughing, they let out an exhausted sigh. Whether they fall asleep or they just don't want to talk to me, it doesn't really matter. I don't have any answers and I don't want to scare them . . . or myself. Better to wait for the experts, as far as we can consider Richard an expert.

The sun goes down and we're still waiting. Jupiter's carved permanent runes in the doorframes, so at least I don't have to worry about candles burning out anymore. Kelly hasn't moved or said anything else, but at least they haven't had another seizure either. I'm afraid to leave them alone. Once, I get up to pace to the front door, like if I do, Jupiter and X might be there, walking up the drive. But I only get to the kitchen before the crackling lightning feel in my chest gets so bad I have to turn around and walk back to the bedroom. Kelly's eyes are closed. Sleeping again. That doesn't make me feel any better. But just the sight of them makes the crackling subside, so I sit down again and wait.

Finally, the front door swings open.

"Ember?" Jupiter calls. "We brought Richard."

Life as a reaper doesn't really involve a dress code, other than the goons who work in quarantine. Each reaper has their own sense of style. Even on their most low-key days, Kelly always looks like their clothes are expensive.

Richard, despite being the founder and chairman emeritus of the whole Afterlife operation, never seemed to graduate beyond

Jimmy Buffet on vacation. Today is no exception. He walks in wearing a wetsuit. Well, half a wetsuit. The top half is unzipped and the sleeves swing around his hips as he enters the bedroom. The zipper has been undone to well below his waist, so a shapely belly hangs over it and teases at what might lie beneath . . . which is not something I want to think about ever, and certainly not when we have bigger priorities.

"This better be good," Richard says. He gives his head a toss and his white hair splatters water in every direction, making us all duck. "I was in Portugal. About to hit the perfect hundred-foot wave. But these two said it was important." He jerks an annoyed thumb behind him toward Jupiter and X.

"Kelly's sick," I say.

Richard bursts into raucous laughter, like he appreciates that at least I've opened with a joke if I'm going to ruin his day at the beach.

"Kelly can't get sick. Reapers are already dead." He pats his belly as it jiggles around his giggling.

"That's what I told her," Kelly says, still in bed. But then they start coughing again. It's an awful tearing sound like it really might pull them apart from the middle. Jupiter winces and X looks like he's considering some infection control measures. Most importantly, Richard's laughter dies.

"Oh, that's not good," he says.

"I'm fine," Kelly says, gasping. "Just tired. I need to rest and I'll be fine tomorrow."

"When have you ever needed to rest?" I ask.

Richard snaps his fingers, and his wetsuit vanishes, replaced with green scrubs and a mask. He's even wearing a green surgical cap and Kelly gives him a flat annoyed look as Richard leans over them. He hums and haws, poking at Kelly while they bat him away, but finally relent to the examination. It all looks surprisingly human. He puts a palm on Kelly's forehead, checks their pulse, then makes them stick out their tongue and say "ahh."

Finally, Richard straightens, pulling the cap off to mop his brow like he's just finished a fifteen-hour surgery.

"Yeah, I have no idea what's going on." He snaps his fingers again and the wetsuit is back. At least he's got the sleeves on and the front zipped up so I don't have to see the top of his ass crack as he walks away.

"That's it?" I ask.

His shrug is infuriatingly careless. "What do you want? I'm a cat, not a doctor. Take Kelly to Afterlife. Someone there will know what's happening. Hang twelve, everyone." Then he vanishes with a soft pop. The only sign he's been here at all is the faint tang of salty ocean air in the room. I'm not good at picking up smells since I died, but this one is unmistakable. Richard is powerful. My heart sinks. If he doesn't know what's happening to Kelly, we're in trouble.

X chuckles to himself. "Hang twelve. He meant hang ten, didn't he?"

I suppress a groan. Jupiter gives him the fond smile she always does when X catches the punchline five seconds after everyone else. Kelly pulls the covers up around them, and it occurs to me I've never seen them actually use the blankets before. If you don't sleep and you don't get sick, and you don't get cold, what's the point of blankets?

"I guess we're going to Afterlife," I say. The very idea annoys me. They'll probably take one look at Kelly and say they're faking it. "*Reapers don't get sick. That's a myth.*" Kelly barely believes there's anything wrong. What are Bang and Minerva going to say?

Like they know what I'm thinking, Kelly groans. "Or you could leave me alone for a few hours. Maybe it's time I try one of those things you call a nap. Jupiter likes them."

"Naps are the best." She nods eagerly, then reconsiders. "But I think you should listen to Ember."

Kelly closes their eyes on a sigh. The rest of us hover, glancing anxiously between one another. Jupiter and X's concern makes me more confident in my own. I'm not overreacting. This isn't like coming home from the office with a sniffle.

"Nope," I say, marching across the room. "We're going."

Kelly pulls the blankets up higher, glaring at me, gaze full of distrust.

"I'll pass, thank you," they say.

It takes some wrestling. X and Jupiter pitch in. Getting a reaper to do anything they don't want to do is nearly impossible, so it's a testament to how awful Kelly truly feels that they finally allow us to drag them out of bed. They shiver, even while sweat drips from their hairline and down the back of their neck.

"Cold," they say through chattering teeth. "I'm cold."

I pull a hoodie from the closet and help them into it. Kelly even tucks the cuffs of their pants into their socks to keep out rogue drafts. They shake violently. I put an arm around them, trying to impart any amount of warmth, but it doesn't seem to help. Ghosts aren't known for their body heat.

"Let's go," I say. "We're taking the subway." Whatever is happening with sliding, it started about the same time Kelly got sick. No way that's a coincidence. I'm not going to chance another blip or glitch or whatever the hell that was, especially not if Jupiter and X are coming too.

For his part, X mutters something about how they've already taken the subway, and I have a moment of remorse because they did just shuttle back and forth to Afterlife to get Richard, who then had the audacity to pop back to Portugal or wherever without so much as a "good luck." But as I help Kelly toward the hallway, their knees buckle, and only Jupiter on the other side of them keeps us both from tumbling to the ground. So we need all the help we can get, and X doesn't complain anymore.

The subway ride is agonizing. It's like the fates know we're in a rush. There's a delay at Old Mill. Something about a pigeon or a raccoon hitching a ride. I'm not sure. The transit PA system has always been garbled and sounds of the living world are muffled to me, which means the conductor's announcement could just be the sound of a tuba being played underwater for all I can understand most of it. Then the train comes to a second stop at Lansdowne Station and sits there for ages. Another announcement is made and I still can't understand it. Kelly's head slumps against my shoulder. Jupiter and X are sitting across from us and she gives me a worried look. I return it with a tight-lipped smile and pull the hood up over Kelly's face. Normally, touching Kelly brings me a sense of calm, stilling the supernatural forces that make lost souls unstable when they're among the living. But right now I feel nothing from them. No comfort. No control.

How times have changed. The first time we took this trip, I'd been dead for only a few days and was sure the answer was to cross over at Afterlife and never look back. Kelly barely tolerated me and only agreed to bring me to Minerva after I hid their phone and half their shoes. At the time, we were both certain our acquaintance was already coming to an end, and now here we are.

Finally, we reach the platform at Lower Bay station. When the train to Afterlife pulls in, Kelly's shivering so badly they can barely lift their feet. What if we don't make it? They're deteriorating rapidly. If Kelly dies waiting for the subway, I'm not sure what will happen to me. I'll probably have to move to Afterlife on a more permanent basis, and the idea of spending all day every day surrounded by their acronyms and bureaucracy is unbearable.

When the train passes over the threshold that divides Afterlife from the living world, Kelly and I both shudder. The unstable part of me always feels easier here. The longer I've spent with Kelly, the less noticeable it's been. But today it's like a warm shower after being outside on a cold day. Even Kelly sits up straighter, though their complexion is still the colour of craft glue and their hairline shines with sweat. I put my hand in theirs, and their palm is cold and clammy, but they give me a gentle squeeze. They still need help to stand when the subway comes to a stop at the Afterlife plat-form, and the reaper waiting to direct souls toward intake only needs to look at Kelly for a split second before they say, "RR, we have a problem."

You'd be mistaken for assuming they're talking to us, but enough time spent among the reapers means I know they're placing a call to another Afterlife department, the way Kelly used to shout Bang's name with no warning, and she would magically appear seconds later.

"What's RR?" Jupiter asks.

"Reaper Relations," I say. "Reaper HR, basically."

A reaper in a pencil skirt and high bun appears, takes one glance at Kelly, and shakes their head.

"Oh no. This isn't an RR problem."

"Then who do I call?" the first reaper asks. They both look us up and down. For once I can't even blame them. Afterlife is the height of "not my job" entitlement, but the subway rarely arrives with a barely conscious reaper on board, so you can't blame them for not having an SOP on these circumstances.

"Infection control?" the second reaper asks uncertainly. They take a cautious step back, like they're worried whatever is wrong with Kelly is catching. Suddenly I'm thinking about things like reaper herd immunity. Just because Kelly has said reapers don't get sick doesn't mean they *can't*. Did I just doom all of Afterlife by bringing them here?

"Minerva," Kelly rasps, swaying even with my arm around their waist. "Call Minerva."

The air gets tense. Minerva may not be the absolute ruler of Afterlife anymore, but she still has a history with the reapers and no one wants to cross her. But I'll take any help I can get.

"Minerva!" I shout at the top of my lungs. The others flinch. I don't actually expect it to work, but just like when reapers do it, she pops in beside us a second later. This time, Jupiter shrieks and the two other reapers recoil. Kelly even takes a wobbling stumble backwards, and I go with them, clinging to their shirt.

"What?" She glares at me with narrowed eyes. Her eyeliner

flicks up in a perfect cat eye, and her black hair is streaked with blue. No wait, those aren't streaks, they're flames. Minerva is not someone you fuck with, but even her vicious gaze turns startled when she sees Kelly.

"Something's wrong," I say.

She looks appalled. "And you brought Kelly here? What are we supposed to do?"

Of course this is her answer. Something inside me slumps. Reapers are not big on problem-solving. They bring a whole new scale to the status quo. Most workplaces can go years without admitting they have cracks in the foundation. Afterlife operates on centuries.

But just as quickly as defeat tries to take me over, indignation beats it back. Minerva's not in charge anymore exactly because she refused to consider change. It's time for her to think outside the box.

"You're going to help them. They're sick. You've known Kelly longer than anyone. You have to help."

"This isn't my skill set. Ask Richard."

"We already did. He took one look at Kelly and fucked off back to Portugal."

Her hair catches fire, circling her scalp like a halo. "What is he doing in Portugal? He's supposed to be meeting with Zach this morning to review the containment room floor plans."

I close my eyes, trying not to grind my teeth. I am not Richard's keeper, and the floor plans can wait.

"Do something, or I'll tell Ziggy it was you who decided to switch the HELL common area playlist to *Yanni Live at the Acropolis*."

She stares me down. Someone behind me—Jupiter possibly, but actually I think it's X—whimpers. Minerva certainly has the power to incinerate us all where we stand. We'd never even see it coming. If she doesn't want to help us, she could make sure we don't bother anyone else in a heartbeat. But I've heard the tantrum

Ziggy threw when he couldn't figure out how to change the music back to his usual mix of avant-garde French jazz and death metal was enough to collapse the barrier that had been erected to seal off HELL from the Other Life. A handful of wraiths and lost souls had escaped, and even found a way through Zach's magical door that sent them back to the living world. The quarantine team needed a week and some extra resources that had been meant for my transition team to round them all up. No one wants to deal with that sort of headache again.

Finally, Minerva sighs. "Fine. But I don't know why everyone hates Yanni. His music is mesmerizing." She puts a hand on Kelly's shoulder. "Let's go."

"Wait. Wait, you can't—" But I don't have a chance to warn her about sliding before she and Kelly vanish with a pop. Actually it's more like a crackle, followed by a snap. A whole breakfast cereal's worth of static. It goes on and on, leaving the air feeling electrified. The two remaining reapers look around nervously.

"Where did they go?" Jupiter asks. Dread settles in the pit of my stomach. I don't trust Minerva. She might have taken Kelly somewhere quiet just to nuke them anyway. Or locked them up in HELL. I should have specified helping them meant not taking them out of my sight.

I close my eyes and concentrate. It takes a second, but finally my senses locate the tail end of Kelly's power. It's moving farther and farther away quickly, and the weird static left from their departure makes it hard to pinpoint where it is exactly. I reach out, mentally stretching until I can nail down which corner of Afterlife Minerva has zapped Kelly off to.

With no warning, the power lashes out, once again wrapping around my ankle like a whip. I only have a second to gasp and look for Jupiter before I'm yanked off my feet. I brace for the impact as I hit the ground, but it doesn't come. It's like being wrenched out of the Afterlife office and catapulted into the unknown all over again.

The static grows louder, until it's a screeching whine that

drowns out everything else. The world goes black, and I'm sling-shotted forward, hurtling through the nothing for a moment. Then just as suddenly, I'm tumbling down a flight of stairs. The world spins end over end and pain shoots through me as I hit each step. Finally, my fall is stopped by a soft, grunting mass.

It's Minerva.

"What was that?" she asks. "I haven't bitched a slide in thousands of years. I wasn't even ready to go yet. What did you do?"

Me? How is any of this my fault? And is "bitched" cool new slang the reapers are using these days, or did she mean "botched"?

Before I can protest, a second soft groan comes from my left. Kelly is lying a few feet away, facedown on the floor.

"Hey," I say, rushing to their side. "All right?"

"Where are we?" they ask as they struggle to roll over.

We're in a hallway. It's poorly lit and fingers of black something twist up the sepia-toned walls. Mould, maybe? Some kind of rot. The floor is institutional linoleum, and doors hang crookedly on their hinges on each side, stretching as far as the eye can see. It's like we're in a hospital. Or maybe an asylum.

To complete the creepy ambiance, a distant cackle wafts toward us. The sound is high. Giddy. I position myself in front of Kelly. Whatever is out there, I'll keep them safe.

But Minerva sighs loudly. The annoyance is practically tangible. If I weren't dead I'd probably be able to smell it. She's got her hands on her hips and she's looking at a faded sign mounted on the wall that says Reading Room #27.

"What is it?" I ask.

"Ah, hell," she says, looking down the hall. "We're in HECK."

chapter
six

KELLY EXPLAINED HECK to me once. It's like purgatory . . . sort of. True punishment makes souls decay, which leads to outbreaks of wraiths, even once those souls have crossed through intake and into Afterlife. But there's always a subset of the dead who, whether for reasons of faith or plain old guilt, believe they deserve some kind of penance before they can walk through the pearly gates. So the reapers invented HECK. As I understand it, souls here aren't punished. More like moderately inconvenienced, sometimes for a very long time.

"We're in HECK?" I ask.

Kelly says, "It stands for Human Existential Cleansing and—"

"Yes, yes. I remember." I help them up to their feet. They sway but stay upright. I hold on to their hand anyway. "How did we get here? Is this where you were taking them?" I ask Minerva, since this is very much something she would do. Drag them here and leave them behind. Reaper with an incurable disease? Make it someone else's problem.

But she glares at me. Her pupils have turned to vertical slits, making her look like a snake.

"I was just about to ask you the same thing. What did you do?

I was going to slide Kelly to infection control." She shakes her head and takes Kelly's other hand. "Never mind. Let's go."

"Where?" I ask.

Her reptile gaze narrows even more. "To infection control. But you can stay here if you like."

"You're sliding?" I pull on Kelly's arm. Hard. They stumble away and Minerva loses her grip. "You can't."

"Why not?" She looks genuinely confused.

Out of the three of us, I'm the least qualified to talk about the mechanics and safety protocols of sliding. But I am confident that whatever is happening to Kelly is making sliding unpredictable at best and dangerous at worst. Not even Minerva can control it. When I went subliminally hunting for their power, it was hard to nail down, but I could clearly feel they were far away. Ugh, are we going to have to walk back to the main Afterlife offices? As much as sliding sometimes feels like getting pureed on a cellular level, it's a whole lot faster than walking. I'm not sure I could go back to the old-fashioned way. It's like finally caving and buying a car in Toronto after one too many nights stuck waiting for a shuttle bus when the subway breaks down. Once you have the convenience of being able to drive, it's hard to revert to transit and its inherent lack of control.

Not that there's been much control with sliding lately either.

"Because we don't know where we'll wind up. Could be infection control, could be the nothing," I say.

"The nothing?" Minerva sneers.

"The black space between slides. I've wound up there twice now."

She rolls her eyes. Clearly, I'm just another irrational human she has to deal with. Can you really blame her for wiping our memories for all those years? It's so much easier when souls don't talk back.

"Let's go," she says, reaching for Kelly again. But this time, they step away, pulling out of her grasp.

"No, I don't think so," they say. Their voice is hoarse, but their position is clear. "Ember's right. I don't know what's going on, but I'm doing something that's making sliding hard. If we aren't careful, we'll wind up in a cell in HELL where no one can find us, or some abandoned place like Zach found that we forgot exists." Kelly coughs, doubling over. I keep a hand on their back, rubbing slow circles. Minerva watches us, clearly itching to get out of here. I half expect her to zap away and leave us to ourselves. Why would she bother sticking around to help?

"So you're suggesting we just walk out of HECK? Hitch heck, maybe?" She asks that last part with a sweet twist of her lip that probably has more venom than a rattlesnake.

"Minerva?" A voice calls from the endless hallway. We all turn to see a man hurrying toward us. He's hunched, with tanned skin and curly hair flying out in wild tufts from the top and sides of his head. He's dressed in a striped vest and a string tie. He looks like an old-timey bartender, especially when he pulls a pocket watch on a chain from his vest. "What time is it? I didn't know you were coming!"

Minerva sighs, taking a nervous step backward. Kelly's hand tightens in mind. They're both uneasy, but the man walking toward us looks positively delighted that we're here at all.

"It's been such a long time." His smile splits his whole face in two and he pulls Minerva into a vigorous hug. I think about hugging Minerva like I might think about hugging a grizzly bear after stealing the last salmon in the river, but he clearly doesn't have any such reservations. He leans back, pulling her right off her feet, and she squawks.

"Earp, put me down." She kicks at the air, and he laughs at her protests.

"Put you down? When I haven't seen you in half a century? I missed you, Nerf."

"Nerf?" I whisper to Kelly, but they're watching the whole

encounter with naked surprise on their face. Not much surprises Kelly, so I close my mouth and let the situation unfold.

Earp spins around, while Minerva flails in his arms. She squeaks and struggles some more, but he keeps laughing. He's not much taller than she is, and his shoulders are thin, but reaper strength is deceiving. Finally, he sets her gently on the ground. Her hair is messed, looking a lot like his now, and she runs a hand through it to smooth it down. It has the opposite effect, though, like her hands are full of static electricity. Her hair rises from her head in wisps as faint blue flames flicker around her like a halo.

She glares at him. "You know how much I hate it when you do that."

But he's already moved on. He directs his grin at us. "Kelly! Oh my stars. The legend arrives." He puts his hands over his mouth in delight and bows a half dozen times, bobbing up and down. Kelly actually takes a step sideways, like they can escape the attention by hiding behind me. When Earp straightens the final time, his gaze meets mine and he gasps. "Ohhh. What are you? I haven't seen one of you before."

"My name's Ember," I say.

He giggles. Actually giggles. Then claps his hands and bounces on his toes a few times. "Ember. Yes. Yes of course. A little spark. That's exactly what you are. I'm so glad you came."

"We can't stay," Minerva says sourly. She turns away, looking down the hall and I think I hear her say something like "Shouldn't be here at all," but before I can ask, Earp loops his arms through mine and Kelly's and leads us the way he came.

"We don't get visitors very often. In fact, it's been downright quiet lately. Not so many souls needing penance, eh, Nerf?"

Minerva's lips are pressed tight, but she trails after us. How long has it been since she's visited HECK? Earp may not know what's been going on in the other parts of Afterlife. While Minerva was wiping memories, there would have been no reason to send souls down here to languish. No reason to let the ones down here remain either, come to think of it. So why does HECK still exist? No point in atoning for your transgressions for a few centuries if you don't remember them.

Earp is still talking, vomiting words at such an intense pace I can barely understand him and certainly can't get a word in edgewise.

"It's stew for dinner tonight," he says, then laughs to himself. "Well, it's stew for dinner every night. We used to have a cook. Crushed by a chuckwagon on a cattle drive a few centuries back. He spent a hundred and fifty years with us before he burned out and disappeared. Didn't even leave us his recipes, so now we just throw everything in a pot and hope it comes out okay. Fortunately, most nights it does." He smiles broadly. I have the brief thought that Earp would probably get along well with Jupiter and X. Shit, where are they? Still at Afterlife? Do they know what happened? Does Bang have some kind of tracking system? Or maybe HECK has CCTV cameras?

We make our way down a long staircase. A sound like shuffling footsteps and a periodic clang of metal against metal punctuates the air. We walk through a wide doorway and into something like a meal hall. Long tables with white tablecloths are arranged in dozens of rows. A line of people moves slowly about the perimeter. Some are serving food. The clanging is the sound of their ladles hitting the side of massive metal pots as they deliver heaving servings of what must be Earp's fabled stew into plain bowls held by detached-looking diners. It's a scene straight out of a Dickens novel. Once they're served, the people wordlessly move to the tables, where they settle and quietly eat their stew. Others who have finished rise and deliver their empty bowls to a second team, who take them and wash them out in vats of soapy water, before handing them back. The people and their clean bowls then get back in the first line, waiting patiently for more stew.

"They don't actually need to eat, of course. But they like the ritual of it. Who's hungry?" Earp asks, finally releasing us.

Honestly, the stew doesn't look terrible. No worse than the things I excavated from Tupperware in the catacombs of my fridge on particularly depressed Monday nights in January. But my stomach is all in knots, trying to figure out what's going on, so the idea of putting food into it makes me gag.

"We'll pass," Kelly says. They've put an arm around me and I'm no longer sure who's holding up who.

Earp points at them, still laughing to himself softly. "You at least need something to shore you up. You're looking a bit worse for wearing there, Kelster."

Pretty sure anyone else who ever dared to call Kelly "Kelster" would find themself immediately on the receiving end of a bolt of lightning and a one-way ticket to HELL. But somehow all Earp gets is a quizzical eyebrow. He winks and cuts the line, walking past everyone waiting for another helping of stew. They rumble and murmur, shooting annoyed looks at Earp's back. Can't imagine why. If my penance was to eat stew for a century or two, I wouldn't mind getting a break if someone jumped the queue.

Earp collects a few bowls and nods for us to follow him along the tables. We get curious looks as we go by, but no one speaks to us. No one speaks at all, in fact. I assumed there were some whispered conversations we couldn't hear, but even though people sit in small clusters, the only sound they make is that of spoons tapping against the side of their bowls. Occasionally someone clears their throat. But that's it. Not a single word is spoken.

"How does this place still exist?" I ask Minerva as we wind through rows of chairs. "Wouldn't you have shut it down when you started wiping memories? Doesn't seem very efficient of you to have let it keep going."

Minerva throws me an irritated glance that would normally have me ducking for cover, but before I can she looks away again, muttering something I can't hear.

"What was that?" I ask.

She flinches, like she's afraid to repeat herself, but finally she says, "I forgot this w . . ." The end trails off. Even Kelly's watching her, the corner of their lip curling up in amusement.

"You forgot what?" they ask. The lift of their eyebrow is the equivalent of a regular person falling over because they're laughing too hard to get oxygen to their brain.

"I forgot they were down here," she mutters. "We cleared the upper layers of HECK, but Earp's always run such a welcoming place we don't see souls come back up to the general population very often. I forgot he was here, all right?"

I snort. Even Kelly makes a soft but amused huffing sound. Minerva looks like if we ask her to repeat herself one more time, she'll obliterate the whole place. No doubt the implication that her operation has ever been anything but perfect is physically painful for her, but if you can't enjoy the smallest victories when you're dead, what even is the point?

Finally, Earp gathers us at the end of one of the tables, setting the bowls in front of four chairs. Minerva looks like she'd rather eat glass than taste his offering. Kelly sits and I settle next to them. They lift the bowl, giving it a suspicious sniff.

"Go on," Earp says. "We put a little something special in it. For the souls, it keeps decay at bay. For you, it just might make you feel a little less . . ." He puts the back of one hand to his forehead and makes a motion like he might faint, but then his smile returns and he motions for Kelly to eat up.

Tentatively, they bring the spoon to their lips, taking a small bite. They swallow, and I brace, ready to leap into action. What kind of action? No idea. But with the way the last few hours have gone, I'm prepared for anything. Instead, Kelly considers what they've just ingested, then goes back for more.

"What's the point in feeding everyone? Not like they need to eat. I thought the whole objective of HECK was because actual torture causes decay, but feeding them is more than just not torturing them," I say as Kelly eats. In fact, after the first few spoonfuls, they start shoving it down their throat like they've been hungry for centuries. Earp watches with a pleased smile. Minerva doesn't touch her food, but that's a her problem. I'm only here to look out for Kelly.

"Decay happens everywhere. Even up there in gen pop." Earp points his spoon toward the ceiling before giving Minerva a knowing wink that makes her stiffen. Something tells me if I spent more time with him, I could get to like Earp. He's the most human reaper I've ever met. "It just happens slowly when souls are happy, or at least when they aren't upset. But even boredom will accelerate and . . . well . . ." He glances around the room, where the people are still standing in their endless line for more stew. "It gives them something to do, and I like mixing up the flavours every few years, just for variety's sake." He shrugs as he eats. "Anyway. What brings you to my neck of the underlife?"

"Afterlife," Minerva says primly.

"If you say so." Earp shrugs again. It's a careless gesture, and it makes Minerva even more uptight. If she grips her spoon any harder, she'll bend the handle. Maybe even snap the metal entirely. No doubt making things easier for the souls in Earp's care isn't part of the official reaper training manual.

But I don't have the patience for another round of meetings and procedural reviews. Into the pause in the conversation, I say, "Kelly's sick."

I expect Earp to dismiss me and remind me that reapers don't get sick. Everyone else has. Instead, he tilts his head, looking Kelly up and down quizzically before he says, "You're not sick."

Kelly nods, glancing down at their bowl. They've eaten all of it and are still dragging the spoon around the bottom like they can scrape up the last few dregs.

"We'll go back up to infection control and figure it out," Minerva says.

"Oh no," Earp says, sounding wistful. "They won't be able to do anything."

I slump, picturing the sight of Kelly's thrashing body on the bed. Will that happen again? Something worse? Is it already too late for us to slide out of here? Are we trapped wandering HECK forever?

"So there's nothing to do?" I ask. My throat is tight from rising panic and unshed tears.

"Not at infection control." Earp's gaze moves from me to Kelly. "You're not sick. It's something more serious than that."

"More serious?" Minerva asks. For once, her perpetually pinched expression shifts to something more like worry.

Earp's grin is sly, like he's been waiting to deliver this punch-line since we arrived. "Kelly, you're being haunted."

chapter
seven

IN TYPICAL REAPER FASHION, Minerva snorts.

"Haunting's not real."

Earp arches an eyebrow. "And you know this how?"

She splutters. "I'm six thousand years old. I'd know if haunting were real."

Her indignation makes me chuckle. "Like anyone would want to haunt you."

The comment slips out before I can stop it. I should be incinerated in the next second, but Minerva only glares.

"Haunting is a myth," she says dismissively.

"Like lost souls were supposed to be a myth?" I ask. "Because I'm sitting right here."

Earp smiles as he waggles his spoon in my direction. "I like you. How long have you been dead for? Don't suppose you want to do a stint in HECK? I could use a sidekick like you."

"I'm nobody's sidekick." Except maybe Kelly's, though I prefer to think of us as partners in after-death reform. It's been a slow process, but what's that matter when you have forever? I go to slip my hand into Kelly's, reminding them that whatever Earp means by haunting, I'm on their side. But they pull their hand free, dropping their spoon from the other and twisting both together in their lap. They won't look at me.

Minerva stands up abruptly. "I have to get back to the office. I have a meeting with Bang and Zach. I can't be late."

"Yes, you don't want to miss that," Kelly says, but their tone is so flat I can't tell if they're being sarcastic or if they still feel too weak to drum up their usual level of snark.

"What about Kelly? You're just going to leave them here?" I ask.

"Of course, of course," Earp says, also rising. He's no more concerned that Minerva's abandoning us than she is about leaving. He collects our bowls, including the two full ones Minerva and I didn't eat. He glances around the room, holding them up, and after only a few seconds a couple souls standing in the endless line hurry forward, take them, then settle down at the next table to eat.

Minerva glances at Kelly. For a moment, her gaze flickers with a dozen different emotions. Guilt. Irritation. Sadness. Maybe regret? She doesn't say anything, though, and a second later, she poofs out of sight, sliding back off to the main parts of Afterlife. I hope whatever thing Kelly's doing to sliding, she finds herself in the middle of Lake Ontario and has to swim for it.

As soon as she disappears though, Earp lets out a long exhale. He undoes his tie, using it to mop his brow, though there's no sign that he's been sweating.

"Phew. Thank gosh she's gone. Hopefully she forgets about me for a few more decades," he says, stuffing the tie into a pocket. He checks his watch, then smiles at us. "Now who's hungry? I hear they're serving stew today." He looks between us and whatever he sees on our faces makes a belly laugh bubble up and burst from his lips. We both flinch and step back like he's just spat on us. I want to reach for one of the cloth napkins on the table and wipe my face with it.

Finally, Kelly takes my hand. The connection between us

crackles, like a phone call struggling to stay connected when service is spotty.

"Thank you," they say quietly. "But we'll be on our way."

"On our way where? Why would we leave?" I say, planting my feet. "What did you mean Kelly's haunted?"

But Earp only waves me off. "I've never seen it myself. There are rumours, even though they don't let me out of HECK very often. Most would say it's a myth, but I find there's usually a kernel of truth in even the most outrageous rumour."

"What *is* it though?" I squeeze Kelly's hand, trying not to direct my frustration toward Earp.

"Let's go," Kelly tugs on me. "Thank you for the food."

"Something to do with reapers spending too long among the living. It takes a lot to keep a soul burning, and humans will latch on to anything that might keep them going for a little while longer. A reaper can't withstand them forever, even one like Kelly. No one's alive here, though. You're welcome to stay." Earp looks around at the silently eating people. "They're not great for conversation, but you get twenty square meals a day, and you'd be better off than you have been among all those hungry living creatures."

The two souls who took our uneaten bowls have finished their meal. Without so much as a glance at us, they take the empty dishes to the wash station, then get back in line for more food. They now have two bowls each, and the idea of having to eat even more of this endless stew turns my stomach. Twenty square meals is not the draw Earp thinks it is.

"We'll be fine," Kelly says.

"But what about—" I start, but Kelly switches our grip so they're holding my wrist to pull me away from the table. Whatever Earp puts in his magic stew, it does seem like it's helped Kelly feel a bit better, but unless it starts talking inside Kelly's stomach, it isn't offering any answers.

"You might go find Buela in the library," Earp says, raising his voice as we walk away. "I've heard she knows a thing or two about reaper illnesses. A lot of books in a library. She's had a long time to read."

Kelly's not much of a reader, from what I've seen. Since they hit the global high score for Mutant Mushroom Relay, they've moved on to other more collaborative town-building games. Last I noticed, Kellyville had a population of 37,000 and Kelly had recruited four other builders around the world as part of their co-op to keep their virtual businesses from running out of stock while each town mayor slept. They certainly have never bothered to check out the books and services Toronto Public Library has to offer.

After we exit the meal hall, Kelly walks like they know where we're going. Does HECK even have one of those *You Are Here* maps? We spiral farther down the staircase where we first landed. Sometimes we see signs that say things like Tech Support and Change Rooms, though the mid-twentieth-century hospital ambiance remains the same. Sometimes we pass souls traveling up or down the hallways.

"Where are they going?" I ask.

"Time in HECK is voluntary. They're free to leave whenever they want. They also have the option to change rooms every few decades. As Earp said, even boredom leads to decay eventually."

"Earp also said you were being haunted," I say. "You're way less freaked out by the news than I am, so you must know what he meant. What is it?"

We're walking side by side and they give me my favourite version of the Kelly Stare. It's the one where they have an answer but they don't want to tell me because they know it will lead to dozens more questions. But it gives me a second to notice some of the colour is back in their skin. Not so much the colour of wet plaster anymore. More like a shade of eggshell. That stew really was magic.

Finally, when it's clear I'm not accepting silence as an answer, they sigh.

"There's a rumour that reapers who spend too long away from Afterlife start to lose their powers. That in being so close to living souls, they start to decay in their own right. That's what Earp was talking about."

It's not unlike what I've seen with lost souls. They're far more stable in Afterlife than they are in the living world.

"So you'll become a wraith?" The idea makes me shudder. So far, there has been no indication anyone knows a way to fully rehabilitate wraiths. Reading hour might calm them, but it's not a cure. Regardless of the book Zach and Minerva finally pick, wraiths are left in HELL to slowly burn out over a few centuries.

Kelly shrugs. The gesture is frustrating when we're talking about something so dire. They can't become a wraith. They're my closest non-living sort-of friend, and they're also the main reason I'm not currently locked up waiting for reading hour right now. If haunting is because Kelly's spent too long on the living plane, does that mean the solution is for them to live at Afterlife like the rest of the reapers? Does that mean I'll have to too? I can barely hack the commute on the subway on my own. If they're here and I'm in Etobicoke, things are going to get rocky quickly, but living at Afterlife among the terminally-superior and still ineffectual reapers is a big ask.

But if it means Kelly gets better . . .

I'm being selfish, aren't I? Pull it together, Ember.

"Okay," I say, taking a deep breath. "So, we stay here."

"In HECK?" They looked shocked. "That stew was tasty, but it's not like I can ask for pizza when I—"

"In Afterlife. If that's what you need to be okay, we'll do it." It'll be fine. Maybe I'll get a place of my own instead of not even having my own room at Jupiter's. Except where do reapers even live? Not like there's a little reaper subdivision that they commute to at the end of a long workday. If there was, you can believe Minerva would be the worst HOA president ever. She'd be on your doorstep complaining how your grass was the wrong shade of green or that the bedsheet ghosts you put on your lawn for Halloween weren't anatomically correct.

But despite my very generous offer of relocation, Kelly isn't reassured.

"It doesn't matter," they say, looking down a hall as we come to a new floor. A sign on the wall says Library.

"What doesn't?" I ask. "If you're sick because you're spending too much time with the humans, then we'll move here. I don't mind." I can take day trips to visit X and Jupiter. Charge my reaper battery before I leave. It'll be like a custody agreement that I enforce myself.

But they only shake their head. "It's too late. If it really is haunting, the drain on my powers and my soul is irreversible." They walk down the hall, toward a set of heavy wooden doors. I don't follow. Can't even lift my feet. What do they mean irreversible? It's not a tumor. They're a reaper. Kelly has existed through wars and plagues, the rise and fall of empires. Surely, they can get better now.

"What are you talking about?" I ask, voice shaking. "Irreversible? Then what happens at the end?"

The floor feels like it's dropped out from under me even before they answer. It's the same sensation I had that day at the doctor's office. Bone cancer. Chemo. Radiation. Low survival. I sat in the chair across from her desk and inside I was plummeting through never-ending space.

I shake my head, taking a slow step backward, but it's not far enough to keep me from hearing what Kelly says next.

"Ember. I'm dying."

chapter
eight

WHAT?

What the fuck, what. The. Fuck?

The dread that's been building for a while finally takes hold, shouting that they've known what was going on for days. Since Kelly walked into that boardroom and possibly before. Reapers don't get sick, so it only makes sense that if they do, the only result can be . . .

"You're joking, right? I mean, you don't joke, but you probably can. Ha ha, Kelly's dying. That's a pretty good first attempt at a punchline." I'm babbling, and they don't reply. When I run out of steam, all I can say is, "What do you mean 'dying'? You're already dead."

Absurdly, I have the thought that we should have found out who they were before they became a reaper. Like that would make any difference. But I know this process. It's not rational. When they first gave me my diagnosis, I wondered what I could have done differently. Could I have exercised more? Eaten more kale? Drunk less coffee? Did the tumor in my leg have anything to do with the time I broke my ankle on a school ski trip? Further conversations with my doctors confirmed my cancer had nothing to do with any of those and everything to do with bad luck. But human brains have an unfortunate habit of attempting to apply logical explanations to the unexplainable.

"Nothing lasts forever," Kelly says. Their smile is rueful. So much for humour. "I've spent half a century among the living and I have no interest in returning to Afterlife. Maybe I *am* being haunted. Maybe it's time to embrace the inevitable."

Their bland acceptance makes me see red. Where are the stages of grief? Where's the sadness and denial? If they think I'm going to do it for them, they're kidding themselves. I already went through it for myself and once is enough for both one lifetime and an after-lifetime.

"And there's no cure?" I can't help myself. Despite my silent declarations, it has to be asked. Everyone asks it. I refuse to believe that reapers, with all their powers, just snuff out like a candle.

Kelly points to the sign on the wall. "Maybe there's an answer here. Can't hurt to check." They walk toward the library doors without looking back. I follow on heavy feet. They just told me they're dying and nothing will stop it. So why are we spending time at HECK's library? This is the worst bucket list ever.

Nonetheless, Kelly opens the door and as we enter, I stop moving again, though this time because I need a minute to take in where we have arrived. The meal hall was big. It could have seated a few hundred people. The library is huge, impossibly so. I can't even see the ceiling it's so high. Bookshelves soar upward, and somewhere above what's probably the hundredth shelf, it almost looks like clouds have collected between them, drifting gently between the stacks.

"How—" I start, but I shouldn't be surprised. Afterlife isn't bound by trivial things like gravity or structural engineering. If they want a library that stretches to the stars, they can make it happen.

"This way," Kelly says, voice soft. My fingers itch to take their hand. So often, we touch each other seeking a weird sort of platonic comfort. Something about solidifying the connection between us makes everything feel easier. But I can't bring myself to touch them right now. It happens when someone is sick. In my case, people would hover, like they wanted to hug me, but also knew any pressure on my brittle bones and too-sensitive skin would be painful. And we'd both grieve a little, knowing we'd already missed our chance for that last moment of contact.

A line of people circulates around the librarian's desk. I'm following Kelly because diving headlong into the shelves feels pointless. I don't even know what we're looking for. I'm very doubtful reapers use the Dewey decimal system to catalogue books.

No one speaks, just like at the meal hall. Slowly, we shuffle forward. As we get closer to the desk, the librarian's voice comes toward us.

"You're welcome to take a look for yourself. Or come back later. Maybe someone will have found it by then."

She says it over and over. Sometimes people turn away, returning to the back of the line. Other times, they walk past her, entering the stacks and moving slowly from book to book.

"So your plan to save yourself is to hope there's a book in here somewhere that tells you how to get better?" I ask Kelly. The woman standing in front of us turns and gives us a sharp "shhhh-hh." I glare at her, but when I don't speak, she seems appeased and faces straight ahead once more.

Kelly furrows their brow. "I knew you wouldn't like my answer and that you'd more than likely exhaust all possibilities to save me. This is a good and harmless place to start."

Harmless? Like we're going looking for reaper self-help books that will tell Kelly they just need to meditate? Like I'm just going to watch them die? I accepted my own death. I've done the work. I'm not going to stand aside and accept Kelly's too.

So . . . maybe they have a point.

We get to the front of the line. The librarian is a tall Asian woman with dark hair cut into a bob and a bright red blouse tied up in a massive floppy bow at her throat. Her lipstick and heart-shaped glasses match the blouse's colour perfectly. As we approach, her eyes narrow and her lips thin in the way all reapers' do because not a single one of them ever likes surprises.

"Kellifern—"

"Hello, Buela," Kelly says, cutting off her suspicious greeting, though not fast enough that I don't hear the beginning of the mysterious next syllable of Kelly's full name. It's something they've never told me and something I've always amused myself with wondering about. I thought I'd have a long time to figure it out. Centuries. Turns out I might be wrong.

"What are you doing here?" she asks, tone flat and clipped. "I have patrons who need assistance."

"I'm looking for a book. Earp said you might have it."

"Earp sent you?" She glances from them to me, then back again.

"Yes. Said you might have some information on how to stop a haunting."

"A book of myths, then," she sneers.

Kelly coughs. The waves of power that roll off them make everything sway. Me. The other souls standing in line. Even the bookshelves, maybe, though it's hard to say for sure since any attempt to look towards the tops of them leaves me dizzy. Buela puts a steadying hand on her desk, and as Kelly's coughing finally stops, she pushes up her glasses with a red-manicured nail before typing on her computer.

"Let's see . . ." she says. "Haunting. Haunting. Hmmm. Harpsichords. Hashbrowns. Hat tricks. Oh here. Haunting. Oh." She frowns at the screen. "Hmm. That's odd. It says here that book has been lost."

Kelly rolls their eyes. "Very surprising."

Her smile is bland. "You're welcome to take a look for yourself. Or come back later. Maybe someone will have found it by then."

This is the answer Earp thought we'd find here? I glance at the stacks. We could truly spend eternity looking for a book in this literary haystack. And Kelly no longer has eternity.

"Can you check again?" I ask, pushing ahead of Kelly. "Surely out of all the books here, there has to be one or two that are in the right place. You would think—"

Kelly puts a quieting hand on my shoulder. "Thanks, Buela. We'll have a look."

"What are you doing?" I ask as once again they pull me away. "You think we're just going to browse? That if we shake enough shelves, the book will just fall on our heads like an apple out of a tree?"

"Your fondness for similes has always been endearing, Ember."

Now they compliment me? Now? It's like they've given up when I've only just found out what's going on. That's unacceptable.

Kelly disappears around the first bookshelf. I hurry after them. Souls dot the way, staring upward at the shelves. Occasionally one pulls a book down, looks at the cover, then replaces it, before moving a few titles down and starting over. In a normal library it would be an effective strategy if you were just browsing. Find the section for mysteries and pick up titles until you find the perfect whodunnit where a tottering old lady with a penchant for gardening solves the murder of the postman buried under her zinnias. Here, though, it's pointless. I pick a random shelf. It has titles like *Kinesiology for Athletes*, *The Mangrove Mangler* and *The Little Puppy Comes Home*. And that doesn't account for the titles that aren't in English but I assume are just as eclectic. Some of them aren't even titled in an alphabet I recognize. Like when you think you can read things in dreams, but really it's just gibberish characters that look like letters.

"This is your plan?" I ask, replacing a book called *The Husbandry of Bovines*. "Browse the shelves until a cure magically presents itself?"

To my surprise, Kelly's voice comes through the shelf. I gasp when I catch their cool eyes watching me from the other side. "What do you propose as an alternative? There are no reaper hospitals. No reaper universities. Anything that ever looked like a research team got repurposed to soul retrieval or quarantine and their records sent to the archives. Would you rather wander the shelves there? Because it will amount to the same thing."

I grind my teeth, making my head ache. Reaper shortsightedness is infuriating. You can't define your entire existence around your job, and yet that's what they did for thousands of years, and this is the result.

Since the alternative is shouting in a library, I growl and stomp away. Let Kelly find a miracle cure. I need a minute to clear my head.

A few rows back, the shelves are basically deserted. Looks like most people spend a few hours—maybe a few days—in the front dozen shelves. When they realize they're not going to find the biography of Virginia Wolfe or the purple penis alien romance that will help them pass a little bit of their semi-eternal time here in HECK, they give up and get back in line, hoping Buela might have better luck.

I wipe a tear from my eyelashes. Nothing in Afterlife is ever certain, other than the reapers will have already found a way to fuck up something that should have been straightforward. They dismiss some of the direst outcomes as myth and take the easy way out without considering longer term impacts, even though they pretty much only exist in the longer term.

My vision blurs and I blink away more frustrated tears. As the bookshelf I'm standing in front of comes back into focus, one particular book stands out from the rest. It's like it's been pushed out a little farther from its neighbours, waiting for someone to notice it. The green spine is marked with gold foil lettering.

On the Haunting of Reapers.

No. It couldn't be that easy, could it? Just once, am I about to catch a lucky break?

"Kelly? Kelly, I think I found something."

"Hey, are you okay?" A worried voice from the front of the library comes toward me. I ignore it and stretch for the book. It's on a shelf just high enough to be hard to reach. I brace my free hand on a lower one and rise up on my toes. My fingers brush the wood, sending dust off the edge. I nearly have it.

"Oh my god. Is she having a seizure? What do we do?"

My fingertips freeze.

"Hey. Hey! Somebody help!" The voices are louder. Worried. One of my fingernails drags over the book spine, but I fall backward when the floor rumbles underneath me. The anxious questions give way to broader sounds of alarm and confusion. The shaking continues, making the bookshelves sway. The green book tumbles toward me, and I catch it just before it lands on my head.

"Should we move her?" someone asks. "This isn't safe. Is there a doctor somewhere?"

Kelly. I clutch the book to my chest and run, weaving through the stacks. The shaking gets worse, like I'm trying to run on a trampoline or one of those floating docks they had at summer camp when I was a kid. Souls rush past me, everyone fighting to get to the exit as more books fall off the shelves, rocketing from such a great height that they drop toward us like missiles. They crash into the floor so hard they crack the floorboards, and the few people who aren't fast enough to jump out of the way drop to the ground like they've been shot.

"Kelly!" Without realizing how close I am, I burst back into the front waiting area. Shit, I've gone too far. Which row were they in? Where did we enter this maze of shelves?

The shaking is getting worse, trembling like an earthquake. The floor undulates and the shelves go from shedding books to rocking precariously, sawing from side to side. The shaking is erratic, meaning the shelves wobble independently, some left and some right. With each roll, they teeter closer and closer together.

Books fall by the dozens, then the hundreds. I hold my green book over my head like it will protect me.

"Kelly!" I call, rounding another bookshelf. A small group of people are crouched on the ground. One of them looks up as I approach.

"Do you know her?" they ask.

Kelly's thrashing like they were on the bed at home. Their heels drum on the floor, kicking out a rhythm that it takes me a second to realize matches the shaking beneath my feet.

I drop to my knees, pressing Kelly's face between my palms. Their eyes are rolled back in their head and as I watch, their features shift. It's a continuous thing. Their nose grows longer, then wider, then shrinks back again. Their cheeks and jaw grow rounder like they're gaining weight, then waste away until the bones beneath their skin are nearly all that's left. The whole time, they shudder and twist.

"What's wrong with her?" someone asks.

Another book drops from the sky, smacking me between the shoulders. I fall on top of Kelly's body and gasp as their power reaches for me, pulling me even closer. It feels hungry, like it will tear me to shreds. Maybe the others around us too. It will take the whole library apart page by page, and Kelly's not awake or aware enough to stop it.

We have to get out of here. This little side trip to HECK has been fun, but we're putting the souls and reapers here in danger and Kelly's getting worse. We shouldn't slide, but what other choice do we have? The bookshelf to my right rocks and tips over. Only its neighbour keeps it from crashing down on top of us entirely, but the remaining books plummet towards us. We're about to get buried. All of us.

"Run!" I shout, hoping the others will listen, but I don't have time to find out.

I grab hold of Kelly's powers. It doesn't feel friendly. Like if I don't hold some part of myself back, it will take all of me. I gasp and squeeze my eyes tight, hoping I can do this. Protect us and get us to safety.

"Hold on," I say, maybe to myself, maybe to Kelly. I clutch the book to my chest with one arm and hold Kelly's hand with the other. I picture the little house in Etobicoke. Maybe Jupiter can find some runes that will keep Kelly stable until we figure out what's wrong with them.

As the library fades and we start the slide, Kelly's power bucks. It's a wild animal trying to throw me off. Suddenly, holding Kelly's hand isn't going to be enough. They're too heavy. I'm going to lose them. The power is going to pulverize me until I can't save either of us.

The book is still against my chest, but as we start to tumble, it slips in my grasp. I grit my teeth, but Kelly kicks and twists. One of their fingers pulls free of my grip and I can't do anything to fix it without having a second hand.

I let the book go. We'll find another way. No one's reading anything if we don't survive. It tumbles away, freefalling in the black nothingness, but it means I can turn towards Kelly, wrapping myself around them. I say a silent prayer, picturing the little bungalow with its flowers that always bloom by the porch. The bay window where Carrot Stick and now Lip Balm like to sit so they can judge the neighbours as they walk by. We can make it. We'll be safe there.

chapter
nine

WHEN I OPEN MY EYES, it's still dark. Utterly black, which is impossible in any part of Toronto. The urban glow means it's never truly dark, even on the stormiest moonless night. My silent heart sinks. Shit. I screwed up. I blink a few times, and slowly my eyes pick out pinpricks of light. Stars dot the sky and somewhere close by is the sound of running water.

Someone groans.

"Kelly." I crawl on my hands and knees, fumbling around in the dark. The ground beneath my palms is cool and damp, hard and uneven. It's rocky and the air is heavy with a smell like sulphur. We're not back in Toronto. I can't smell anything there. So I don't know where we are. Outside, somewhere. Maybe in a forest. But once again, Kelly's powers went rogue and we're off course.

"Ember?" Their voice is soft and hoarse, coming somewhere from my left.

"Kelly?" Stones cut into my skin, but I keep moving.

"Where are we?" They cough. Finally, I find them in the dark. I touch a leg first, then follow it along until my fingers touch theirs.

"Are you okay?" I brush their neck. Their skin is slick with sweat and they're shivering.

"Not really. What happened to the library?" they ask.

How do I explain it? One second we were arguing and the next they were on the floor and the whole place was coming down around our ears.

"I tried to slide us home," I say instead. "Looks like I took the wrong turn at Albuquerque."

They grunt. "Why would you take us to New Mexico?"

The question makes me smile. Same old Kelly, despite everything.

Ahead of us, a point of light shines brighter than the others. Maybe we're in a tunnel? A hall? I attempt to stand and am rewarded by a blinding pain as I hit my head off the top of a ceiling much closer than I expected.

"Are you all right?" Kelly asks as I moan and rub the top of my head.

"Fine," I say. "Stay here. I'm going to have a look around."

"Ember." Their voice is full of warning. "We should stay together."

We're definitely in a tunnel. When I put my arms out, I can touch both sides without having to lean very far in either direction.

"I don't think we can get separated," I say, moving forward more carefully this time. "You rest. I'm just going to see where this leads. I won't be gone long."

Whatever they might say is cut off in a new cough. Their power pulses at me weakly, but at least the wild hungry feeling is abated. They can follow if they want to, but after a few minutes of crawling it becomes clear I'm alone. Good. I meant what I said. I won't go far and Kelly needs some rest. And I need some breathing room too. I'm worried. Scared, even. The way home is not a straight line and I'm only making things worse. We need to understand what's happening both in terms of Kelly's power and their health, though increasingly the two seem related. Step number one: figure out where we are.

My hands and knees ache as I crawl, but when I get closer to the mouth of the tunnel, a sound reaches for me, urging me on. It's faint at first, but as I move forward, it becomes clearer. A woman's voice sings a wordless melody, familiar but not something I know. Or do I? I stop, closing my eyes so I can listen. Her voice soars and winds its way like a hawk on a thermal draft, stretching to the horizon and all the way into the tunnel, echoing oddly off the walls around me.

"Ember?" Kelly calls. Their power tugs at me, though not in any physical way that stops my progress.

"It's okay," I answer. "I'm almost to the end."

The singing grows louder. It's beautiful. Melancholy. I should probably be worried, right? Afterlife isn't exactly known for its appreciation of the arts. Assuming we're even still in Afterlife. No one's ever explained the limits of sliding. Just like they don't think I should be worried about winding up in that in-between nothingness, why would a reaper ever worry sliding might take you anywhere else but the worlds of life and death? But as I reach the opening at the far end of the tunnel, it's like someone is singing a welcome just for me. The space beyond the tunnel is wide. I'm kneeling at the edge of a long slope that drops away slowly toward a shining pool of water. The sky overhead—if it is a sky—is dotted with hundreds of thousands of small white lights, and so is everything else. The rocks glow, like they're covered with luminescent paint, but when I look closely, the streaks are actually endless tiny dots, each one placed so close to the next they look like continuous lines and shapes. They go on and on in all directions, like they're being reflected in an infinite set of mirrors.

The singing is closer now. The song is so beautiful it brings tears to my eyes. I slide down toward the water. Something says if I can find the singer, I will find the answer to everything. Answers and peace. Calm. Relief. The melody promises me all the things I wanted when I first died. Maybe I still want them. It would be better than this. The uncertainty. The half truths. The way reapers talk to each other in a shorthand I will never fully understand until

I've also lived a thousand years . . . and probably lost all my humanity in the process.

The water ripples as I approach the shore. Something flashes just beneath the waves, maybe a fish. The power inside me tugs again, more urgently this time. I'll go back in a second, but first I creep closer, peering at the water. The voice is coming from beneath the surface. Is that even possible? I shouldn't be so doubtful. I'm dead and still making memories like the living. Anything is possible. What's an underwater aria?

Far away, a voice like Kelly's calls my name.

"I'll be right back," I say, without looking behind me. I can't look anywhere but at the water. Who is it? Will she let me listen a while longer? I have the sense that if I do, everything will be all right.

The flash comes again. It's bigger now. Not just a little fish like the ones that would nibble on my toes at summer camp. Something longer. An eel, or maybe a carp. I'm so close to the waterline my knees are getting wet in the sand. The water laps at my fingertips. It feels like the voice is coming from inside me. Like if I opened my mouth, the song would flow through me and out into the darkness.

"Ember!" Kelly's voice is closer now.

I put a hand in the water, reaching down. It's only a few degrees cooler than body temperature—or dead body temperature at least—so it almost feels like I'm floating through nothing, but when I twist my wrist the water sparkles as it swirls. Tiny glittery sparks dance between my fingers and I smile. Everything will be fine.

There's no warning before something breaches the surface, shooting straight up from the depths. It coils around my wrist, squeezing tight and I scramble back, falling away from the water. The tentacle comes with me, though the rest of whatever it's attached to stays hidden in the water.

The singing is gone. Instead, there's nothing more than a

scream. Oh, it's me. I'm screaming. Can't really blame me, what with the way the tentacle is wrapped so tight my hand throbs while suckers the size of bottle caps cling to my skin. It pulls, dragging me toward the water, even as I dig my heels in. Doesn't do much though. Not with the sandy shore that gives way beneath my feet. Not with the inhuman strength pulling at me. As much as the song was irresistible, the strength of this monster is more so. My free hand skitters in the dirt, but there's nothing to hold on to. I push my senses out, desperately reaching for Kelly's power, like it can pull me back to the tunnel, but all I get is the same feeble warning tug, then nothing. It's no match for whatever monster is lurking beneath the waves. I won't survive whatever is pulling me away from the land. This is it. Finally. Death. For real this time.

As I slide into it, the water turns cold. Freezing. It makes my bones ache. Another tentacle rises up, grabbing my ankle. I'm slipping in faster now. Only a few more seconds and it's like I'll have never been here at all.

"Kelly!" I call, even though it's too late. Water soaks through my pants. I kick with my other leg because despite everything I'm not going down without a fight. But the pull on my arm and leg doesn't slow for a moment. I might as well be a doll for all the difference my resistance makes.

The water is up to my chest. A third tentacle grabs my other wrist. I gasp as my lungs recoil from the cold. It's so senseless that even dead my body still wants to breathe, but that really is the least of my worries now.

"Kelly!" I tilt my head back, gasping as water spills into my mouth. It tastes nothing like the lakes of childhood swimming days. It's harsh. Burning. It will corrode me from the inside and—

Strong arms wrap around me, pulling back toward shore. The tentacle thing redoubles its efforts, swinging farther up my limbs, sucking deeper into my skin. But the arms around my chest are just as determined. The grip is crushing. Supernatural. They're the arms of someone who has lived for thousands of years and won't let anything as insignificant as a pissed-off octopus take me from them. Whatever unkind things I've ever said or thought about Kelly, about their stubbornness or their habit of hiding things from me when they think I'm too human to understand, it doesn't matter. At the end of the day, we're friends. Partners. They will always come for me when I need them most.

The tentacles snap like elastic bands, and the monster shrieks. It flails in the water, but it doesn't reach for me again as Kelly pulls me back up the hill. We're moving too fast for me to turn and see them. Rocks tumble down the slope as we climb, splashing into the lake below. The singing is gone, replaced only with the sounds of the monster thrashing in the water and the shifting dirt and stones around us.

Finally, we reach a flat spot, about halfway up from where I first climbed down. We're well beyond the reach of the monster and I sprawl backwards, closing my eyes as I gasp. Adrenaline courses through me and when I lift my arms, they're covered in welts. Perfect concentric circles like those awful suckers have burned me.

I laugh, just once. It shakes off the last of the fear and I'm left feeling better.

"Sorry about that," I say. "I don't know what happened. There was something singing to me. It was the sweetest sound. I needed to know what it was, but I think maybe—"

"It was a siren."

My nervous chatter skids to a halt. The voice behind me is not Kelly's. Not that Kelly can't change their voice, just like they can change their appearance. But right now doesn't seem like the right moment for them to randomly decide to look and sound like a young woman with a soft lilt to her voice.

I scramble around, feet sliding in the rubble and stare up at the figure sitting behind me. She smiles down. Her hair shines, white and iridescent in the gloom, with little elfin ears that poke up from the strands. Her grin, as she gazes down at me, is bright and childlike, as though we haven't just narrowly escaped a ravenous tentacle monster.

I thought that face might be a friend once, or at least an ally. And she was, until Zach blasted her out of HELL and I never saw her again. Don't even think about her most days because my head is full of acronyms and questions and frustrations about things I'm increasingly sure I'll never be able to change.

"Cerise?" I say, voice hoarse with strain and astonishment.

Her smile widens as her fairy features dazzle me. She was sent to collect a bus crash full of children once. They looked at her like she might be an angel, and maybe she is, after all.

"My name is Sareesha," she says. "What's yours?"

chapter
ten

DEAR SPARKS, if you're new here, allow me to provide a quick recap:

Cerise is a reaper. She's one of the closest things to a friend I've seen Kelly have at Afterlife. But she was also helping Zach build his Other Life, and whether she knew it or not, being a part of that meant releasing lost souls back into the living realm under the pretext of promising them reincarnation, only to actually be using them as bait and a distraction for the quarantine team so the reapers didn't notice Zach creeping closer and closer to HELL's back door. But being the sidekick comes with risks, and the last time I saw Cerise, Zach wasn't happy she'd told us his plan, and she was getting blasted out of HELL to parts unknown.

Guess we're in that part now. It's still dark, with only the gentle glow on the stones to light the way. The singing is gone and with its departure, I feel clearer. Something about the voice had taken control of me, to the point I could ignore everything else.

I gasp. "Kelly."

Cerise's placid gaze turns into an excited smile.

"Who's that?"

"Ember?" Their voice comes from above. They're kneeling in the tunnel opening. I can't see them so much as they make a dark outline that blots out some of the glowing lights. I scramble upward, kicking rocks back down toward Cerise, though she quickly overtakes me, moving faster than a human—or even a reaper, that I've seen—can. Kelly recoils at her approach, and I hurry to catch up.

"Hello!" Cerise sounds delighted as she pulls them into a tight hug. Their arms stick out straight, like they're afraid to touch her. "What are you doing here?"

They grunt, straining for breath. "Where exactly is here?"

She releases them, spreading her hands and spinning in a precise circle, which is an impressive feat considering we're still standing on the hillside.

"It's the Other Side," she says, voice trilling with joy. "Where did you come from?"

Something weird is going on.

"What's the Other Side?" I ask. Afterlife, Other Life, Other Side. The naming conventions make my head hurt.

Cerise laughs again. It doesn't sound like she's laughing at me so much as she finds the whole situation amusing. Has she been here this whole time? It might explain the giggling. I'd be a little delirious too if I'd spent the last however many months by myself on the side of a dark hill with nothing but a tentacle monster for company.

"The Other Side doesn't exist," Kelly says. "It's a m—"

"If you say it's a myth, I'll push you in the river myself," I say. Kelly is no longer the authority on what is and isn't real.

Cerise tsks and shakes her head. "I wouldn't do that. The siren will be angry you didn't join her. She'll be extra hungry now and very happy to devour you, especially since"—she gives them a considering glance—"you don't look like you'd put up a fight. Are you okay? Do you need some soup?"

The dark cavern spins around me, lights whirling. An arm wraps around me, and this time when my vision clears, it's Kelly. We're both on the ground, and if I look half as bad as they do, we're definitely worse for wear. My fingers are tangled in their sleeve and I feel like if I let go, I'll wind up rolling all the way back down the hill.

But Cerise doesn't seem at all worried about our struggling state. In fact, she doesn't seem to know who we are or really care about what we're doing here. Her gaze is upward, toward the top of the hill, and she drums her fingers on her stomach to a rhythm I can't hear.

"Are you hungry? I'm hungry," she says. "Come on. I know a place."

There's a softness to her posture and her smile that doesn't match the harried and passionate reaper I met. She might have made some unfortunate choices along the way, but she had convictions and empathy. Now it's more like she's not even really aware of us or her surroundings. We could be anyone and she'd still be thinking about the all-hours Other Side diner just out of sight.

As if to prove the point, she climbs without even a backward glance.

"That's not Cerise," I say.

Kelly makes a wordless noise of agreement, eyes on Cerise as she scrambles up even higher.

"You okay?" I ask. "To climb, I mean. We probably shouldn't stay here." At some point, the siren tentacle thing will start singing again. I don't know if I can resist it, even knowing what it is now, and even if I'm dead, I'm very sure I don't want to know what happens when the water in the lake closes over my head.

Kelly breathes heavily as they get to their feet, but they nod. "After you."

In fact, we go together. Even I'm flagging now. We climb and stumble, keeping one hand on each other and the other for stability. While the incline from the tunnel to the shore was gentle enough, the pitch from here to the top is much steeper. Cerise is more than halfway to the top while we're still only twenty feet from the tunnel and for a minute, panic returns, telling me this is a bad idea. Aren't you supposed to stay where you are if you get lost and don't know the way out? But that advice is meant to make it easier for someone to find you, and no one even knows we're here. Minerva left us in the meal hall, and even if someone goes looking, Earp will say he sent us to the library, and Buela will have no more information than that, assuming she isn't buried under all those books.

Shit. The book. *The Haunting of Reapers* or whatever it was called. I couldn't keep it and Kelly, but I regret not having it right now. I'd much rather sit down and do a little light reaper reading than follow after Cerise who is taking us who knows where. But the book is gone and we can't stay here. Wherever Cerise is headed, there might be others there. Maybe someone can help us.

The climb is excruciating. We spend more time resting than making painfully slow progress to the top. When we finally reach the last ridge, Cerise is sitting on a low flat rock. She has one leg crossed over the other, and one of her feet bobs an impatient rhythm.

"Are you coming?" she asks. "It's jerk chicken today. They always run out. We have to hurry."

I have so many questions. It's like someone completely different is wearing Cerise's face. And who lives in this place? Why would they need to eat? And where the heck are they getting the ingredients for jerk chicken? At the top of the hillside, we're standing on a long sandy path that drops out of sight beyond the next rocky ridge. The landscape on either side is barren, like the set of a sci-fi movie on some distant planet. No one's planting crops here, or there's definitely not anything that would keep a flock of chickens fed until they were big enough to become dinner.

But my stomach is indifferent to these issues and lets out an unexpected growl. Literally the first sound it's made since I died. Even Kelly takes an astonished step away from me, but Cerise only smiles, clapping her hands excitedly.

"See? You're hungry too. Let's go." Once again, she hops to her feet and sets off, leaving us to follow or not.

I glance at Kelly, but they give me a shrug and say, "I could eat."

At least the walking is less treacherous than the climb. And a path signals some kind of civilization, doesn't it? Like Cerise isn't the only one out here after all.

The ground beneath our feet is silent. At a distance, the singing resumes and reflexively I take Kelly's hand.

"I suppose sirens are a myth too?" I ask, shuddering at the memory of how I'd followed the song down a strange hill without a single thought for my well-being or what would happen to Kelly after I went for my swim.

Kelly huffs out something that might almost be a laugh. "Are you going to push me in the river if I say yes?"

A long time ago—on the same day I last saw Cerise actually—Zach was facing down Minerva with an army of radicalized lost souls at his back and he asked her if she thought reapers, wraiths and ghosts were the only things that existed. His tone implied he had seen some shit in the years he'd been left to wander alone after falling through the many and incredibly wide cracks of Afterlife administration. Did he mean sirens? I'm still not entirely even clear on what a siren is. Nothing in the living world's legends about beautiful women dragging sailors to the deep mentioned tentacles. Or is there something else? Maybe the price for a good plate of jerk chicken out here is a couple unwitting souls—or one confused lost soul and an ailing reaper—and Cerise is luring us to our doom after all.

But as we round another curve in the path, lights appear on the horizon. Real lights, not just more glowing rocks. They flicker and dance until it becomes clear they're torches mounted on polls, lighting the way into an actual settlement. It's rudimentary, with canopies strung over more posts. As we enter the encampment—how many tents do you need to make a village?—curious faces peer at us. A few even venture out to watch us pass. Cerise waves and greets some of them and they wave cautiously back. They're people, or at least they're human-shaped, though some flicker around the edges, or they appear to float above the ground, with only the top half of their bodies showing. Some are illuminated with the same glow as the rocks. A few others hobble forward on twisted limbs, and their skin is streaked with black ooze like you see with wraiths, though they don't make any move toward us, and a few even speak coherently to Cerise as she passes. Lost souls, then.

"Where are we?"

For once, the question is Kelly's, not mine. It's cute they think I have any answers.

"The Other Side, I guess. The other side of what remains unclear."

"The other side of the dark river," Cerise says over her shoulder. She makes a hard right turn into one of the tents and we follow after her. There's something to be said for reaper literalness. No need to guess how they came up with that lake.

"So how do we get back to the other side?" I ask. Didn't look like there was a boat anywhere close by. Or a bridge. "I mean the first side. The *other* other side. Back to Afterlife."

"You don't," a new voice says. A tall man is sitting by a small fire. His face is hidden in shadow, but when he leans forward, his skin is grey. And I don't mean pale like he's unwell. Slate grey. The colour of a winter sky before a storm. It's like he's made of stone, but when he gives us a cunning smile, his face is too smooth and supple to be anything but skin. "You brought guests, Sareesha?"

She nods eagerly. "Kelly and Ember. I found them on the hillside." As we get closer, Cerise—though apparently, she uses a different name now?—rushes ahead, collecting bowls and spoons from a woman standing behind a wooden counter. It's like a more rustic version of the HECK dining hall. Cerise pulls the lid off the pot cooking on the small fire, and the space fills with an aroma that has my mouth watering.

"OMG, you really did mean jerk chicken," I say, watching transfixed as she spoons stew into each of the bowls before passing one each to me and Kelly. My stomach growls again, and I nearly collapse onto a low stool. My hands shake in my haste to get the spoon to my mouth and it's only in the last second that I catch the watchful gaze of the man and remember he had a question.

"You crossed the dark river?" The grey man's voice is a rumble like a thunderstorm.

Regretfully, I set my spoon down. No free meals, I guess. I'll have to answer his questions.

"I don't know. We were in HECK and we slid here. I mean, not *here* here. Just away from there. I was trying to get back to Toronto and—"

"You're a reaper?" he asks, arching an eyebrow. The man could be anywhere from forty to four thousand. He carries the same gravity that Kelly does . . . or at least the way they did before they got sick.

"A lost soul," I say. "Kelly's a reaper, like Cerise."

"Who's Cerise?" he asks.

I blink, trying to piece together the puzzle in front of me, but I might as well be fumbling for pieces in the dark. I point at Cerise. "We know her. Or knew her, I guess. Her name is Cerise and she is a reaper."

"I'm not a reaper," Cerise says, sounding indignant like I've just accused her of being a worm.

Kelly's attention snaps to her with a frown. "Not a reaper? Then what do you think you are?"

She smiles, before putting a finger to her lips on a quiet "shhh."

"Okay." I spring to my feet, nearly upending my meal in the process. Cerise makes a diving catch to save it. "Enough with being cryptic. I'm Ember. I died last year, bounced back and forth between Toronto and Afterlife and now I'm a lost soul. This is Kelly. They're a reaper and have been one for thousands of years." I point at Cerise. "You're a reaper. We met not long after I died. At a bus crash."

She's still smiling at me with a childlike innocence that is becoming increasingly creepy, but she says, "I don't remember a bus crash."

"Don't remember?" I ask, my voice creeping up higher. It would be hard to forget. "Nearly fifty children died."

Her smile drops away. Her hands go to her mouth and a tear slips down her cheek.

The tent gets quiet. Along with the seated man and the woman at the counter, there are a half dozen others gathered around a small wooden table close by. Once again, I have to wonder how this desolate moonscape has things like wood to make furniture—or to burn.

When Cerise doesn't say anything else, I turn on our host, because I'm on a roll now.

"And you? Who the heck are you?"

The man smiles his predator's smile again. He's not someone to be messed with, but increasingly I find I don't give a shit. He studies me for a minute longer, and I force a spoonful of chicken in my mouth to keep from talking.

He says, "You can call me Smith. And this is the edge of the Other Side."

Smith. Great. John Doe would have been more helpful.

"And you're a lost soul?" I ask.

"A shade," he says, sitting back with satisfaction, like I've passed some test. I eye Kelly, expecting them to declare shades are myths, but they don't say anything. In fact, before I can ask more questions, Kelly coughs, making their power ripple out erratically. Then they cough some more, harder this time. I put an arm around them, holding on tight. I half expect them to accidentally zip us away to somewhere unfamiliar yet again. What comes after the Other Side? The Other Place? The Next Place? But we stay put as the coughing racks Kelly over and over again.

The lost souls—or shades, or whatever they are—around us shift nervously, like they're afraid Kelly's plague might be catching. Even Cerise takes an uneasy step away. Only Smith doesn't move or even blink. If anything, he leans in closer, watching as I slowly help Kelly lie down when it's clear the coughing won't stop. Are they going to have another seizure? How much longer will this last? How much longer can *they* last? They don't get to leave me alone with these weirdos.

Smith watches us shrewdly, though he doesn't make any move to help. Fortunately, Kelly doesn't seize. The coughing fades, but they remain lying on their side, curled protectively around themself. I keep one hand on their shoulder, rubbing gently in a circular motion, though whether I'm comforting them or myself is unclear.

"Very interesting," Smith says.

I hang my head. I wanted to keep this quiet, but there's no hiding what's going on.

"Kelly's sick," I say.

"For how long?" he asks. His gaze is intent. It's the opposite of our visit with Richard, who barely even looked at Kelly before fucking off to Portugal or wherever it was he went.

"A few days," I say, though I'm not even certain about that. How long since we left Toronto? How does time work here? A few hours at the Other Life with Zach was the same as a few weeks for Kelly and Jupiter.

"And how long have you two been together?"

Heat creeps up my cheeks and I pull my hand away from Kelly. Jupiter's question about whether I was in love with them rings in my ears. I'm not. The last thing I need in my afterlife is a hopeless crush on a reaper who practically views humans as a separate species.

"Oh no, we're not . . . We don't . . . I'm a lesbian."

Yeah, Ember. Real smooth.

His lips twist with amusement before he shakes his head. His tone is patient when he says, "I wasn't asking if you were involved romantically. I meant how long had you been living in close proximity?"

Is it possible to die of embarrassment if you're already dead? I'm certainly doing my best to find out.

"Almost a year," I mutter. "We're roommates."

"And when did you decide to start haunting each other?"

My head snaps up like it's on a spring. Even Kelly pushes up to their elbows looking astonished.

"Decided?" they ask. "Haunting isn't a decision."

Smith smiles knowingly. Pretty sure he's about to tell us a joke I won't find funny in the slightest because we're the punchline.

He lifts his chin, staring Kelly down. On a good day, when Kelly was at full strength and dripping with their usual aloofness, their confrontation would be a clash of titans. Today, it's more like a Great Dane staring down an aging dachshund with back pain, though even sick as they are, Kelly won't appreciate the comparison.

"I've heard that some of the old lore has been lost at Afterlife," Smith says. He might as well be stroking his chin as he speaks. The sage on the mount watching his creation struggle to understand the scale of their existence. "What do you think haunting is?"

"It's contamination," Kelly says quickly. "Reapers aren't meant to spend too long among the living. We're incompatible. Their energy wears us down and—"

"If that were true, would you not be improving now that you've returned to Afterlife?" Smith asks. He gives me a wink, like we're both in on a joke I've never heard before. Or is he teasing me because I'm the contamination in question?

Kelly's brow furrows stubbornly. They don't like to be laughed at and they're mustering for an argument. Maybe I should be taking cover after all.

"What is it?" I ask, mostly to head off any potential fireworks. I put a hand on Kelly's chest, placing myself between them and Smith. "Reapers have a bad habit of dismissing what doesn't fit their standard operating procedures or filling in the gaps with half answers."

Smith chuckles, fingers curling on his knee.

"You're strong, aren't you?" he asks. "That's why you've lasted this long, even though Kelly's soul was missing a piece from the start."

I don't respond to the compliment. He's mastered the reaper art of letting people expose themselves by leaving trailing sentences dangling in the silence. He smirks, clearly recognizing I know his trick.

"Let's take a few steps back, why don't we?" Smith says finally. "Sareesha." He lifts a hand and she scurries toward him. There's a lightness to her movements that is still so completely different from all the reapers I've seen. They're always so restrained. After hundreds and thousands of years, nothing gets a reaper excited, but Cerise's expression is ecstatic as she crosses to his side. He pats her hand as she kneels next to him. "Do you know these two?"

She giggles and shakes her head.

"But you know her?" he asks us.

"Yes. Cerise," Kelly says. "She worked with me at the SRU."

"My name," she says on a petulant inhale, "isn't Cerise."

"We know," Smith says, patting her. "I think what we have a case of is mistaken identity. You knew a reaper named Cerise, and this"—he smiles down at her again—"is the child that reaper was before she died."

chapter
eleven

I'LL BE the first to admit that in the months since my life ended, I have experienced some weird shit. Ghosts, wraiths, cats that might be gods, and immortal managers who have clearly never heard of the Peter Principle. Being promoted to the level of your incompetence takes on a whole new meaning when you have that job forever.

But when Richard said that reapers were humans without the memories that defined their humanity, I believed those parts didn't exist anymore. When the reapers went to the archives in search of lost identities, I assumed they'd find them in an old ledger. A name and some facts on paper, but nothing more tangible than that.

And now Smith, whatever or whoever he is, wants me to believe that those missing pieces are out here walking and talking like this is how they've always been? That they can climb mountains and eat jerk chicken? If Cerise (or Sareesha? It's interesting how close those two names are when the person in front of me doesn't know the reaper existed) wasn't sitting right here, I'd laugh and say clearly Smith's got his facts wrong.

To prove the point, Kelly, of course, snorts dismissively. "What do you mean, the child she was? That's not possible." Because why ask questions when you can just dismiss the thesis outright?

Smith catches me rolling my eyes and raises a fresh wry eyebrow in my direction. I don't like that he thinks we're on the same side. Who wouldn't be exasperated in the face of Kelly's obstinacy? That's not a fair test.

"You know how reapers are made?" he asks. His verbal merry-go-round is making me dizzy. And what does how reapers are made have to do with haunting? Is the part of who Kelly used to be about to pop out from behind a tent flap and shout "boo!"?

I glance around. Kelly is still staring stubbornly. Cerise—though apparently that's not the Cerise I knew—is humming softly to herself. The others have abandoned their conversation and are watching intently. Some new arrivals have gathered by the tent's entrance, inspecting us curiously. The dim lighting and the heavy cloth overhead make me think of an old-timey mining camp, and of people gathered around campfires telling stories because there are no phones. No streaming. We are the most interesting thing to happen to them today, and they want to hear all the surprises and revelations.

"Reapers are the souls who don't burn out," I say. "Richard takes their memories so they don't get hung up on human feelings when they're collecting souls."

That's what Richard said, anyway. Though right now, I'm not sure that's true. Or the whole truth. Because if reapers dismiss things left, right and centre as myths, Richard probably doesn't even think about the words that come out of his mouth half the time. He's like an AI text generator that just puts the words in an order that makes sense, without any real confirmation as to whether they're factually accurate or not.

"Is this the part where you tell me reapers really emerge from slimy pods like aliens or something?" I ask.

Smith's grin turns catlike, reminding me of Carrot Stick.

"You're fun. I like you." He clears his throat as he stands. "But you're correct. Their humanity is taken and the memories come here. Some of us anyway, Sareesha included. I believe she had what you call scarlet fever. The part of her that remembered that life was discarded as worthless by Afterlife and found its way to the Other Side. We're a haven for those cast-offs, whether they are the total person or only pieces of them."

Sounds more like a cult to me, but Kelly once described souls as batteries on the landfill of humanity. Have we now tumbled into Afterlife's landfill? Or is it more like a thrift store? Animal shelter? My gaze shifts to Cerise. She's toying with the hem of her skirt, like she doesn't have a care in the world. It's unnerving. I didn't get a chance to know her very well before the whole debacle in HELL. But aside from her fairy-like appearance, everything about her is different.

"And you," I say slowly, because trying to come to an understanding of what Smith is telling me feels like walking through heavy snow. "You're all that? Memories?"

Smith presses his lips together in disappointment. "I already told you. I'm a shade. My soul is missing a piece, but it's not my memories."

"So you're a reaper?" I say, but I'm already sure I'm wrong.

Kelly makes a disapproving noise. I take their hand, silently telling them not to argue.

"Making reapers is only one of the possible outcomes when a soul loses pieces of itself. A shade is another. Some of those you see here are shades. Some are memories and carved-out identities. Still others aren't incomplete at all, but were the souls of powerful humans that Afterlife couldn't handle. Witches. Mediums."

Outcasts in life, outcasts in death. We'll discuss the fact witches are supposedly real later. If mediums like Jupiter and X exist, I supposed I have to believe Smith about witches too. Regardless, I can totally believe Afterlife might look at some of the newly dead who arrive at intake, the ones who don't fit the parameters for one standard human unit, and basically go "does not compute" before punting them off to parts unknown. Out of sight, out of mind. Not their job, not their problem. Is this Other Side where X and

Jupiter are going to end up someday? On the outskirts of life after death with the bits and bobs Afterlife didn't want to deal with?

"You're using a lot of words," I say with mounting impatience, "but not giving a lot of answers. She's a child who died of scarlet fever. You're missing a piece of your soul but you're not a reaper. This is all very interesting if I wanted to go to a seminar, but what I want is help for Kelly. If you don't know how to do that, we'll be going." Since we're already holding hands, I turn to leave. The gathered people (souls? Memories? Whatever. I don't have time to get into the nomenclature) part to make way for us. I'm pleased with my dramatic exit, but I have to swallow hard to keep from crying. Where are we even going to go? I don't know where we are and if we can't slide without hurting Kelly, I don't know how to get us out of here. The best we can do is follow the shoreline. Maybe we'll meet someone who was a supernatural doctor in a past life. Even I know we're reaching the end of what's plausible, much less possible. But I refuse to give Smith the satisfaction of being in charge a minute longer.

He calls after us. "If you don't stop the haunting, Kelly will be dead within days. Maybe tomorrow. Even now, you're draining the existence out of them."

Smith's voice is heavy. Satisfied. He's been waiting to share this verbal gut punch since we arrived. I stiffen, but instinct—or maybe a stubbornness I've learned from Kelly—tells me to keep walking. We don't need his help. But Kelly stops, feet dragging. They let go and step away. I feel the separation like a wound.

"Can you help Ember or not?" Kelly asks. It's the first time they've spoken in a while. Maybe they were waiting for the verbal jousting to be over. I kick myself for falling into Smith's trap of digressions. Also I'm annoyed that Kelly phrased it like I'm the one who needs support. I'm doing fine. They're the one who can't be left alone for fear they'll have another medical crisis.

"You can feel it, can't you?" Smith says with a flash of teeth, also apparently understanding to read between the lines of Kelly's question. "Maybe you even knew it from the beginning. But these days, just the closeness of her must feel like such a load. You're carrying it, but barely, aren't you?"

Kelly's jaw tightens and they ball their hands into fists.

"I'm managing," they say.

They aren't, though.

"Kelly, what is he talking about?" I ask, but they don't answer. They're having a wordless conversation with Smith. His smile is growing, like he knows he's winning their subliminal fight. I go to put an arm around Kelly, offering support, but when I touch them, they flinch in pain and step away. A shock emanates from my chest, like it has a few times lately. I gasp, putting a hand over it, but when I look at Kelly again, they're watching me too, and guilt flickers in their gaze like they know something they don't want to share.

The others around us shuffle, putting a little more space between us. I want to tell them it's not contagious. Whatever is happening, we're no threat to them. I'm no threat to anyone. As long as I have Jupiter's runes and I'm close to Kelly, then—

The world drops out from under me. Not literally, though of course that's always possible too. But in this case, I'm consumed with the falling sensation that comes the minute you get steamrolled by a terrible realization. Because Kelly said haunting happens when a reaper spends too long with people, and I assumed they meant *living* people. But my assumption could be wrong, and just because they said it doesn't mean it was true. I only believed them because it was similar to what Earp said. What if haunting isn't a general kind of thing? It's not broader humanity rubbing off on them, or using up their energy. What if it's just one human? A dead human.

What if it's me?

Kelly is speaking, but their voice sounds like they're underwater. Or maybe I'm the one drowning. I've been relying on them to keep me stable since I came back from Zach's Other Life. I stumbled back to the house and tried to attack Jupiter. The next thing I knew, Kelly was lying on top of me, telling me everything would be all right. And I believed them. I could feel it. They were going to protect me.

I focus inward, on the spot the pain came from in my chest. This time, instead of trying to calm it, I poke at it. Nothing happens. I concentrate, giving it a hard tug. Beside me, Kelly jerks and their eyes go white for a second before returning to their normal grey.

I didn't expect their protection would come at a cost. Reapers are powerful, and Kelly especially. I expected they could watch out for me with minimal effort. It's not like they ever put any real labour into anything besides beating their personal best score in their gaming obsession of the month. Maybe I believed they didn't even notice how much they were helping me. I've been thinking about using their power the way someone might sponge off a neighbour's Wi-Fi because they didn't bother putting a password on it. Convenient, maybe a little morally dodgy, but no one actually gets hurt.

Smith's gaze drifts toward me, watching as I rub the spot on my chest.

"I see you found it," he says. "Haunting is when two entities attach themselves to the same soul. Sometimes it's temporary, necessary even, to safely move a soul from one plain to the next. But if it goes on too long, it becomes a permanent connection. It's meant to work with two souls that are intact. Not if one soul is damaged or incomplete, like Kelly's became when you were made a reaper. Eventually, the deficient side of the connected souls loses the struggle for balance and the entity attached to it ceases to exist."

Death. The real death. That's what he's talking about. And he means Kelly. Days, Smith said. Within days, it will be like Kelly never existed at all.

I expect Kelly to protest at being called deficient. I certainly would. But instead they're standing motionless with their hands clasped behind their back. I desperately want to take hold of one. It's been our thing since the beginning. A little comfort for both of us. That's what I thought anyway, but maybe I've been kidding myself. Maybe I was the only one getting relief out of it, while all it's done is cause them harm. And that means I'm not better than a leech or a tumor, slowly taking what I need without a thought towards the other party. Despair threatens to crush me to the ground, but just like I've been underestimated over and over since I died, I'm stronger than that. If Smith is telling the truth, and I'm more parasite than partner, I know exactly what to do.

"So we sever the connection," I say, putting more confidence in my words than I feel. Let's be real, what I feel is terror and a shame so bitter I can practically taste it, even with my dead senses. "We go our separate ways and everything will be okay." I'll go live with Jupiter. Kelly's presence has always been more effective at keeping me steady than the runes, but they work. Jupiter and I can figure it out. And Kelly can . . . stay at Afterlife, I guess? Though that's hardly fair. They had a perfectly decent life in Toronto before I came along and started siphoning off them. I'm the one who was supposed to go to Afterlife. I can't take their home from them along with everything else. Doesn't matter though. Someone hand me a scalpel and let's get on with this. If I have to sit in an eternal waiting room listening to death metal and New Age music or go hang out with Earp and eat his endless stew for a few centuries, I'll do it.

Smith shakes his head. "It's not that simple. Disconnecting two haunted souls is not an easy process, especially when the two of you have been in close proximity for as long as you have. Every day you've spent together has knit the bond tighter. To undo it, you would need to be surgical, or it could fundamentally change who both of you are, or even destroy you both to the point there are no pieces left to put back together."

I can't help myself when I glance at Cerise. She's lost interest in our whole conversation and is drawing intricate patterns in the sandy floor. But that wouldn't be so bad, would it? One of us becoming our childlike selves is better than Kelly dying altogether, isn't it?

"How do we fix it? There must be a way," I ask, desperation rising up my throat like bile. I can't make myself look at Kelly, but I can still feel them, the way I always have. It's like a heartbeat. A pool of light that always stretches just far enough to wrap around me. The longer I can think about it, the more I can picture it. Every touch. Every brush of their fingers on mine. The overwhelming wash of their power as they came down the hall that first morning. I was looking for strength in an unfamiliar and unwelcoming world and they provided that. And in return, I undid them.

"I might be able to do it, but I would need help," Smith says slowly. "And of course, there would be a price for my assistance."

"Why would we trust you?" Kelly asks, gaze on Smith.

But we're running out of time for trust and negotiation. "Yes. Yes, anything." I don't even know what I'm promising. How bad can it be? A hundred years in HELL? Letting the siren slowly squeeze the life out of me with its tentacles? In case Smith has forgotten, I'm already dead. What's the worst he can do to me?

"I need you to find someone," he says, and his expression hardens, turning intent. This is serious to him. Whoever it is he wants found, they're someone who matters to him. "She's in the living world."

"Sure." If I had a pulse, it would be picking up speed. He wants help finding a living person? Does he not know about Google? I'm certainly not going to be the one to tell him. Let him think I have super people-finding powers.

"She's dead," he says. "She died in 1837."

Oh. That will be harder.

"So, she's a wraith?" I ask.

His jaw tightens, muscles rippling beneath his skin.

"She's not," he says.

"That's impossible," Kelly says. "No ghost could stay in the living world for nearly two centuries without decaying completely."

Smith's gaze flashes a warning. He doesn't like to be contradicted. I can't help myself when I put a hand on Kelly's shoulder, guiding them behind me. As soon as their out of firing range, I let them go, already mourning what I'm about to lose when our connection is gone.

"She was a resident here, but she left over a hundred years ago. Said she needed to go home. She wasn't supposed to be gone more than a year, but she never returned. Something must have happened to her. She's trapped among the living. If you can bring her back here, we can help you."

"I'll do it," I say. Whatever it takes, I'll do it.

"No you won't," Kelly says, sounding surprisingly resolved.

"Yes I will. You stay here. I'll get Jupiter and X to help. You stay safe and I'll be back as soon as I can." Why are we even arguing about this? They certainly can't go. Kelly looks like they're about to collapse right here. If they stay here, maybe Smith has some kind of reaper medicine they can take that will buy us a little more time. Or maybe there's an Afterlife equivalent of Uber Eats and we can get Earp to send more of his stew. That certainly helped Kelly, even for a little while. I'll be off to find Smith's missing woman and back before they can get any worse.

Smith shakes his head. "It's too late for you to go alone. You must know that, or at least sense it. Are you even able to be apart from each other? How much distance can you put between yourselves before—" His expression softens as he looks toward Kelly. It's so odd. Sometimes he looks like a benevolent father figure, and other times a cutthroat predator waiting for us to lower our defenses.

But I don't need him to finish the sentence. I can see it. We can't be apart and it's getting worse. The first seizure was when I went to Afterlife without them in Barrie. How far is that? It can't be measured in feet or kilometres. The second though . . . I was only a few shelves away in the library. How far could I go now? Feet? Maybe only a couple steps?

"We can't go back to the living world," I say, still looking for ways to keep them as safe as possible. "Not easily. Kelly can't slide."

But Smith waves a careless hand, like after everything else, that obstacle isn't an issue. "I can put a patch on your connection. A bandage, of sorts. Keep the worst of the symptoms at bay, and Kelly will be stable for a few days longer. Long enough for you to run this little errand."

"And if we succeed?" I ask. "If we find your friend and bring her back here?"

The leonine smile is back. The tension in his jaw is gone.

"If you succeed, she can help me undo your haunting. You'll both be good as new."

It sounds so easy, though nothing in Afterlife ever is. There's bound to be a catch. A quid pro quo that means the terms are never equal.

But if it means saving Kelly, that's what I'm doing. We can navigate the fallout later. No doubt Minerva, Richard, and maybe even Bang will be very interested to know Smith's out here, wherever *here* is. They may not have wanted these discarded bits and souls, but they also won't want them building a little community in the outer reaches. Eventually communities get ideas. Ambitions. So I have leverage. But also I'm the reason we're in this mess at all, thanks to my thoughtlessness when it comes to using Kelly as my personal backup generator.

I don't have room for more recriminations right now. First things first. Do Smith this favour. Save Kelly. Then get everything back to normal, whatever it takes.

"Fine," I say. "We'll do it."

chapter
twelve

SMITH'S "PATCH," as he called it, is nothing like a bandage. It's more like a ritual, and it hurts like hell. Actual hell, not the sanitized Afterlife version where everyone is kept separate for their safety and yours.

We're led out of the tent. Smith is at the head of our little procession and Cerise—I guess I should be calling her Sareesha—skips alongside, humming to herself. The others follow after, murmuring to each other.

"Do all memories wind up looking like the person they were, even though they're only a small part of that person?" I ask, more to distract myself from how every step Kelly takes beside me sounds like it's excruciating. Their breathing is laboured and the rigid way they carry themselves makes me think one hard push and they'd crumble into a million pieces before they even hit the ground.

"Sareesha is special. Sturdier," Smith says. "Maybe that's why the rest of her was made a reaper." Smith gives Kelly a knowing glance. "The fragments you saw on the hillside are where most of the reaper memories go. Sareesha is surprisingly vital. Most are barely bigger than a speck of light in the darkness."

I am about to say we didn't see anyone else on the hillside when his last words finally catch up to my thoughts.

"The specks? You mean the glowing bits on the rocks?"

"They aren't all from reapers. There are lots of ways to lose parts of a soul. Witchcraft. Possession. Some people willingly trade them away while they're still alive in hopes it will bring them special favours. Either way, they all seem to wind up here. More plentiful than stars," he says, gaze trailing off into the distance. I swallow down a mix of emotions. A little awe, because now that I know what I was looking at, the expanse of it is mind-boggling. A little dismay, because all those reapers who have gone off for the archives, like their old lives might have been kept a precious record, don't know they were really cast aside as cosmic junk.

"Does that mean the missing bit of Kelly's soul is out there too?" I ask, a new plan already hatching. Smith said haunting could be stable when both members had their full soul. We could find Kelly's. Reattach it . . . somehow. A little reaper reconstructive surgery. Watch out for infection, do the physiotherapy and boom! Problem solved.

There's a gentle tugging sensation in my chest, like something pulling at me from the inside. Now that I know what it is, the link between me and Kelly feels substantial, like a weighted chain that pulls me down. Have they been carrying this the whole time and I'm only just cluing in now? My muscles strain with the effort of holding myself up. Maybe I'm still holding Kelly up too, even if we're not touching. Joined souls. It should be romantic. My fifteen-year-old self would have swooned. I just feel guilty. I give them a furtive glance, but once again they're waiting for me, and when our eyes meet, they shake their head, silently telling me what I already know. We'll never find it. Smith said we had days left. We'll never find Kelly's little missing soul piece. It's not even a needle in a haystack. It's a needle in a stack of needles.

"Have a seat." Smith guides me to a flat stone. I sag onto it. Smith leads Kelly around to a second stone twenty or so feet away.

Their movements look like they're feeling every one of their thousands of years of existence. We don't have time for pointless scavenger hunts on the hillside. Smith has to help Kelly sit, and Sareesha joins them, sitting by their feet and patting Kelly's knee in something like reassurance.

The others who have followed us arrange themselves so that we're all in a circle. They all bow their heads and join hands and a rushing sensation spills over me. The hairs on my neck stand up straight like iron filings stretching for a magnet and I gasp when the connection between me and Kelly pulls taut. They sit up too, and I can practically see it, like a cable running from my chest to theirs. Around us, the circle of joined hands glows, intensifying until it's a band of light encircling us. Feels like someone should be chanting or playing some ominous music. But it's completely silent, which only makes it worse.

I try not to move, so of course an itch forms on my nose, followed by the feeling like a fleck of something has gotten stuck in my eye. Kelly frowns, then coughs. It starts more like a gentle clearing of the throat, but when that doesn't help whatever tickle they have, they cough again, and the sound quickly turns wet and hacking. The cord between us tugs, making me jolt, then gasp as pain shoots through me. My sternum feels like it's being pulled away from my ribs and I brace my hands on the rock, swallowing a scream.

"Patience," Smith says. "We have to find the point of contact and put the patch on. If it's uneven, it won't last as long."

The link between the two of us turns white hot. Kelly stops coughing, grimacing instead. The pain in my chest burns so hard my vision blurs and the world goes topsy-turvy for a minute. When it clears again, the circle around us has turned bright blue while a line of searing white cuts through the middle. I squint, and slowly, the line turns the same shade of blue, and the shattering agony inside me finally cools. There's a sizzling sensation, like hot metal quenched in a bucket of water. Kelly shudders. My nails drag over stone. The connection tightens, trying to drag me from my seat. Cerise is still sitting by Kelly's feet and she whimpers.

The line snaps, yanking me forward. The motion is familiar now, being hurled through time and space with no control. But just as suddenly as I was flung into motion, I stop. I'm back on the rock. And I'm looking at . . . me?

It's been a while since I've seen myself properly. Can't take a selfie and reflections aren't a thing when you're dead. But there I am, still sitting on the same rock across from where I am now. Red hair, ponytail, sweater and leggings. I—the other one, the one I'm looking at—am not moving. Her face is contorted in a grimace and even from this distance, I can see the white of her knuckles where she's gripping the edges of the rock.

"Kelly? Is that you?"

I glance down into a pair of childlike eyes set in a fairy princess face. Sareesha. Sareesha is sitting by my knee and she scrunches her brows into a frown as our gazes meet. Her hand is on my thigh, and when I put mine on top of it, the fingers are unfamiliar. Long, elegant. The skin is gently tanned, and the mole on the back of my wrist is missing. I'm looking at—

With no warning, I'm flung backward and, even dead, the impact of my head on the smooth stone surface makes my senses reel once more. It takes a moment to remember how to make my arms and legs work, and pushing myself back upright is one of the least graceful things I've ever done. When I do though, Kelly is watching me. They're staring from their rock and look like they've just been through the same thing, but their gaze is steady, and they even manage a smile and a shaky wave. It's so out of character for them that I laugh. My chest aches with the sound and I rub the space between my breasts, but the discomfort is temporary. Mentally, I nudge at the link. It's still there, but the weight isn't so heavy anymore.

What just happened? One second I was worried the weird

culty group was going to do something I'd regret, and the next I was looking at myself like I was having an out-of-body experience.

"Everyone okay?" Smith asks, the question rising like we've all just stepped off a terrifying but hilarious rollercoaster ride. I beg to differ. At the end of the day, rollercoasters teeter at the edge of control but are fundamentally safe. The details on what just happened are sketchy, but I don't think the safety bar—if that's what the others and their blue ring were—could be considered very reliable.

I haven't replied. Not sure I can. I'm shaking. Maybe I feel better. Hopefully Kelly does too. But I'm going to need another minute before I start forming sentences. Kelly bobs their head in something like a nod, then swallows hard like they're trying very hard not to throw up.

Smith chuckles. "Maybe we'll give you two a little time to recuperate."

I shake my head. "I'm okay. Tell me about who you want us to look for." But when I go to stand, my knees buckle and I crash down again.

"We should rest," Kelly says, voice soft. After a few more moments, I find it within myself to get to my feet. Kelly needs a minute longer, but when I hold my hand out to them, they take it and stand. I brace, ready for new pain, but the threat has passed for the moment. It's like it used to be. Relief. Comfort.

"Not that I want to do this again soon," I say slowly, "or possibly ever, but how long will the patch hold and why can't we just keep putting new ones on?"

Smith joins us, considering the question. The longer he takes, the more I think he wasn't sure it was going to work at all in the first place. Finally, he says, "A few days? I haven't had to make one in centuries. And it's like patching clothes in that we can't keep putting new ones on. Eventually, there's nothing left for it to hold on to."

I glance to Kelly. We're both looking a little threadbare.

Urgency thrums under my collarbone. We need to go. Find whoever it is Smith wants us to find.

But I take a step forward and my feet are like lead. Maybe we do need a little bit of downtime. A few hours. Reapers don't sleep. Neither do ghosts. If Kelly says it's time for a nap, it's time.

Smith leads us to a new cluster of tents. The interior is simply furnished. Wood, cloth. Everything is brown and grey. It's not a lot of ambiance, but there are two small cots with crocheted blankets like my grandmother used to make, and that's good enough for me.

The last thing I think as I lie down is I wonder if Kelly even remembers how to sleep.

When I wake up, I don't know how much time has passed. It could have been a few minutes or a couple centuries. For a moment, as my mind whirs back to life, I start my daily checklist of the things I need to do today. Make some calls. Update the content calendar. Is today a filming day? Or is today the day Lindsey and I were . . .

I open my eyes and I'm in the tent in that strange Other Side where the memories of reapers are scattered on the hillside like tiny sparkling diamonds no one will ever pick up. Lindsey, my best friend from my living life, is not here. Instead, I'm looking directly into Kelly's eyes. They're grey and quiet, but there's more colour in their cheeks than I've seen in a while.

"Were you dreaming?" they ask.

My ears get hot. Did they not sleep at all? The idea they've been watching me feels too personal, which is wild considering we're literally sharing a soul right now.

I stretch. My body still feels tried, but instead of the existential exhaustion from earlier, it's more like the day after a tough workout. The protest of worn-out muscles, rather than the mental strain of wondering what the future holds.

"Where's Smith?" I ask, swinging my legs over the edge of the cot. "We should get going."

"We don't have to," they say. "Go back to sleep."

Suddenly I'm very awake. Kelly has never been one for consideration. They'd tell me to get lost, but not to go back to bed.

"What do you mean?" Because they're not telling me to hit the snooze button. This isn't about five more minutes and then we'll get going.

Kelly sits up too. They look better. Stronger. They aren't using the cot frame for support. I should be relieved, but the improvement makes me wary. Harder to win this argument if they're running at full strength, and I'm pretty sure whatever they're about to say next is going to leave me no option but to win.

"We're not taking Smith's deal," they say.

Yup, there it is.

"Don't be ridiculous. He's the only one who has offered any kind of help. What are you talking about?"

They sigh. "We can go find whoever it is he's looking for. But not to undo the haunting. I've decided I don't want that."

Oh, for god's sake. Now is the time Kelly develops a sacrificial streak?

"Don't want it? Kelly, you're dying. I'm—" I nearly say that I'm killing them, but I don't want to make this about me. I've been selfish enough as it is. "You know what's happening to you. Smith says he can help us, and you're saying no?" Without any real thought, I rush across the small space of the tent—it's hardly more than two steps to get from my cot to theirs—and sit down. Let them tell me up close that they're done with this.

"I don't trust him."

"I don't trust him either, but that's not a good enough reason. We can't fix this ourselves, and no one else knows what to do either. So we're taking our chance with Smith while we can."

Their jaw has a familiar stubborn set to it as they say, "What if it's not me who dies?"

I laugh. "Who else would it be?"

Their expression shutters. They're withdrawing. Too close to some big feeling for their own comfort and they're protecting themselves. But I won't let them. Not now. Not when I'm the reason they're sick in the first place. I turn inwardly, finding the hot spot in my chest and tug gently. They stiffen, no doubt feeling the answering pull and the silent prompt for honesty that accompanies it.

"What if you die?" they ask. "Really die. Not like you are now."

The answer is a shock. I let go of the link, remembering at the last second I can't really escape it. And now it's Kelly's turn to pull on it, forcing my attention back to them. Their gaze is almost too sad for me to look at. We aren't having this conversation.

"No one is dying," I say firmly. "We'll fix this."

"Ember."

"No. No." I stand. The tent is too small for me to pace, so I walk a tight oblong shape between the cots instead. "No. That's not the answer. We're going to give up. That's what you're saying. Then what? You're just going to die?"

And that's when I hear it. The question. My question, but also my sister's.

You're just going to give up and die?

We were in the hospital. It was the day after my latest round of scans showed nothing was getting better. No amount of treatment moved the needle. The tumors were bigger than ever and there were more of them. The medication they were giving me was just as likely to cause a stroke as it was to save me, never mind the risk that I might get some random hospital infection and go from alive and fighting to septic and dead in the space of a day.

I was done. The remaining options were unacceptable. I gathered my family around me and told them the fight was over.

It went about as well as expected. My dad stayed silent, keeping his face turned to the window in the vain hope no one noticed him crying, but we definitely did. My mother sat in the ugly vinyl recliner next to my hospital bed, flipping through her phone whispering desperately about a clinical trial in Ireland. So it fell to my sister to deputize herself and speak on behalf of the family.

"You're just going to give up and die?"

That was exactly what I was going to do. And there was no shame in that. There's no shame in forfeiting when even the best remaining outcomes are all unpleasant. More pain. More nausea. Being too drugged up to communicate with the people I cared about. What was the point of sticking around for that?

But I'm not going to give Kelly that much grace. Is it hypocritical? Sure. Unfair? Probably. But this situation is different. I knew what was left for me. The cancer had won and now all that was left were the choices that would make my death less awful. That's not what we're facing here. Smith said Kelly was the one who was sick because their soul is the incomplete half. Why would they be worried about me? They can't be. It must just be a cover for their own fear.

They don't move away as I sit again and run my fingers through their hair. I study them. Grey eyes. Unlined skin that hides the stories of their millennia of existence. The hooked nose that made me think of a bird of prey when we first met. The thin-lipped mouth set into a grim line. Grim reaper. Kelly is scared, and that's understandable, but we're not at the end yet.

I put a hand to their chin so I can turn their beautiful face to look at me.

Then I kiss them.

I don't mean to. Or . . . right now I mean to. It's not like my plan was to bite their nose and at the last minute I swerve for their lips and soften the approach. I kiss them because I can't think of anything else to do. Because I need all their attention and some deep prehistoric part of my brain shouts this is the only way to do it.

Kissing Kelly is . . . well, it's not romantic. This isn't one of those movie scenes where we're both startled and freeze, maybe brush noses for a moment before they gather me up in their arms and soft music plays. But it's not as bad as I thought it would be . . . if this were ever something I'd thought about. It could be like kissing a mannequin, or a picture in a magazine. Cool. Unresponsive. And it's not that. Their lips move against mine. Their skin is surprisingly soft. The patched connection between us thrums, getting bigger, like it could even hide us away if we wanted to explore this a little more. Who knows if we would ever find a way to climb out again?

They don't follow when I sit back, though. Slowly, they roll their bottom lip between their teeth, making the skin turn a darker shade of pink. Their gaze turns inward, like they're trying to identify an unfamiliar flavour that triggers a long-buried memory.

"Why would you do that?" they ask without looking at me, but there's no accusation in the question. No heat or anger. Only utter bewilderment.

I can't explain, but I don't want their altruism either. That's not who we are to each other.

"Nobody is dying," I say, walking to the tent opening. "Let's go."

MY FACE IS on fire as we walk through the silent paths that make up the Other Side. More than once I trip over an obstacle that isn't there. Kissing Kelly has scrambled my brain. Not that I can show it. I can't answer questions, from them or anyone else. Or think about why that was the only solution I could come up with. All I can think is that Kelly was ready to die. It's hard to come back from that. I hurry down the path, assuming Kelly will follow. We don't have much time. Whether I meant to do it or not, I'm responsible for this. Kelly survived thousands of years before they met me. So I have to fix this.

Smith is back in the tent Sareesha initially took us to. He's reading a book. The cover shows a woman in a half-undone gown, embraced by two shirtless men in questionably snug trousers.

"*The Duchess Takes a Groom,*" he says, lifting the book in our direction as we enter. "Have you read it?"

How the hell do they get romance novels here? Or anything? My questions are endless, but only one matters right now.

"Who do you need us to find?"

His eyes narrow with pleasure. "Viola."

Viola. A name. That's the first step. Not a common one either, unless you're at an audition for *Twelfth Night*. Hopefully a little research, a little recon, and we can get this done ASAP.

"Anything else?" I ask. "Any other details? Maybe a last name, for example."

Smith huffs on a bemused smile. He's definitely the kind of guy who finds authoritative women amusing. Like it's cute when we speak up, but not something to be taken seriously.

He rolls his eyes and says, "Just Viola. She never told me her last name. They don't serve much purpose here. She died in 1837 in a town called Brockville."

"And you think she's still there?" At least a name and a town narrow it down. I've been to Brockville. Or at least, I've passed through it and maybe stopped for gas or a donut on my way to Montreal. It's not very big. Only so many places for a ghost to hide.

"If you know where she is, why haven't you gone to retrieve her?" Kelly asks.

Smith winces, looking uncomfortable for once. "As a shade, I can't leave the Other Side without risking a haunting among the living, at which point I'd be trapped there too. And even if that weren't the case, my last encounter with Viola didn't end well. If I show up there and tell her to come back, we won't get very far."

This is getting worse and worse.

Smith clearly sees my growing reticence because he claps his hands and makes a shooing motion. "That's all the information I can give you. Off you go."

Kelly and I glance at each other. I ball my hands into fists. I can't even touch them anymore, both out of fear it will make the haunting worse, and also because if I touch them, I'll look at them, then maybe want to kiss them again, and we don't have time for that.

"How would you suggest we get back to the living world?" I ask, though it doesn't come out loaded with sarcasm like I'd hoped. "Unless you want me to call a cab?"

He winks. Sareesha is close by and laughs like it's the funniest joke she's ever heard. I feel shitty to say, but I'll be glad to be away from her at least. The uncanny pairing of her familiar face and a stranger's personality isn't something I'm going to miss.

"The patch should hold for a few slides," Smith says. "You need to stay as close to each other as you can and limit sliding to only when absolutely necessary." He rubs at his chest dramatically. "Don't want that thing wearing out prematurely."

"Thanks for the warning." I think he's made his point. Find the ghost, get back here. No detours. No funny business.

No kissing, my brain adds helpfully. Kelly makes a soft noise beside me, but whether it's because they had the same thought or they're just trying to muffle a cough is unclear.

"Let's go," I say. If we stay much longer, I'm going to convince myself this is a bad idea, which will just send us through another round of Kelly's "let me die" speech and that's still a hard no.

"The patch should hold for another two days," Smith says, looking pleased we've agreed to his deal. "If you're not back by then—"

"Yeah, yeah, we'll turn into pumpkins." I pull Kelly's arm around me. Their palm against my hip is warm, and I have a split-second memory of my lips against theirs before the world goes sideways and we slide.

▭

Our landing is less than smooth. We crash into cool wet grass, rolling over someone's lawn. Kelly's got their arms wrapped around me, which softens the impact, but somewhere along the way one of their fingers gets caught in the shell of my ear, which is an experience I'd prefer not to repeat.

We lie still for a moment. Kelly's on their back and I'm on top of them, nose buried in their hair.

"You okay?" I ask.

"I will be when you stop grinding your knee into my hipbone."

I scramble up to my feet, apologizing. Kelly follows.

"Ember?" The front door of the house bangs open. "Kelly?"

Jupiter rushes into the front yard. X is close behind. The relief that rushes through me at the sight of them makes me sink to my knees again. How long have we been gone? Hours? Less than a day, surely. It feels like weeks.

"What happened?" Jupiter is asking breathlessly. "One second Minerva and Kelly slid away, then you were gone too."

"Then Minerva came back. Didn't say anything about where you were," X adds. "She just said she was late for a meeting and walked off."

Of course she did. Typical.

"You brought us to Toronto?" Kelly asks, looking horrified at our psychic homecoming party. "I thought we were supposed to go somewhere called Brockville."

"I figured we could use some help. We don't have much time. Put a few heads together and—"

"Not much time?" Jupiter asks, looking between us worriedly. "What do you mean? Where did you go?"

I close my eyes, waiting for the last of the spinning from our slide to stop, though the avalanche of questions isn't helping. A hand settles in the middle of my back. Kelly. They've done it before. Regularly, even. I've grown used to the small comfort, but now I yelp involuntarily and step away from their touch. Fear that any contact might make the patch wear out mixes with embarrassment that I kissed them—kissed!—earlier. What was I thinking? What are they thinking? Nothing I've ever seen from reapers indicates that they have any interest in kissing, sex or any sort of physical intimacy. They must know it exists, but no doubt they view it as just another silly human custom that they shed along with their old lives.

Unfortunately, X and Jupiter have stilled at my unexpected cry, so there's no way for me to play it off. Even Kelly is watching me with a worried expression. I can't meet anyone's gaze for more than a second. The neighbour who always seems to be out walking her shih tzu passes by on the sidewalk.

"Let's get in the car," I say, pushing to my feet. "Pack some stuff."

"Stuff?" Jupiter asks, still sounding confused. "What kind of stuff?"

"Snacks?" X asks hopefully, then his eyes go big with excitement. "Are we going on a road trip? Yes!" He doesn't wait for confirmation as he pumps his fists in the air. "Roommate road trip!"

He rushes back into the house without another word. Jupiter stays a bit longer to work out the logistics. Yes, we'll need snacks. Clean underwear and a toothbrush too.

"What about Kelly?" she asks, glancing at them. "Are you okay? You're feeling better?"

"It's a long story," I say, being careful not to touch them as I herd Jupiter back toward the house. "I'll explain once we're on the way."

It takes longer than I'd like. X tries to bring pretty much everything including the kitchen sink. Jupiter overthinks everything and tries to pack clothes ranging from a sundress to her winter coat.

"But if you won't tell me what's going on, how will I know what to wear?" she howls. Lip Balm appears in the doorway, joining in her wail. That makes her panic more, scooping him up and rushing to the basement.

"Where are you going?" I ask.

"I have to find his carrier."

"We're not bringing the cat." I should have taken the direct route to Brockville and called Jupiter and X to join us.

Finally, we get in the SUV. Kelly is in the driver's seat. Lip Balm is still in the house. I convinced Jupiter to text a friend who agreed to cat-sit. So that's one hurdle cleared.

"Are you sure you should be driving?" Jupiter asks. "What if you have another seizure?"

"It's fine," Kelly says impatiently. "The patch should prevent seizures."

"Should?" Jupiter doesn't sound confident.

"Yeah," X says. "Some of us are still alive and want to stay that way."

"And what do you mean by a patch?"

There's some explanation, and even more grumbling and negotiation, but finally we get underway. Kelly will only accept a demotion to the passenger seat. Jupiter drives. X and I are in the back. We're barely on the 401 before he's already busted open the veggie straws. They're like chips in that they're crispy and salty, but you can convince yourself they're healthy because the word "veggie" is printed on the bag in big letters. Man, I miss those things. They're basically savoury Styrofoam, but I used to be able to stuff about a hundred in my mouth before I realized maybe I was just bored instead of hungry.

We fill Jupiter and X in on our little adventure while we drive. Traffic is painful getting out of Toronto, but once we're beyond the communities that have slowly been swallowed by the GTA over the last half century, things circulate more freely. Lake Ontario glistens to our right, and slowly the subdivisions and big box stores give way to farmland.

"So you have to find this ghost who's been dead for almost two hundred years and missing for more than a hundred. She somehow isn't a wraith, she might be trapped, and you get to break her out of whatever supernatural jail she's in. After that, she'll break the connection and give Kelly their soul back?" Jupiter asks, sounding a little awed.

"Something like that," I say, laughing weakly. Beside me, X has his phone out and is searching through screens.

"Did Viola have a last name?" he asks, already sliding into research mode. I shake my head. "Because when I search 'viola

Brockville' all I get is a bunch of people advertising kids music lessons and obituaries for people with Viola as a last name. That's not much to go on."

"She died in 1837," I say. "Add the date and see if anything comes up."

He frowns, squinting at the phone for a moment, but then X's face lights up into his characteristic smile.

"Oh, here's one. Viola Reynolds. Wow, she has a Wikipedia page. Looks like her father was some bigwig rich guy. They had a mansion in Brockville, and when she was twenty-three, she fell down the stairs and died. Woah, that's super sad." He holds up the phone, showing me a picture of a serious woman in a Victorian-era gown. "Is that her?"

"I didn't even know her last name, you think Smith told us what she looks like?" But it's as likely as anything. The timing works at least. I glance at Kelly. Their head is bobbing, like they've fallen asleep again. Even with the patch, they're not well, so we're going with what we've got. "Does it say anything else about the mansion? Is it still there? Maybe she is too."

"The house was called Manor Rock," X says. "Oh hey, it's for sale. Looks like there's an auction happening. They're selling everything inside."

"When?" Jupiter asks.

"This weekend."

I snort. "That's very convenient." Not that I'm complaining. Operating on so little information, I'll take the fortunate coincidences when they come.

"No, really." He shows me the phone again and sure enough, a website shows a picture of a stately home and proudly announces a content sale and property auction. The house is straight out of a period piece film shoot, with grey stone walls, peaked gables, a wide porch that wraps around two sides, and a tall turret on the other side, keeping watch over the property. I can almost imagine men in stiff collars and women in corseted gowns walking around the front, remarking on how fine the weather is and gossiping about who called on who this afternoon. It's funny to think about those kinds of things happening in small-town Ontario, but they must have, just like they happened in places like London and New York.

By the time we roll into Brockville, it's midafternoon. X has exhausted his entire selection of snacks. Jupiter kept up a steady stream of questions the whole way, and Kelly napped.

"Do you think we're going to be here long?" Jupiter asks. "Should X and I find a hotel or something? And Kelly . . . I mean . . . Do you need to sleep some more?"

One step at a time. We passed a few chain hotels right off the highway when we drove into town. It's not a very big place, just like I remembered, and if we get stuck here for more than the afternoon, I doubt there will be any real difficulty finding a bed for the night. And with any luck, Smith will have sent word—how is irrelevant—that we're coming and Viola will be waiting for us on the verandah. A quick "hi, how are you? I love what you've done with the place" and we'll be back on the road before it gets dark.

The town centre is lined with old two- and three-story buildings, many of which proudly display their construction dates. 1851, 1899. It's a lot of stone and brick. The ground floors have been converted to storefronts, while upstairs looks mostly like apartments. It only takes a few blocks though before the commercial buildings give way to more space. Old homes with mature trees. A few have been modernized, but most still bear the gabled windows and gingerbread trim that denote architecture from more than a hundred years ago.

Manor Rock faces the water—we're beyond Lake Ontario and now staring at the St. Lawrence River—at the bottom of a winding road on the town's east end. Cars are parked on both sides of the street. Viewers coming to scope out items before the auction, I guess. They make the road so narrow that Jupiter has to creep past them, careful not to hit our mirrors on either side, and X looks like he's holding his breath. Finally, we come to a wide semicircular driveway, where an attendant in a reflective vest makes us go back the way we've come. We park almost all the way back at the main road, and walk back to the house. I keep an eye on Kelly, but they seem capable enough of moving under their own power for now.

"Yikes," X says as we approach. I have to agree. Manor Rock in front of us looks nothing like the auction post. The basic framework is the same as the picture we saw. The gabled windows and turret are still there. The wraparound porch is too, though it slumps ominously on one side and mortar between the concrete steps is cracked in some places or missing entirely in others. Perhaps most egregiously, some previous owner decided it would be a good idea to cover over the original stone facade with peach-coloured stucco.

"Yikes is right," I say. The stucco has fallen away near one corner of the roof. Beneath the windows, it is stained with mouldy-coloured streaks that run down the walls. Some of the windowpanes are boarded over with plywood. The paint on the shutters peels. The place looks half abandoned.

"Guess they're not looking for top dollar in the auction," Jupiter says. "What a dump." She rubs at her arms, even though the afternoon is sunny and clear.

"You feel it too?" X asks. For once, his expression is uncertain. He's staring at one of the windows on the top floor.

"Something," Jupiter says. Her gaze has gone unfocused, the way it does when ghosts are close by. "It's not happy."

If I were still alive, I'd probably laugh. Her statement is hilariously ominous when you don't know what creatures go bump in the night. But I do. Technically I'm one of them.

"You think it's haunted?" X asks.

"Would you like it to be haunted?" The question comes from an elderly woman standing at the front door. Her snowy hair is cut short, and she wears a plaid shawl over her shoulders. A silver name tag is pinned to it and reads "Brenda." She hands Jupiter a thick copy of the auction catalogue. "Some people don't like the idea of buying a haunted house."

"So, it *is* haunted?" Jupiter asks.

Brenda grins. "It can be if you want to. Do you believe in ghosts?"

Everyone glances at me. Well . . . everyone except Brenda, since she can't see me or Kelly. If only she knew there was a real ghost right here.

"We're interested in the family that lived here," Jupiter says.

Brenda shakes her head. "The family doesn't want to be bothered. If you have any questions about the auction, I'd be happy to—"

"The Reynolds family?" X asks.

Brenda pauses in her sales pitch. "No. The Emmanuelle family. They're the sellers. They moved to Vancouver after their grandfather died in 2005. He was the only one living here. The Reynolds were the original owners, but they haven't lived in this house since the mid-1800s. It changed hands a lot until the Emmanuelles bought it in 1997."

Another wordless glance between our little group. Do those hands include any Reynolds family ghosts?

"If you're interested," Brenda says quickly, clearly noticing we're not here for real estate chitchat, "I believe there are some old paintings and jewelry that belonged to the original family up on the second floor."

Good enough. We're doing all this on a wing and a prayer right now anyway. Maybe we'll be lucky and find Viola hanging out upstairs telling people to stop touching her stuff.

We make our way through the house. While the exterior is marred from neglect and unfortunate updates, the inside is perfectly preserved. Everything is dark wood and chandeliers. The stairs creak as we follow their winding path upwards. The walls are decorated with carved leaves and woodland scenes. It may not look like it from the outside, but someone spent a lot of money on this place once.

Unfortunately, while the woodwork and interior decoration is expensive, it's entirely mundane. In the upstairs room Brenda mentioned, there's a small collection of landscape paintings the auction catalogue says belonged to Mr. Reynolds. A crystal ring holder that belonged to Mrs. Reynolds. An old rocking chair with a curved wooden frame and splintered whicker seat. No sign of the ghostly Viola, or anything supernatural.

But the whole time we're inside, Jupiter shivers. X pulls off his hoodie to drape over her shoulders. She gives him a grateful smile, but it doesn't stop her teeth from chattering. Without his hoodie, the hair on X's arms also stands up.

"What's wrong?" I ask.

"I don't know," Jupiter says. "I'm freezing and my head is killing me. It's like when we're close to wraiths."

"I haven't seen any wraiths," Kelly says. They hold a silver locket in one hand. The two halves are open, but when I peek over their shoulder, the insides are empty.

"Me neither," X says.

"Something's here," Jupiter says, walking a slow circle, before her gaze rises upward. "Maybe on the third floor?"

Yet when we go back to the stairs, a man with a shiny name tag like Brenda's is standing there. The staircase is cordoned off and he gives us a polite smile as we approach.

"I'm sorry," he says. "The third floor is closed. It's not structurally sound."

So what? Everyone looks around, trying to figure out what to do next. I roll my eyes. This is obviously my time to shine. I put a finger to my lips, then slip through the rope. The man with the name tag doesn't so much as turn in my direction.

"I'll be right back," I call over my shoulder.

"We'll be closing the house for the evening soon," the man says.

"If there's anything else you want to take one last look at, you've got another ten minutes, then . . ." His voice fades away as I pass through a door at the top of the next floor. The attic beyond is dark, full of cobwebs and dust. It's also entirely open, like it has always been unfinished, or else someone once knocked out all the walls, then either ran out of money or interest to complete whatever renovation they had envisioned. Abandoned sawhorses and disassembled scaffolding lean against the walls. Old paint cans with no lids lie on their sides.

I poke around, but aside from old paintings with torn canvases, a couple desiccated mouse carcasses and some disgruntled spiders, I don't find anything. No sign that anyone's been up here in the last decade, much less the ghost of a deceased heiress.

A sound like a door shutting and a lock sliding into place comes from behind me. I whirl, expecting to find a grinning jailer telling me I've fallen into their trap, but there's nothing there. Not even a door. Just more dark emptiness.

Sighing, I go back to the stairs. This better not be a wild goose chase. Wild ghost chase. How would a reaper say it? Wild duck pursuit, probably. Whoever or wherever Viola is, we aren't going to find answers here. I shouldn't have got my hopes up. It was never going to be this simple.

Jupiter is still chatting with the man at the bottom of the steps, and Kelly raises their gaze as I descend, which unfortunately means they see the exact moment I hit the barrier. One second, I'm about to step off the last stair, and the next, I might as well hit a brick wall. My nose and cheek smush against it, and I must look like a mime as my hands smack against an invisible blockade. X certainly sees me, because even though he's standing behind Jupiter, I still see him clap a hand to his mouth to hide a laugh. Yeah, thanks a lot, Alexander. That's really helpful.

Kelly clears their throat and nudges X, who, for once, takes the hint and pulls himself together. He starts into a very loud series of questions about jewelry design in the Victorian era and points at something down the hallway. The questions actually sound legit, and even the attendant perks up and allows himself to be led away.

"What's wrong?" Kelly asks.

"I don't know." I run my hands over the thing in front of me. It wasn't there when I went upstairs, but now it goes on as high as I can reach and from one side of the stairway to the other with no breaks.

I have no idea what happened or what's going on, but I know one thing for sure.

I'm trapped.

chapter
fourteen

I BANG on the barrier with my fist. It makes no sound, but it's undeniably there. Kelly puts a hand forward, and their palm slides through it like it's not even there.

"Wait," I say.

"What? We have to get you out." They dart their gaze all around, like they don't see what I see. The fact they can't makes me even more uneasy. I take their hand, the contact making me breathe easier, but when they pull me back, it's like we're dealing with two completely different things from our respective sides. Kelly's hand escapes easily, so they can drop their arm at their side. My hand touches the barrier and my knuckles crumple up against it.

When Kelly raises their hand a second time, I shake my head.

"Stop. We don't know what this is. What if you get stuck in here too?"

Their expression is serious. "You want me to leave you here?"

"Of course not. But we need to find out more about Viola. Where she might be. *What* she might be that Smith wants her." Me getting stuck here is not nearly as important as finding out if Viola is even close by. What if she's somewhere in the Amazon rainforest? Or on a meditation retreat in Tibet? What if she started her own cult somewhere farther down the banks of Smith's dark river and we're chasing our tails out here in the living world? "Take Jupiter and X and see if there's anywhere else in town you might learn more."

Their lips press into a thin line—which is saying something given Kelly's never been particularly well endowed in the lip department. Not that it stopped them from being a pretty decent kisser when I—

Stop, Ember. Now is not the time.

"What about the bond?" they ask. "We can't get too far apart."

I don't like the word "bond." It sounds personal. Intimate. It's a link. A point of contact. That's all. I study them for a second. Dark eyes, flowing hair. Somewhere on our road trip, since the patch has perked them up, they shifted appearances so that now they look like an emo beauty queen out for a weekend in the country. If I get stuck here for a long time, will they miss me?

Speaking of emo . . . Maybe I'm the one revisiting my teen years. Next I'll be slumped against the wall writing lyrics to songs that will never get played.

"The patch should mean we can be farther away from each other. Just don't leave town, okay?"

Kelly's watching me too, though the pinch between their eyebrows says they're in problem-solving mode, not cataloguing my features in case we never find each other again on our cosmic voyage through time and space.

They say, "Wait here."

I tap on the barrier. "Not going anywhere."

Then they leave. Jupiter and X reappear from one of the rooms with the attendant. X gives me a worried look, but Kelly corrals them and they all head back downstairs. Their voices trail after them. A few moments later, the lights on the second floor go out, and I'm left alone in the dark.

Just great.

Halfway up the stairs is a landing. I peer through a window

that shows the front driveway. Most of the cars are gone. I watch, Jupiter, X and Kelly emerge. One at a time, they look up toward me, but they keep walking. The link tugs in my chest as Kelly gets farther away, but not painfully so. More like a gentle reminder that it's there. How did I not notice it all these months? Then again, I walked around with tumours growing in my body and assumed I just needed to stretch more after Pilates. I can't be trusted when it comes to these things.

Below me, the sounds of the rest of the auction staff wrapping up for the night come and go. Doors closing. Questions called and answers given. The last of the lights go out and a heavy slam like the front door shutting follows. I am alone.

"Are they gone?"

I'm not ashamed to admit that I scream at the voice behind me. Nor that I feel some satisfaction when she screams too. She's young, white, with brown hair braided intricately in loops around her ears before being tied back behind her head. Her dress is nearly as wide as I am tall, belling into an enormous hoop at the floor. She stumbles backward and crumples into it, hands stretched out like she might have to fight me off.

"Please don't hurt me," she says, voice already verging on tears.

If her Victorian dress didn't give it away, the fact that I can see her in crystal clarity is a surefire indicator that I'm looking at a ghost.

"Viola?" I ask. Is it this easy? I nearly rush up the stairs again, ready to bang on the window and signal Kelly before they get too far. If she was just waiting for the staff to go away to present herself, we only needed to be a little more patient. But at the mention of the name, the girl on the stairs shrinks back even more, letting her massive skirts practically swallow her.

"Don't say her name," she says, frantically shaking her head. She's wearing drop pearl earrings and they swing wildly around her ears and throat as she does it. "She'll hear you. Don't wake her up."

Viola is grumpy first thing after a nap. I make a mental note.

We should have brought her a latte, and instead I'm empty-handed. Better and better. Every so often, I'm reminded that all I wanted was a peaceful afterlife with no more pain and inconvenience. Instead, I have . . . whatever this is. I never did get around to filling out that comment card about my post-mortem experience. Now I have even more things to add to it.

"Okay. Okay." I crouch, holding my hands palms up so she can see I don't want to hurt her. "I'm Ember. What's your name?"

She sniffs, looking at me with watery eyes. She's unnervingly pale, except for two pink spots on her cheeks. Her dress has a wide neckline that stretches over her shoulders. It should be pretty, but it's an unfortunate shade of green and the ruffles that adorn it make me think of organic leaf lettuce. Maybe she died at a costume party.

"Isabelle," she says. "Isabelle Brown."

"Okay," I say again, still trying not to scare her. "How long have you been here?" I put a hand out to touch the barrier. "Do you know what this is?" I bang my fist against it. There's no sound. Not even a muffled thump.

"One hundred and forty," Isabelle says behind me.

"A hundred and forty what?" I ask, without looking back.

"Years," she says. Now I turn, and she's wringing a handkerchief between her hands. I lick my lips in an attempt to steady my suddenly prickling nerves.

"A hundred and forty years?" I ask, just in case I misheard, but she nods, braids bobbing. I study her again. As far as I can tell, she's a ghost. Based on everything I've learned, if she'd been here in the living world for over a century, there is no way she shouldn't be a wraith by now. "Did you go to heaven?" Maybe she got taken up to Zach's Other Life at some point, then booted out as part of his bid to create more lost souls. But she only shakes her head, looking down at the frilly hem of her wide skirt.

Before I can ask any more questions, a rustling sound comes

from the floor above us, preceding another young woman in a ball gown who appears at the landing, her face pinched in a frown.

"Isabelle, are you coming? She'll be awake soon and—" Her eyes narrow when she notices me. "Who are you?" Her hair is brassier than Isabelle's but twisted up in a similar style. Her dress is a soft lavender and more elegantly decorated than Isabelle's lettuce ruffles, which is maybe to offset her harsher features. Her nose is too big to be conventionally pretty, and her eyebrows meet in the middle of her forehead with a ferocity that would make Frida Kahlo proud. A mole twitches on her chin as she pinches her lips together disapprovingly.

Isabelle, who by comparison has the kind of face you'd paint a portrait of if you wanted to marry her off to a titled landowner in England who only wanted her for her fortune, says, "Tiffany, what are you—" But she freezes, whirling back toward me with wide eyes. Her gaze fixes at something behind me and she gasps. "Someone's coming. Someone will see us. Hurry. We can't—" But the sentence is cut off as she and Tiffany both vanish, blinking out like they've both just slid off to Afterlife. But they weren't reapers. Or at least, not like any reapers I've seen before. Even though only Kelly has ever had that overwhelming aura I can feel from rooms away, all reapers have a signature. They're powerful, even the newest among them. But now that they're gone, I don't feel anything from either of those two girls. Not so much as a zing or hum in the air.

My musings are cut short though as pain seers through my chest. It makes my vision go white and I gasp, doubling over. There's the sound of something heavy hitting something solid behind me, followed by a muffled "oof." I yelp and hop up two steps before I turn to find Kelly sliding down the invisible wall like a bug getting smeared down a windshield.

"What are you doing here? Are you all right?" I ask, rushing back to them. They're on the other side, so I can't touch them, which is unfortunate, because a red mark like the beginning of a bruise is already forming just beneath their eye and I want to make sure they're okay.

"Plummy," they say as they settle on the carpeted floor with a muffled groan. They probably mean peachy.

"Why is it solid on your side now?" I ask. "And why did you leave the others?"

"It wasn't exactly." They roll to their knees, shaking their head and working their jaw like they've been punched. "One moment we were in the car, the next I was falling through space and running into"—they fumble until their palms are flat with the barrier—"this." Kelly rubs at their chest like something hurts. Somewhere along the way, their goth girlfriend persona is gone and they're back to the reaper I'm used to. Blue hair. Leather jacket. But the welt that's rising on their cheek is new and unnerving. Reapers aren't prone to bruising. Kelly's not as all-powerful as they once were.

"The patch," I say.

"Not as strong as we hoped." They wrinkle their nose and flex their jaw like they're making sure nothing is broken. "Did you make any progress on finding a way out?"

I shake my head, knocking in silence against the barrier. "No. But I met some ghosts. The place must be haunted after all."

"That's not what haunting is," they say.

I wave an annoyed hand. "The other kind of haunted. Not like me and you, tethered together on an invisible and unbeatable bungee cord. The human concept. Where ghosts linger in the places they died because of unfinished business."

"That doesn't happen," Kelly insists. "If they become wraiths, quarantine is dispatched."

"Well, these two must have slipped through the cracks. They were dressed like Viola was on Wikipedia, but they were—"

"If they died in your Victorian era, they would certainly be wraiths by now. Even Goran would—"

"Just listen for a second," I say. Now really isn't the time to debate reaper collection efficiencies. We have bigger problems. "They were afraid of her. Whoever she is. Getting Viola to come willingly might be even harder than we thought."

"Where did they go?" Kelly asks, looking behind me like they might suddenly reappear. "These ghosts who aren't wraiths, if that's what they are."

"They vanished. One moment they were here, then they said someone was coming and vanished, then you . . ." I mimic flinging myself against the invisible wall. Kelly doesn't look amused by my reenactment. Tough cookies. If we can't find the humour in this ridiculous afterlife, what even is the point of soldiering through it?

"They slid?" Kelly asks.

Something like that. I shrug. "It's not like they stuck around for me to ask more questions."

Kelly snorts. "They're obviously not ghosts. Ghosts can't slide."

For once, their insistence on absolutes gets on my last truly frayed nerve. One of us is dying, and yet somehow they insist on wasting time with semantics. They're not even trying to find an answer.

"Are you sure of that?" I ask. "Just like lost souls don't exist. Just like haunting is a myth? What is it exactly that you really know?"

"I know many things." They tilt their head, looking genuinely confused, but how can that be true when they think they know everything? I kick at the barrier and pain burns from my toes all the way up my shin. I swear in response before pressing right up against the thing, jabbing a finger at Kelly.

"You really are worse than no help." Anger makes my skin go hot, and the pain in my chest pulses a furious rhythm, like it's cheering me along. "You know that? No help whatsoever. You add nothing, you only dismiss ideas and observations that turn out to be true or useful later. When I tell you I saw a couple ghost ladies who can slide, what you should say is 'Wow, Ember. That's really interesting. I wasn't aware that was a possibility, but since you've witnessed it and I haven't, we should trust your observations. What else did you see?'" I can't help it when my voice lapses into a terrible approximation of their otherworldly accent. "Would it kill you to be just a little inquisitive about the world around you instead of thinking you've seen everything in the realm of possibility? No wonder you're dying."

The old house falls silent after my rant. Kelly's mouth has dropped open slightly. Their cheekbone is swelling noticeably now, making it look like they're squinting at me. Far away on another floor, the chime of an old grandfather clock rings. Once. Twice. We stare at each other until the clock strikes six.

Finally, Kelly says, "Since it appears I can't leave this house without you, I'm going to explore more. Perhaps there are more clues about the original family now that we no longer have the supervision of the auction staff. I'll leave you to investigate your new friends." Without another word, they turn, once again disappearing down the winding stairs that lead to the ground floor. It's almost like I've hurt their feelings, but how can that be possible when it's never clear if Kelly has feelings in the first place?

The link tugs as they get farther away, which only annoys me more. What a pain. Though the unexpected jolt in my chest right before Isabelle and Tiffany disappeared must have been the paranormal version of getting snapped with a spiritual elastic band. The idea of Kelly suddenly getting yanked out of the car and being hurtled through the ether just to get back to me is pretty funny. Romantic and slapstick at the same time.

It's possible I'm losing some marbles. The sooner we find Viola and convince her to come see Smith with us, the sooner I can be free of Kelly and this thing I accidently birthed between us. I will be my own ghost, haunting (the human kind of haunting, not the parasitic kind) ancient sites and tourist hotspots. There are so many places I never crossed off my bucket list. The pyramids. Vietnam. Christmas markets on the Rhine. If I finally decide to check them out while I'm dead, I won't even have to pay museum admissions.

But all of that requires me to get out of here first.

"Hello?" I call out to the quiet house. "Isabelle? Tiffany? Are you still there? My friend is gone." Hah. Friend. More like eternal pain in my undead ass. "You can come out now."

A fluttering sound comes overhead, like many skirts brushing over a hardwood floor. There's a tap-tap of someone in heels walking, followed by several more as others join her. The eerie sound of a single violin tuning winds toward me. Despite all my big feelings and brave thoughts, fear grips me and I look toward the empty hallway, half hoping Kelly will reappear so I can ask if they hear it too. But I'm a big girl ghost. I can fight my own battles and do my own exploring.

Slowly, I creep up the stairs. The violin is joined by other instruments, their sound part melody and part chaos as they prepare for a performance. As I get closer to the door at the top, hushed voices become audible.

A cobweb that spans the entire width of the space hangs in front of the door. It wasn't there before. I push it aside and grimace as it sticks to my skin. What on earth? Nothing's stuck to me but the stink of Kelly's disdain since I died.

As I wrestle with the spider web, the door swings open. A man in a coat and tails is standing at the top of the stairs, and when he sees me, he bows gracefully.

"Good evening, madam," he says, his voice deep and formal.

"What the hell?" I ask, no doubt sounding super classy.

He blinks but doesn't respond to my question. Instead, he says, "But that's not what you're wearing to the ball, is it?"

I should be afraid. With the door open, the music from instruments and the mingled conversations are clear. There are a lot of people up there. More than a couple scared girls playing dress-up. I have no idea what I'm walking into and I have no backup. Kelly's annoying, but they command respect, whereas I'm standing here looking like I just fell off the back of the potato truck.

Just like a kindly fairy godfather, the man snaps his gloved fingers, and a fresh cobweb falls over my head. It's even heavier and stickier than the first one. I fight to be free, but the more I struggle, the more it clings to me, wrapping itself around my arms and my waist, making it hard to breathe. It swirls around my legs and up the back of my neck. I try not to freak out at the sensation of tiny pairs of legs crawling over my skin. I have never done well with spiders, and even death hasn't relieved me of that fear.

Finally, just as my options become scream or claw my skin to ribbons, the crawling feeling subsides, and the webs stop suffocating me.

Oh.

When I glance down, my leggings and sweater are gone. In their place, I'm wearing a shimmering dress. It's the colour of wispy clouds on a moonlit night. It weighs nothing, but when I shift my feet, it bells out around me with the structure of light-as-air petticoats—stitched by spiders, apparently?—just beneath the skirt.

Okay, no, seriously. What the fuck is this?

The man on the stairs smiles. "That's better." He holds out a hand. "Won't you come in? Our other guests have already arrived."

chapter
fifteen

I NEVER REALLY HAD A PRINCESS PHASE AS a kid. I remember reading fairy tales and watching princess movies, but they were no more significant than making mud pies in the backyard or the week I wanted to be a cat when I grew up.

Joke's on six-year-old me, because I am every inch the cobweb princess now.

Turns out the way women in old movies and photos hold their hands so gracefully isn't a choice. It's either holding your hands demurely in front of you at the place where the dress makes its tumble to the floor, or else out to your sides like a Barbie doll. Anything else, and your arms get consumed in metres and metres of fabric and you wind up stomping around like you're trying to keep your feet from getting muddy in a wet field.

The attic has been transformed. The abandoned construction site is now a flickering ballroom. Candles burn from sconces on the walls, and a giant crystal chandelier, more spectacular than anything in the rest of the house, glitters overhead.

"What the fuck?" I ask, drawing each word out slowly as I look around me. The question is met by more than a few shocked gasps. The room is busy, with forty or more young women clustered in small groups. Their dresses vary from the huge hoop skirts like

Isabelle and Tiffany wore, to the fitted skirts with elaborate bustles that were more popular later in the Victorian era. There are even a few women dressed in shorter calf-length dresses and wearing their hair bobbed, like they might break out in the Charleston at any moment. Their conversations are hushed, and many cast furtive glances towards me as I enter. At first the whole thing feels very mean girls, which makes me sigh heavily, because if I hadn't managed to escape catty looks and whispered rumours by the time I was in my thirties, surely there must be respite once you're dead. But when I look around again, the looks aren't nasty. They're nervous. No. They're scared. No one makes eye contact, and the way the little circles tighten in on each other as I approach isn't about keeping an outsider on the periphery, it's about protecting those inside. Hands are taken and squeezed reassuringly. Arms, clad in gauzy gloves that reach to the elbows, are slung around corseted waists, pulling friends or allies in for comfort. The gesture reminds me of Kelly, in those early days when my soul was disintegrating . . . and me selfishly leaching their existence away without knowing. It's better to put a little space between us. Hopefully Kelly's in the basement, discovering that Viola's actually locked away in a cursed painting.

I shake my head, bringing myself back to the situation at hand. The women around me aren't snobby. They're not judging my appearance or my modern vocabulary.

They're terrified.

Well, it's been fun, but I gotta go. Things that terrify ghosts are none of my business. Figuring out how to get past the barrier is a far better use of my time. I spin—nearly falling over because the spindly heel of my historically accurate footwear can't be more than the size of a pencil and I'm very much a sneakers and Crocs sort of girly—and make for the stairs, but the same man who ushered me into the room steps in front of me and wordlessly shakes his head. No exit that way. I'll have to find somewhere else.

Another man stands by the wall. In fact, there's one every ten feet or so. They all wear the same coat and tails, and I've watched enough period dramas to know they're not guests at this ball; they're servants. The one closest clears his throat. Skirts shift and the little circles tighten inwards even further, until silk is pressed against silk and shoulder against shoulder. Close by, someone starts crying. It's a ragged whimpering sound, which is quickly shushed by a neighbour. I'm left standing alone in the middle of the room, feeling very exposed. There's no shelter to be had among the groups, but I do my best to duck in behind the closest one, a little trio of dark-haired girls in frothy gowns. They shift uncomfortably at my proximity, but before they can adjust to either accommodate me or push me away, the music starts up for real, playing a synchronized rhythm that makes me think of trumpets announcing the arrival of the king.

The servants along the wall bow deeply at the waist, and the women all drop into elegant curtsies. Mine is more like a squat, but the goal is to keep my head in line with everyone else's as slow footsteps come up the stairs, and it's not like you can see my lack of grace under the hoops and material anyway. The crying gets louder. It's not from my trio, but the next cluster over. A girl in a baby pink dress who can't be more than fifteen or sixteen gets shuffled back to the wall, and a taller girl in a pale yellow gown whispers to her harshly.

"Pull yourself together. Do you want her to see you?"

The question only makes the girl cry harder.

Finally, the person on the stairs appears. I gasp. Her dress is a heavy black, and her skin is sunken against her bones, but the narrow face and scornful brow are familiar, at least as much as they can be when all you've seen of a person is a single portrait on Wikipedia.

Viola.

"Shit," I whisper, but even as softly as I say it, the word attracts more furious glances as people silently beg me to be quiet. Where the heck is Kelly when I need them? My personal feelings aside, it's always good to have a reaper in arms when you find yourself in uncertain supernatural situations, and I'm like ninety percent sure the way Viola glowers around the room and everyone shrinks even further to avoid her serpent's gaze says nothing good is going to happen in the next fifteen minutes. No one's passing tiny snacks, and I will not find myself dancing in the entrancing arms of Lord Belvedere Bevonshire or whatever his name might be . . . or his hot butch sister Lady Bevonshire's arms either, for that matter.

Despite my trepidation, I can't help but peek over the shoulder of the shuddering debutante in front of me. A heavy velvet curtain at the far end of the room, where there used to be nothing but old scaffolding, is pulled wide, and Viola ascends to a small throne. She needs the help of one of the servants to make the last step and to sink gracefully onto her seat. As she does, the music cuts out, fading to silence as she surveys us.

Her cheeks are sunken. And I don't just mean the hollow-cheeked appearance of a couture model. I mean like the way mine were sunken in my last months as a cancer patient. If she were alive, she'd be dead anyway. Never mind the raspy breath she takes when she finally opens her mouth. Her hair is coiled around her ears like Isabelle's was, but as she turns her head, making her braids glisten in the candlelight, I realize they're not braids at all. They're snakes, winding their way slowly about her head. Similarly, the heavy black necklace around her throat that I assumed was dark stones is shifting, swirling in a steady line from one collarbone to the other, before disappearing around her neck. Spiders, making a slow loop. Now I'm the one shuddering and the desire to pull the spiderweb dress from my skin nearly has me flinging myself to the floor in the middle of the room.

No wonder Smith sent us to get her instead of coming himself. We're not brave agents on a secret mission. There's a very good chance we're sacrifices. Get us off Smith's case and make sure no one finds out about the Other Side. Two birds, one paranormal stone. Well played, sir.

Viola lifts a single gnarled finger; a wordless signal to the musicians who are positioned just to her right. They lift their violins, and the strained chords of music that hasn't been popular in probably a hundred and seventy years fills the room. Like puppets on strings, the girls and women move forward, filling the dance floor. Since there are no male partners, they dance with each other. Panic engulfs me as they pair off. It's like watching classmates choosing partners for an assignment and realizing you're going to be left as the odd kid out if you don't act quickly. Not that I know this dance or anything like it, but pretty sure I don't want to find out what happens to those who beg their way out of this situation by pleading ignorance. But as I whirl, I trip over the hem of my ridiculous skirt. Everything is about to come crashing down around me, before an arm catches me around the waist, pulling me back to my feet.

I sigh. Kelly. Of course, they would show up when I needed them most. They wouldn't let me down.

But when I open my eyes and fall into step with the spinning women around me, I find myself looking into a different disdainful gaze. Not Kelly. Tiffany. She glares furiously at me from beneath the dark line of her unplucked eyebrow, and the tight pucker of her mouth makes her look like she's either just eaten a lemon or is about to spit in my face.

"What are you doing?" she asks.

"Does it look like I have any idea?"

She's a good dancer. Or better than I am. Her hold on me is firm, and even if I don't know where we're going or what I'm supposed to do next, the push of her palm on my side or the not-quite-gentle press of her fingers against my ribs is enough to guide me from one figure to another.

"How did you get in here?" Her questions are a furious whisper. I don't answer a second time. Simply bobble my head. What does she expect me to say? Tiffany sighs, sending me spinning away from her without letting go of my one hand. When I reach the apex of the turn, the women around me have already begun to spin back into their partner's hold, and I follow.

"What's happening?" I ask. "How long have you been dead? Are you a ghost or a lost soul?"

"Quiet," she hisses. "She'll hear you."

That's what Isabelle said earlier. Unconsciously, I scan the dancing crowd, looking for the lettuce green dress. I think I catch a glimpse of it, but the effort makes me stumble, and only Tiffany's expert maneuvering keeps me from falling.

"What happens if she does?" I ask. "What is she?" With the next revolution, I look towards Viola. She's watching us all, eyes narrowed in a squint. The corners of her mouth are turned up in something like a smile, but it might also be a painful grimace. Her gaze is intent, while her spiders and snakes make slow revolutions around her, their path mimicking the swirling dancers around the room.

Tiffany doesn't answer. Her nails dig into my skin, even through the spiderweb material of the dress.

The music ends, the players waving their bows with a flourish. Tiffany releases me for a moment, before Viola lifts her boney finger a second time. A ripple of fear washes over the women, but the musicians begin a new piece without any further prompting. It's faster this time, livelier. In sneakers and leggings, it would make a great cardio workout. In a hoop skirt and shoes that pinch my toes, I can barely keep up.

Tiffany is also concentrating hard on the intricate steps of the dance as we bob and whirl between other pairs. Her grip on me is firm, basically dragging me along as she moves in time with the music. By the time the second song finishes, if I could still sweat, I would be dripping inside my corset.

"Continue!" Viola calls from her throne, and muffled sounds of dismay fill the room. The man by the stairs coughs loudly, just once, and the women all subside, while the musicians start all over again, even faster than before. What the hell is this? Whoever Viola is, she could give the reapers some tips about fun new ways to orchestrate HECK. This creepy little ball makes me think of old fairy tales about princesses sneaking out and dancing until their shoes fell apart, or the devil dancing until he burst into flames. At the same time though, it brings to mind Depression-era dance marathons, where exhausted couples struggled to hold each other up after dancing nonstop for hours, all for the opportunity to win a ham or a few pounds of ground beef.

The thought makes me giggle, and despite Tiffany's careful guidance, on the next turn, my small lapse in concentration is enough to break me out of her hold and crash into the next woman closest to me. Someone steps on my skirt, and I flail as I tumble to the ground. No one catches me this time. Instead, a body lands on top of me with a frightened "oof."

"I'm sorry," I say, because even in death I'm still Canadian. "So sorry. This is my first time. Are you okay?"

It's the girl. The one in the pink dress who was crying before. Her eyes are wide with terror as she scrambles away from me.

It's only as I get back to my feet that I realize the music has stopped. The girl trembles as I help her up. The dancers have parted, leaving the two of us alone in a sparkling pool of light beneath the giant chandelier. I glance around, looking for Tiffany, but she's melted into the sea of silk and frightened glances.

The *tap tap tap* of heels on the hardwood is my only warning as Viola walks across the silent dance floor toward us. If it's possible, she appears to have aged even more. She's hunched, like even the weight of her dress is almost too much for her frail body to bear. But her gaze is diamond sharp as she stares us down. The girl slides behind me, clinging tightly to my bodice until it pulls uncomfortably at my shoulders. I shift, but every time I move, she goes with me, determined to keep me fully between her and the approaching horror. The others around us all duck their heads, curtsying again as Viola passes without acknowledgement.

Finally, she reaches me. Her hands are tinged bluish in the way it becomes sometimes with the elderly. Poor circulation and skin so thin it's practically paper. But her touch is confident as she puts one pointy fingernail to my chin and lifts, forcing my head up to meet her gaze. The snakes continue to coil lazily around her brows, but the spiders still on her collarbones, legs quivering in anticipation.

"You're new." Her voice is a rasp, like dry leaves tumbling down a windy street. I don't answer. I've read enough dark fairy fantasy books to know names are powerful and until I know what the hell is going on here, I'm not sharing more information than I have to. A snake hisses, and her nail pushes painfully against my skin. "Where did you come from?"

Between the trembling girl pressed against my back and the terrifying woman in front of me, I have nowhere to go. A snake rises from her brow, staring at me with cold eyes. The spiders make a strange clacking sound as they begin moving again, scrambling about her exposed skin before disappearing into her bodice. I can't help it when I shudder, but for a moment, she looks even more uncomfortable than I feel.

"You're from Afterlife," she says accusingly. She peels my hand from her with surprising strength. She turns it over, twisting my arm to a painful angle. "Jules!"

The man at the stairs strides up, nodding his head in a sharp salute.

"Yes, madam?"

"Hold her. Let me deal with the other one."

I struggle, but for all his fine clothes, Jules the butler must go to the gym in his downtime, because as he wraps his arms around me, he's built like a wrestler. I scuffle, kicking my legs up, but he doesn't move.

The girl behind me does, however. Viola closes in on her. She screams when Viola grabs her arm, looking wildly at the other women around us, but no one moves to help her. If anything, they all take another cautious step away. Viola grins, showing sharp pointed teeth.

"You're a pretty one," she says, pulling the crying girl toward her. "So young. So bright."

Viola pulls the sobbing girl to her as she struggles, but it's for nothing. Viola's eyes flash, turning pure white. The girl's crying becomes something more like a moan, but she stares directly at her captor, transfixed.

There's only a momentary hiss of warning before the snakes uncoil themselves from Viola's head, and the spiders reemerge from her dress. The snakes stretch forward, reaching for the girl's terrified face. The spiders scurry down Viola's arms, then make their way over the girl's, before once again disappearing inside the fabric. I gasp, and the gathered dancers all retreat even further.

The girl screams. It's pure terror. I can't really blame her. Without the snake wig and other creepy accessories Viola looks straight out of a late-night low-budget horror movie. The kind of monster that slowly crawls out from under the bed and slides under your covers while you sleep, then devours you as you scream. The snakes are now coiling over the girl. Around her throat and across her shoulders. Viola releases her, and she falls back, desperately clawing at herself to be free of the creatures that swarm her. She kicks and tears, howling, and even if I wasn't being held tight against Jules, I would have to look away. Her fear and pain are too much. Everything you don't want death to be. She may already be dead, but this is it. Her true end. I don't have to know exactly what's happening to understand what's going on, and just like every other human being, I have to look away when faced with this kind of torture.

Eventually, the screaming fades. When I open my eyes, I'm looking at Tiffany, who watches implacably from the edge of the crowd. Her gaze lingers on mine, and there's anger there. Accusation. I've failed some test of hers, and I didn't even know there would be one.

Slowly, I look back to the centre of the room. The girl is gone. All that's left are the shredded remnants of her pink gown, lying in a heap on the floor. The snakes and spiders slither over the wood until they find the hem of Viola's skirt. The spiders disappear into the material, and the snakes make slow circles around the hoops. As they scale her body, she stands up a little straighter, and when the spiders reemerge above her neckline, she stretches her neck up, tipping her head back. Her smile is ecstatic.

I can't help but be amazed as I watch her transformation. The creatures curl around her, moving over her chin and around her face, like they might suffocate her. Slowly though, the spiders perch again on her collarbones into the most unsettling of necklaces, and the snakes take their place once more about her ears and around her head like a crown.

The crone is gone. The skeletal features hidden beneath newly rejuvenated skin. Here is the woman I saw in the picture online. She's young. Fresh. Beautiful. Her smile as she runs her fingers over her cheeks is delighted. She is the heiress reborn and the power it took to make this happen must be massive. She's not a reaper, but she's definitely something, and that something is very, very formidable.

This isn't someone I can club over the head and drag back to Smith. He clearly left out some important details. And if I can't do that, how am I going to save Kelly?

AFTER VIOLA'S HORRIFYING GLOW-UP, she gives me a knowing look.

"The old crop was getting stale. Let's invite her to stay," she says to Jules. He nods, and releases me. I stumble forward, tumbling to the place where Viola stood only a moment ago. She has already lost interest in me. In all of us, really. The mood in the room is understandably tense. Everyone is back into the nervous clusters they were in when I first entered. It all makes more sense. Who would be excited for a ball when they know someone's going to get eaten by the end of the night?

Also, whatever Viola may say about inviting me to remain, no one makes the offer. The way Jules and his buddies continue to line the walls and block the stairs says there would only be one acceptable response in my RSVP anyway. Got it. I'm a prisoner.

Viola returns to her seat at the head of the room and cues the musicians. The music is calmer now. Stately waltzes that send us turning around the room. Jules lets me go and for a moment I'm frozen to the spot, but then Tiffany grabs hold of me and we're dancing again.

"What did she mean you're from the afterlife?" she asks,

without so much as a "wow, that was weird wasn't it?" How many times has she seen that happen before to not even blink now?

"I'm not *from* Afterlife," I say, sounding like Kelly. But their love of semantics comes from an irritating belief in their superiority. Mine is based on a desperate need to make sense of what's happening. "I'm from Don Mills."

Tiffany won't be distracted, though. "But you've been there? You've been"—for once, her stern gaze becomes uncertain as she glances around the spinning room—"not here?"

I snort. "Of course. Haven't you?"

She gets quiet. We're at the head of the room, close to where Viola sits, and Tiffany gives her an apprehensive glance before dancing me away again. She moves us to the centre of the room, so we're turning in faster circles than the others who dance closer to the edges. So many women. For a moment I think I spot Isabelle's lettuce green dress. Then the woman who had comforted the crying girl, moments before she gave up the rest of her existence to Viola. No wonder she was upset.

"Once a year," Tiffany says in a low voice, "she gathers us. Chooses one to help her. Keep her beautiful."

"What is she?" I ask.

Her eyes narrow and she says, "A monster."

That goes without saying. The vibes have been off since Viola walked up the stairs. But while I have no doubt she's not some guardian angel for the dead, I don't think "monster" is an official classification of the supernatural at Afterlife.

"Like a lost soul? A reaper?" I prompt, but the words only make her squint in confusion, so I try a different path. "How did you die?"

"Fever. My family lived in this house. Viola was waiting for me, saying she was going to take me to heaven. Instead she brought me up here."

It's not hard to envision Viola standing at the foot of someone's deathbed, pretending to be a kind angel, only to trap unsuspecting souls in the attic. Why does everyone who has their hands on life after death have to be such a dick?

"Does no one ever escape?" I ask, hoping against hope, but Tiffany shakes her head. Whatever Viola is, she's powerful. Strong enough to keep not only herself, but everyone else from turning into a wraith for more than a century. However she's doing it, keeping that invisible barrier up at the bottom of the steps feels like the easiest part.

"At first she was able to come and go, bringing new ghosts up here. But about a hundred years ago, suddenly she couldn't leave either. So now she preys on those who are unfortunate enough to die in this house, or those foolish enough to come exploring when they should be on their way to heaven, or wherever this afterlife you speak of might be."

And, yet again, Afterlife fails to save the day. If they were any good at picking the newly dead up in a timely manner, there would be fewer girls and women falling into Viola's undead day spa. I make a mental note that, as soon as everything else is settled, I'm going to tell Bang to up the SRU coverage here in Eastern Ontario. It may be rural, but that's no excuse for poor service.

"We're going to change that," I say. "All of it. I'm getting us out of here." Doesn't matter that I don't really know Tiffany. Or anyone else here. We are now part of the sisterhood of ghosts who got royally screwed by forces bigger than us. So now we're going to work together to stick it to them.

Her laugh is dark, practically daring me to try. "Just because no one's ever escaped before doesn't mean no one's ever made the attempt. We're trapped. When the ball is over, we leave."

How can they leave if they're trapped? And, now that I think about it, where the hell were they all when I first checked the attic? Jupiter and X knew the vibe was off, but you can't hide this many scared women behind some old paint cans, any more than Viola could do a complete redecoration in the time it took to get stuck behind the barrier.

"I'm going to need a little more to go on," I say.

Tiffany shrugs. It's an elegant gesture, but everything is elegant when you wear fifteen yards of silk. I wonder what she was like when she was alive. She seems older and more mature than a lot of the women here, but she still can't be more than twenty-four or twenty-five. European beauty standards being what they were, she probably wasn't seen as much of a catch visually, but if her father owned enough railroads or had a title, that might not have mattered.

"When the ball is over, everything goes dark. I don't know where she takes us. There's just nothing, until the next ball," she says. "All I know is we're not here, but I can't move or see anything."

Yup. We're not letting that happen again. What a shitty life. Or afterlife. Worse than mine, with all its annoyances and inconveniences.

"And you've never tried to fight back? There are dozens of you and only one of her." But even as the question leaves my lips, I know how silly it sounds. I may have been piggybacking off Kelly's powers for the last while, but before I figured out how to do that, I wasn't any more special dead than I was alive. What could these women do against Viola, when she can tear them down to dust and threads?

Tiffany's grimace is pained. I squeeze her in silent apology, careful not to let the momentary kindness interfere with the way she leads me through this dance.

"I have friends," I say. "They'll know what to do." I try to make my smile reassuring, even if I'm far from sure myself. Because how do I even tell Kelly or Jupiter or anyone where I am and what's going on? Second, how do I get them to believe me? I can already picture Kelly's scowl and their dismissal.

"She's a ghost, Ember. Or a lost soul. There's nothing else she could be. And spiders don't do that. Anything else is a myth."

This is how we got into this mess. Their obstinate refusal to learn. I've been on a learning curve the size of Everest since the minute my eyes closed in that hospital room. Kelly, meanwhile, has just continued to be themself. The reaper who has seen it all and isn't touched by any of it. They were even ready to walk into their own death and—

My throat is tight. I shouldn't have yelled. I miss them. Wish I could help them. Instead I told them to go away. When Viola decides she's had enough paranormal Botox for the night and the musicians pack it in, will I go off to the black too? Smith's patch will only hold for a few days. In a year, when Viola needs a pick-me-up and I suddenly find myself free for a few hours for this nightmare dance, Kelly will be long gone.

"Do you have someone?" Tiffany asks. "A husband?"

I snort. "No. No husband."

She frowns, the unibrow bunching together. "But you must be older than I am. How can you have no husband?"

I blow out a breath. How am I supposed to explain all that to someone who probably died a century before I was born? No, I don't have a husband, but I did have a bank account and was able to vote and own property. I'm actually a lesbian and not only is that—mostly—socially acceptable, I would have even been able to marry another woman eventually . . . if the cancer hadn't gotten me first.

So instead, I say, "My friend is a reaper. A powerful one. They'll know how to get us out of here."

"They?" she asks. "There's more than one?"

See? Kelly's refusal to buy into human gender is one more thing to explain when we're running out of time. Has Tiffany ever even considered the idea that male and female might be arbitrary? My guess is not.

A sensation around my ankle makes me glance down, just in time to see a black snake with silver-edged scales disappearing under the enormous width of my skirt. It winds itself around my calf and I bite down on a scream as I try to kick it away. Others around me do the same.

Tiffany gives me a rueful look. "It's been very nice meeting you tonight. I'm sorry you got caught up in all this. Will you save me a dance next year?"

No fucking way. I won't be here next year. I'm getting out now, whatever it takes.

The women around me stop dancing. The musicians begin to pack up their instruments. Slowly, they are consumed. Spiders skitter over the floor and begin to weave webs around each. Not a single person fights back. Why would you, after a hundred years or more? The fight's gone out of them.

But I do. Without intending to, Tiffany and I have stopped towards the back of the room, as far from Viola as we can be. I watch as the others are encased and mummified, then begin to vanish one by one. The snakes around my ankles hold me in place, but when the spiders come, I won't let them take me. I kick, and scratch, pulling them off as they climb up my legs and inside the dress. I'll be naked by the time I'm done, but who cares?

"There's no point," Tiffany says. Her dark gown is already turning white with webbing. "We've all tried it. They just keep coming."

Not this time. I kick and claw. The spiders go squish under my shoes, hard shell bodies cracking beneath the soles. I throw the ones I can reach against the walls and towards the unmoving men who guard us. Across the room, my gaze catches Viola's. She watches me with a gleam in her eye as I keep tearing at the webs and killing her creatures.

"I appreciate a little defiance," she says, approaching. "These girls here were taught from such an early age to bow and scrape and do as they're told. Your generation is so much more direct. So focused on your own goals and desires. Go on," she says with a wicked smile. "Let's see what you can do."

What can I do? The spiders pour from her sleeves, rushing over my shoulders and around my throat. I gasp and try to scream, but the sound comes out strangled. The webs are so thick around my shoulders and middle they're like rope and I can't lift my arms to tear them off anymore.

Viola makes a disappointed sound. "A spirit like you, I thought you'd be more of a challenge. But you're just like them. Weak. Frightened. You're of no more use than any of them."

Being frightened isn't weakness. Who wouldn't be scared in this situation? But also, I'm angry. What a stupid way to go. And how dare Viola trap me along with everyone else for her own uses? She should know better. Care more, especially for women who had so few choices when they were alive. I won't give in to her selfishness. Not when I have to get back to Kelly and save them before it's too late.

The webbing closes over my mouth, muffling my ability to scream. I struggle against the bonds, even though I know it's hopeless. A year. What will a year get me? No one at Afterlife will look for me. Jupiter and X will have no idea how to get through the barrier. And Kelly will be dead. Even deader than I am. I will never get to bicker with them again. Complain when they're being too literal. I will never get to roll my eyes when they mangle an idiom. I will never get to apologize for that awkward kiss, or find out if there's a way to make it less awkward, maybe with a little more warning and practice.

The webbing surrounds my eyes and ears, sending the world into blackness.

I will never get to tell them I'm sorry and I'll miss them, and maybe that I—

"Ember?" A familiar voice comes from behind me, so close I should be able to feel them pressed against my back, but I can't through all the spiderwebs. "Ember, what's happening?"

I can't speak. Can't move. It's just like Tiffany said it would be. I'm trapped.

"Ember?" Kelly's voice is clear. Worried. Too late. I don't

know how they managed to get here, into the black empty place, but what are they going to do, weak as they are, against Viola?

Yet strong arms grab hold of my waist. Familiar arms. I've been tricked before, but this time I know. They tighten their grasp around me, anchoring me to the world—my world, with all its inconveniences and irritations—in a way I feel all the way to my soul. Because they're not holding on to me physically. They can't. But the connection between us is strong. We've been strengthening it for months without realizing what the repercussions might be. It can't be broken by a few spiders and some fear.

"What are you doing?" Viola asks, sounding surprised. I can't answer. Can't even see where she is. Instead, I send every ounce of my awareness to the anchor, following the line from my chest all the way down to the bottom. To the point where I am me but not anymore. The place where we have become an us. Bonded. Connected. Maybe a little toxic. The knot there is intricate, wrapping around itself and crisscrossing over and under until it's pulled so tight I can't see how we're ever going to undo it. Not with Viola. Not with Smith. It's so tangled and woven together there's no beginning or end.

I grab hold and pull.

"Ember."

The voice isn't Viola's. It's not Kelly's either. Or not entirely. It's mine but also theirs. Ours. Here at this point, there's no difference.

I pull harder. Something tears. Someone screams. Maybe me. Maybe Viola. Maybe a hundred spiders watching their work be undone. I pull, even when the current tries to sweep me away.

"Ember. Hold on to me."

seventeen

IT'S DARK. Nothing to see, not even the sparking colours behind my eyelids. Is this the nothing? If I reach out a hand, will Tiffany be beside me, encased in an unbreakable web for the next three hundred and sixty-five days? Except I can't move my hand. Can't move any part of me.

The spiders begin to spin again, starting at my ankles and crawling over my body. I can feel them, even if I can't see them. So many tiny eight-legged bodies spreading over my skin. I squirm. Writhe. Even death hasn't cured me of my fear of them and now they're everywhere. *Get away. Get away.*

"Ember. Ember, hold on."

"Get away. Get off of me."

My hands are free and I tear at my skin, trying to find the spiders and rip them away before they suffocate me further. I can already feel them, little legs just beneath my lips and over my neck forcing their way inside me. I'll be nothing but web and creature and—

"Ember!" The voice in my ear is loud. Frightened. Someone is shouting. No, screaming. Two people. One of them is screaming like they're being eaten alive, the other to be heard over the terror.

"Ember, open your eyes."

I kick at the spiders.

"Get them off!"

"There's nothing there. Ember." They take hold of my wrists, pulling them away from my skin. "Ember!"

I open my eyes, surging to new awareness like I'm rising up from the bottom of a lake. Someone is breathing hard in my ear. My skin throbs. My clothes—my leggings—are torn, shredded in long lines like the tears were made with animal claws. The skin beneath is scratched and seeps blackish red blood.

"Stop. You're hurting yourself." The voice is desperate. We're sitting on the floor in a room I don't know. Electric lights burn overhead. The walls are high Victorian, wood panels and crown moulding. The floor is pure '70s, with shag carpet that—if it isn't infested with spiders—must host an entire civilization of dust mites and other creepy crawlies.

Kelly is behind me, caging my body between theirs, still holding my hands apart. Their eyes are wide with fear, and their breath on my cheek is coming in great gusts like our fight has gone on for a while.

"Kelly?" I whisper. My voice is a wreck, just like the rest of me. They let go of my wrists one at a time and I pull up onto my knees, turning. My nails are caked in blood. Kelly puts their palms on either side of my head, holding me in place so they can study me. Their inhuman disinterest has been replaced with profound worry, so I hold still, watching as their eyes dart over my face and around the rest of me.

"I'm okay," I say when they can't seem to confirm that fact on their own. They put a finger to one of the scrapes on my forearm, touching gently like they're afraid of hurting me. I put my hand over theirs, squeezing. "I'm okay," I say again.

They pull me into a tight hug. The movement is so sudden, I only have a second to gasp before my cheek is pressed against their ear and their strong arms are wrapped around me, trapping my arms against my sides. Panic threatens to well up as the feeling of

Viola's webs lingers, but I stuff it back down. This is Kelly. I know them. Trust them. Just a few minutes ago I was listing all the regrets I had about my time with them. I'm safe.

"How did you find me?" I ask when they finally let go. They help me to my feet and lead me to an ancient cracked brown leather sofa. We're in what looks like some kind of old rec room, and also a holding ground for every piece of furniture the auction staff deemed impossible to sell. The cracked sofa is just the beginning. High-backed wing chairs with water-stained cushions so worn the material is frayed at the seats. A couple farmhouse-style wooden dining chairs with an odd number of legs or missing spindles in their backs. I sink an uncomfortably long way into the sofa when I sit, and even if my legs didn't feel like jelly right now, I'd still probably need Kelly's help to stand again.

"You called out," they say, though they don't sound very sure about it. "I was down here looking for more information on Viola and suddenly I could hear you. You were screaming." They sit next to me, closer than they normally would, like they're not convinced I won't pop back out of this plain at any moment. They keep my hand in theirs, running their thumb over my knuckles. I don't know if the gesture is meant to reassure me or them. Though when has Kelly ever needed reassurance? I still feel ragged. Twitchy. The scratches on my arms are healing, but I can't shake the remembered sensation of creatures on my skin. My foot bounces where I have it crossed over one knee, and without meaning to, I brush a nonexistent spider from my ankle. The gesture doesn't escape Kelly's notice and they give me another worried frown. Even though I'm the one who nearly fell captive to the queen bitch heiress from hell, I feel like they're the one who needs a hug.

"I could feel you," I say. "She was trying to take me away to the nothing, but you wouldn't let me go." I put a hand to my chest then, trying not to shake, put one to theirs. "Whatever this is between us, it saved me."

They give me a tentative smile. They smile so rarely, it's like the sun coming out on a cold and rainy day. Between that and the hug, I could pretty much fly.

But just as quickly as the safe feeling settles over me, it vanishes as Kelly's smile is marred by a thin rivulet of blood that appears in their right nostril before slowly dripping down until it meets their lip.

"Oh," I say, not wanting to move, like I could somehow scare it and make it worse. Kelly, who had just lifted a hand to mimic my own tender gesture, instead puts their fingers to their nose, then stares at the blood like they've never seen it before.

I gasp. "Oh no. Did I slide? Is that how I got out of there? Did I make you worse?" My voice rises with fear. I was so scared, so desperate to escape, but did my desire for self-preservation lead to more harm, when I've already caused so much?

The distress must be evident on my face, because Kelly shakes their head, wiping off the blood with their sleeve.

"I'm all right. See?" They wipe again, and no further blood appears from their nose. "Nothing to worry about."

"Nothing?" I've been trying not to cry pretty much since I came to in this abandoned room, but I can't hold it back anymore. Hot tears spill over my cheeks. I twist my hands in the hem of my sweater. "Kelly, you're dying. You're—I'm killing you. I've been killing you since we met. It's all my fault."

They tug me into them again. It should be comforting. Instead all I feel is bone-deep sorrow and regret. I never wanted to hurt anyone, but even without meaning to I've made it worse over and over.

"It's not your fault. We didn't know this would happen. No reaper has ever spent such a long time in the company of a single ghost. And no ghost has ever been tenacious enough to put up with a reaper's disinterest for as long as you have."

My sob is an embarrassingly wet messy sound, but it only makes Kelly hold me tighter. This is a level of consideration I've never felt from them, but staring death in the face makes people—and reapers, apparently—behave in unexpected ways.

I sit back a little, but they keep their hands on my shoulders, so I can't pull away completely.

"I'm okay," they say, echoing my reassurance from earlier. It makes me want to start crying all over again. It's grief. I'm grieving. Crying for a loss that hasn't happened yet. They don't tell you the grief starts before a loved one dies. It happens in a million little ways as you start to recognize the small defeats. The last Christmas together. The last time they can walk themselves to the bathroom or get into bed unassisted. The first day they don't get out of bed and you worry they might never get out again.

I study Kelly, looking for signs, the little clues that say we're out of time. But this isn't human disease. There's no way of knowing when Smith's patch will fail. There's no way to predict when will be my last chance to say goodbye or I'm sorry. To look at their face and remember the stubborn narrowing of their eyes. The hawkish nose that never approves of me. The thin mouth that contradicts and infuriates and—

I lean forward. Maybe they do too. We're a mess, the two of us. Bloody noses and scratches. But I called and they pulled me free and maybe that's what really matters.

"Em—" they say, pressing their lips into the perfect shape to—

A distant banging shatters the air. It shakes the foundations of the house. Even Kelly must feel it because they dive on top of me, like they might be able to protect me one more time. I hit the floor with an "oof" and we lie there, frozen for a moment. They're a heavy weight on top of me. The link between us pulses almost like a heartbeat, reminding me of that moment as I got pulled from the attic where the line between Kelly and me didn't exist. Only a we. An us. We didn't intend for it to happen, but maybe it was always going to work out like this, from the moment I first saw them on the sidewalk outside the hospital.

The banging comes again. Oh. It's not a threat. Not an immediate one anyway. Far away, someone is pounding on a door.

We don't look at each other as we rise to our feet, but Kelly takes my hand as we climb up the basement steps. I don't let go, even when we reach the top of the stairs, and keep behind them as we approach the shuddering front door. I know I should be all brave girl boss, but quite frankly I've had enough tonight. It's Kelly's turn to face the monster.

"Ember? Ember, are you in there?" Jupiter's muffled voice comes through the heavy wood of the front door. "If you can hear me, open up. Kelly disappeared and we need to talk to you."

Her eyes go big as Kelly flings the door open. X is standing behind her, but at our appearance, he yelps and flings himself back down the wide front steps to the circular drive, like he might need to outrun a demon or the devil himself. Can't really blame him. He doesn't even know about Viola upstairs, but something is seriously messed up with this house.

"Something is seriously messed up with this house," Jupiter says.

Oh. Maybe they do know.

"What happened?" Kelly asks.

"How did you get here?" Jupiter asks without answering them. "One second you were in the car, then—" She puffs out her cheeks and makes a sound like *ffft*.

Kelly puts a hand to their chest, the same place I did back in the basement. They rub, like maybe it's tender. I step a little closer to them. We're still holding hands, so I wrap my free one around their arm and rest my chin on their shoulder, offering what comfort I can. I let my consciousness drift down the invisible line between us. When I find the anchor point, I mentally poke at it, like I might be able to notice weak spots or assess how Smith's patch is holding up. Kelly tilts their head toward me, a wordless acknowledgement of what I'm doing. I squeeze tighter. Maybe I can hold us together a little longer.

Jupiter's watching us with an arched eyebrow.

"Did I miss something?" she asks.

We pull apart immediately, once again not making eye contact with each other . . . or Jupiter and X. Even still, I can feel their scrutiny, and when I finally do look up, they're sharing a wordless glance of their own. It's the kind that says we're too cute, and my cheeks nearly burst into flame. I don't want their amusement or their interference.

"What did you mean about the house?" Kelly asks, taking a decent-size step away from me. The space between us suddenly feels huge and the desire to close it is nearly unbearable.

Jupiter gives us one more thoughtful look, but finally says, "We did a little more researching. This town isn't very big, you know. There's a museum and a library, but they were both closed by the time we got there."

"So you didn't find out anything?" I ask, heart sinking.

"No, we totally did," X says. His lips are trembling like he's trying to hold back a proud smile. "There's been a bunch of women who died in this house and even more in this town. For over a hundred years."

"They were murdered?" I ask. I wouldn't put it past Viola to kill unsuspecting young women to add to her little collection.

"Maybe?" Jupiter says cautiously. "Some of them definitely would have loved things like vaccines and antibiotics. But a lot of the earliest ones were young women who died suspiciously. They'd fall down the stairs or drown in the river. Some flat out disappeared from their bed. There were so many. We stopped counting after a while and just kept reading."

"Counting?" I suddenly realize there must have been so many more. If there are still forty scared girls in the attic—or wherever they are now—how many more must she have taken in the time since she left the Other Side? But why? It can't just be so she can stay beautiful, can it?

Though I was happy to hopscotch the dimensions hitchhiking on Kelly's power, so I probably shouldn't be so shocked.

X waggles his phone at us. "Wikipedia, baby. They may not have late hours at the library, but this place has good cell service everywhere. Who knew? I sort of thought once you left Toronto, the signal disappeared."

Kelly makes an impatient sound.

"If you follow the related articles," Jupiter explains, hurrying on, "it tells you about a lot of the women who died. One after the other. After Viola, it linked to an article about a woman named Isabelle something."

"Isabelle Brown?" I ask. X is already searching on his phone, and when he holds up the screen it's her, right down to the elaborate hair and lettuce dress. Even the portrait that is used as the key photo holds the same fear in her eyes, even though she couldn't have possibly known her fate when it was painted.

"It says she fell from a cliff one night. No one knew why she'd even left the house. There was a snowstorm," X says.

Jupiter is breathless as she says, "You guys. I think this house might be haunted by a seriously fucked-up ghost who is killing people."

Yup. They do know what's going on. And now we have to find a way to get that fucked-up ghost to come back to the Other Life with us.

eighteen

AT LEAST JUPITER and X's return means I only need to relay the story of my evening with Viola and her horrible ball once since I didn't get around to conveying all the details to Kelly. We were too busy doing . . . whatever it was we were doing—or about to do—before Jupiter interrupted us.

I'm equal parts annoyed and relieved she did. Maybe she was right from the beginning. Maybe somewhere along the way I fell in love with Kelly. But that doesn't mean they've fallen in love with me, or that they're even capable of falling in love with anyone.

Also, who says it's love? Not like the way humans feel it anyway. We are literally joined at the soul. Mushy feelings probably come with the package. It's not love. Empathy, maybe. I'm over-thinking things and we have bigger priorities than me and Kelly knuckling down to define the relationship.

For example . . .

"So she's kidnapping women and turning them into her personal skincare regime?" Jupiter asks when I finish describing what I know about Viola . . . which isn't very much. Somehow X and Jupiter have found out more, which hurts my pride, though I try not to show it.

"And she's definitely not a wraith?" Kelly asks, for once sounding genuinely curious.

"If you say she's a myth—" I start, but they hold up a hand to stop me.

"I'm not saying that. I don't know what she is."

My pride revives itself. Just because I was pissed off at Kelly when I told them to grow some curiosity doesn't mean my words weren't true. If they've taken them to heart, maybe there's hope for us finding common ground after all.

"She's not a wraith. She was aware and in control the whole time," I say. "She knew about Afterlife. But she didn't sound like she'd been there, so she's not a lost soul. If she's a wraith, she's figured out how to avoid decay. And the whole spider and snake minions is not very wraithy either."

X gasps. "Did we just discover a new species? Are we like Charles Darwin but for ghosts?"

I laugh. Loud. Sharp. I can't help myself. For once, X's enthusiastic nonsense is exactly what I need after everything. The others watch, throwing me nervous glances, which only makes me laugh harder, until I'm wiping tears from my eyes and holding my sides.

"Yes," I finally say as the giggles subside. "A new species. You can name her. *Violus horribilus*." The name cracks me up all over again, and by the time I'm done the second round, my cheeks hurt and I'm wheezing. Somewhere along the way, Kelly has put a concerned hand on my back, but they don't move away when I calm. I lean into the touch, and their fingers flex gently against my muscles. It's nice. Nice enough. Maybe we just get to be touchy friends. The kind who perpetually confuse the others around them without ever admitting to being more. The feeling in my chest gets warmer, almost like Kelly's agreeing with me. The sensation of the link is equal parts comforting and disarming, like I can never fully keep my thoughts to myself while we're still connected. Having someone who knows when I need a hug is nice. If Kelly can read my mind? Not so much.

"If she's the one killing the others, trapping them in some parallel attic dimension, and slowly sucking the life out of them, how do we catch her and take her back to this Smith guy?" Jupiter asks, because of course she does. She's not swirling in existential questions. And we have a killer ghost to catch. "It doesn't seem like she's going to help us out of the goodness of her heart . . . if she even has a heart anymore."

I nudge Kelly. "What are you feeling?"

They give me a funny look, before they say, "Not bad overall. It helps when you're close like this. It hurts less."

Jupiter lets out a little happy sigh. X makes a face like he's seeing a puppy for the very first time.

"I meant, do you feel anything weird here? Anything dead? You know. Like the time at the bus crash where you knew something bad had happened."

Pink stains Kelly's cheeks at my correction. They finally move their hand away from my back and I silently curse my big mouth for embarrassing them and losing their touch in the process.

They say, "No. Nothing out of the ordinary." But they lift their chin, tilting their head to hear something far away. "Maybe more before, when you were caught upstairs. It was like the air got heavier. But it's gone now."

This is why the ghost hunters on TV are always making up weird stuff about floating orbs that are really just dust on drafts, or assigning words to random ambient sounds in an effort to make their paranormal undertakings seem legitimate.

"I don't suppose Wikipedia has anything to say about the different types of ghosts and spirits and what Viola might be?" I ask with a heavy sigh. The question is half a joke, but X and Jupiter immediately start scrolling, and without a better suggestion for what to do next, Kelly and I wait to see what they come up with.

"Kinds of ghosts," Jupiter says, reading off a title. Kelly lets out a soft groan, like they can't believe their illustrious career has come to this: two sunshiny mediums and Wikipedia. Can't say I blame them, but we're working with what we've got. X peeks over Jupiter's shoulder, checking to see what page she's on, then taps quickly on his phone and must come to the same place.

"Apparitions," he says, reading out loud. "Apparitions are the presence of a long-dead person, usually tied to a physical place or event like a battle. They're believed to be harmless to living people. That doesn't sound right, does it?"

"Banshees," Jupiter says next. "Banshees are believed to be the spirits of spurned women who are left to wander . . . Oh. They're mostly in Ireland. That probably doesn't have anything to do with us either."

Kelly pinches the bridge of their nose. I pat their arm sympathetically. Never mind their soul dying. This investigative technique has to be excruciating for them.

"Corpse bride," X says excitedly, but then frowns. "Oh no. That's only in movies. Moving on."

Considering how very little the living actually know about Afterlife and what happens when we die, we really have come up with a lot of different classifications for the restless spirits who linger. All of them are wrong, unfortunately. After corpse brides come D, E, F, and garden variety ghosts. None of them provide any real clarity on Viola. Eventually the words start to lose meaning; they're just going through a thesaurus for ghostly synonyms without gaining any additional knowledge. Kelly slumps down on a red velvet settee in the front hallway. They tip their head back against the wall and close their eyes.

"You all right?" I ask, settling beside them. I let my head drop onto Kelly's shoulder. In turn, they let their cheek rest against my hair. I lean into it, letting myself relax and almost forgetting for a minute that I was the one asking if everything was okay.

"I'm tired," they say softly, too quiet for the others to hear. Their tone makes my throat get tight. Kelly would never make even an admission as small as that lightly. It's like the coworker who never takes a sick day announcing they might be in a little late tomorrow if their headache doesn't go away. Call the paramedics. We have an emergency situation on our hands.

"Just hold on a little longer," I say. It's like we're in our own little cocoon made of spider silk, while Jupiter and X chatter away. "We'll figure something out soon."

They don't answer. Only lift their head from mine, and when I straighten too, their eyes are closed. It's a sight I'm far too familiar with. The moment when sickness wins over everything and there's nothing you can do but let your body rest, even while other conversations—like the doctor relaying the latest round of test results to your stricken family—float around you.

"Malicious spirits are believed to be—" Jupiter is saying. I lean my head back too, letting her words wash over me. Kelly's shoulder is pressed against mine. Maybe this is the last time we'll sit like this. I try to bat the thought away, but it bobs in my consciousness with the tenacity of a late summer wasp at a picnic.

"Does your family still miss you?" Kelly asks. The question comes from so far out of left field I actually jerk back to sitting up with my eyes open.

"What?" I ask, startled.

They open their eyes slowly. Their gaze is heavy. Tired. There's strain in their face I haven't seen before. Whether it's the time we've already used up, or the extra burden from sliding to save me from the nothing, they're flagging.

"You don't talk about them much," Kelly says. "Do you think they talk about you?"

I blink rapidly, trying to understand what they're asking.

"I . . . think they do? Probably?" It's barely been a full year since I died. Hopefully they still talk about me sometimes. Honestly, my greatest wish is that they have stopped talking about me with sadness. I don't want to be an unhappy memory for them. Before the cancer, there were so many years of good memories and inside family jokes to share. I hope they're getting to a place where those are the things that come to the forefront, rather than the days and weeks of doctor's appointments and hospital stays.

"How come you never had a partner? A romantic one, I mean?" Kelly asks, which is even more shocking than their first question. It takes me a second to pick myself up off the metaphorical floor before I can even begin to respond.

"I had partners. I dated," I protest, struggling to cover up a hundred different feelings all at once. "I just never . . ." I shrug. What do I say? There were a few girlfriends. Nubia and I were together for over a year right after undergrad, but then she got accepted into the year-at-sea training program for young adult educators, and by the time she came back she was engaged to a woman from the crew. Margot and I even lived together for a bit, but that ended suddenly when she decided to become a militant vegan and refused to allow me to keep any leather products in the apartment, including the leather jacket I had found at a thrift store the previous fall. And yes, it's silly to break up over a jacket, but it was her third "lifestyle makeover" in the seven months we shared a lease and I couldn't keep up with the emotional whiplash of constantly having to give up whatever of my possessions she suddenly felt objectionable, and throw out whole fridges full of food because she believed they were contaminated by whatever had lived in the same Tupperware before.

"Do you wish you'd been married when you died?" Kelly asks, clearly impatient for me to wrap up my mental rationalizations. "Many of the souls I've collected always spoke first of their husbands or wives. Like they were the most important people in their world and the ones they would miss the most after death. Are you sorry you didn't have someone like that to remember you once you were gone?"

Maybe this isn't Kelly? Maybe I really am in the nothing. Is this how Tiffany and the others spend the year between balls? Having impossible conversations with people who look like their friends and loved ones but are really facsimiles dressed in their clothes?

"What are you talking about?" It's not the most elegant response, but I can't think of anything else to say.

Kelly watches me wordlessly, gaze darting over my face. Are they doing the same thing I'm doing? Looking at the features so I can print them in some permanent memory that lingers beyond death?

They say, "If we don't stop this . . . If the patch fails and the bond . . . I was wondering if you would—"

Jupiter leaps between us, waving her phone. "You're not listening! I think I found it!"

chapter
nineteen

MURDER IS WRONG. Murdering your medium friend who is the only reason you didn't get left on a street corner in Toronto to turn into a slavering wraith is especially uncharitable. But I wouldn't be mad if a paranormal spider spun Jupiter up into a web and dragged her off to the nothing—only for a few minutes, of course—so that Kelly and I could finish our conversation.

But even as she takes a step back, watching us both with flushed cheeks and bright excitement in her eyes, Kelly's face has already slipped into its usual mask of impassivity. The moment of strange vulnerability has gone, and we are back to the business of kicking Viola's ass.

"What did you find?" I ask with the barely disguised impatience of a parent whose four-year-old has just interrupted a very important conversation to announce that they farted. Jupiter, even though she is the more perceptive of our human sidekick duo, doesn't notice that she's just completely crashed the party. Instead, she pulls up her phone and reads with delighted pride.

"A spectre is a subtype of malicious ghost that uses the life force of other spirits to supernaturally extend its own existence among the living. It can be separated from wraiths, lost souls and—"

"Wait," I say, momentarily drawn out of my sulk. "Wikipedia knows about wraiths and lost souls?"

"The article on lost souls was wrong," X says, sounding apologetic like it's his responsibility to monitor all the afterlife-related entries on the world's largest free digital encyclopedia. "It said lost souls were the ghosts of unbaptized or unconverted indentured servants from the Middle Ages, who were responsible for—"

"So why do we think this definition of spectres might be accurate?" Kelly asks. They don't look at me. We will have to resume our private—and weird as fuck, if I'm being honest—conversation later.

"Because there's a section in the article where it talks about famous spectres, and it includes a picture of this house," Jupiter says. She holds the screen out, and sure enough, there's a grainy photo of Manor Rock, taken back in the grand old days before the stucco and years of neglect. The caption underneath says *Manor Rock in Brockville, Ontario is believed to be the residence of a malignant spectre who has caused the suspicious deaths of young women in Eastern Ontario in the late 19th and early 20th centuries.*

"Woah," I say.

"Right?" X asks, sounding pleased. He and Jupiter stand shoulder to shoulder with twin expressions of pride on their faces. I want to give them both a cookie, but X ate all our road trip snacks. "She's a spectre." He punctuates the end of the statement with a little exhale that's probably meant to make it sound spooky, but it only makes me smile. He's unflappable. I was skeptical about his place as a long-term partner for Jupiter. His openness can easily be mistaken for ignorance and naiveté. But he's got a heart of twenty-four-karat gold, and I have no doubt if Viola came to take Jupiter away to the nothing, X would fight tooth and nail to keep her among the living.

And that's what I have to do for Kelly. Whether I'm in love with them, or just love them, they are my ally and my reaper in arms, and we are not letting a mistake we didn't even know we were making end this.

"Does it say anything about how to stop a spectre? Maybe how to subdue one and drag it off to the far outer reaches of a completely different undead dimension?" I ask. Wikipedia is hardly a source of academically rigorous reference information, and clearly they're also not an authority on the wide variety of post-life entities that might visit this world, but it's the best shot we've got right now.

Jupiter frowns as she scrolls through the screen, but finally she shakes her head.

"It says spectres typically disappear once their wrath has been sated or they run out of victims. Do you think Viola is sated?"

Not even a little. Whatever she does in her down time between nomming some poor debutante at her balls, she's not ready to call it a night just yet.

"Who wrote the bit about this place being haunted?" X asks. Without asking permission, he takes Jupiter's phone and taps at the screen. "Leeds & Grenville Paranormal Society."

"What's that?" I ask.

"The bit about the house and the spectre links to an article on a blog for the Leeds & Grenville Paranormal Society. There's an address on the website. Looks like it's in town." His smile is so proud it makes me blush. "Maybe we can go ask them if they know more about it?"

God bless crowdsourced reference material. So often since I died, I've felt like I've been in a life raft with no way to signal for help, or climbing a mountain without the necessary gear. If even one detail on Wikipedia is correct, maybe we don't have to go this alone.

On cue, and like they can read my mind, Kelly snorts. "People like that are the worst. I've collected a few of them. Know-a-lots. Won't stop talking, but everything they say is wrong."

And normally that would be my cue to roll my eyes and be

annoyed at Kelly's perpetual negativity. But somehow the mental image of them trying to stay patient and professional while a recently dead supernatural fan boy trails after them going "Is it true that—" or "I had a bet with Dave about—" while every one of their random theories and beliefs is so profoundly incorrect Kelly won't dignify them with a reply, but also can't get away from the endless questions until they turn their charge over at the gates of Afterlife is incredibly funny. The look they give me as I muffle a giggle is even funnier. Even Jupiter's lips are twitching, while X mutters about this so-called Paranormal Society.

I slip my hand into Kelly's, smiling sweetly. "Let's just hear what the weirdos have to say. It's not like we've got any better ideas." Poor Kelly. If I were a millennia-old reaper who had accidentally hitched my soul to a dead life coach who couldn't even get a joint ghost-reaper task force off the ground, I'd be feeling pretty grim about my survival prospects, even though being grim isn't even in my job description.

The sun is just coming up as we exit the house. Viola's ball must have done some physics-defying time-bending thing, because it doesn't feel like we've been here that long.

The office of the Leeds & Grenville Paranormal Society isn't an office. More like a house at the end of a long dirt road about ten minutes north of town. An ancient golden retriever on rigid arthritic legs gives us a few half-hearted barks as we get out of the car, but all it takes is X crouching down to ask who's a good boy, and the dog clearly recognizes a kindred spirit. He rolls over, exposing his belly, while his tongue lolls out of his mouth in ecstasy and X offers endless affirmations that, yes, in fact, this dog really is the very best goodest boy there ever was.

Kelley, Jupiter and I make our way to the front porch. It's technically too early for a business call, but that doesn't mean much right now. I'm ready to march right up to the door and even walk through it if it means finding one person with an inkling of knowledge about how to get me and Kelly unhitched before it's too late.

So of course, I lift a foot to climb the first step to the old wooden porch, and it's like kicking a concrete block.

"Oh, for god's sake, not again." I curse, hopping up and down on one foot as I try to figure out if it's possible to break a toe when I don't really have bones anymore.

"What's wrong?" Jupiter asks. She's two steps ahead of me and clearly didn't run into the same obstruction. Kelly does, which makes me feel less alone, though my gymnastics mean they approach it with more caution, putting a hand out until it lies flat against yet another invisible barrier. Or, mostly invisible. When Kelly touches it, the light ripples like gasoline on water.

"Woah, that's cool," X says, coming up behind us. He's followed by his new golden retriever best friend, and both of them walk past us like nothing is there, his face squashing into a pout as he comes to stand next to Jupiter. "Oh man. That was going to be really fun if I ran into it."

The front door swings open and an elderly woman in a purple sweater and dark green pants with dirt stains at the knees stands in front of us.

"If you don't have a pulse, get off my property," she says. Her hair is a frizzy grey mass pushed to one side like she's just woken up, but the narrowing of her gaze is very sharp. And it's particularly unnerving because it's aimed directly at me. I take a step back, until I'm pressed against Kelly's chest. Don't know if I'm looking for protection or trying to protect them, but either way, a little distance feels like a good idea.

"Can you see Ember?" Jupiter asks. She and X are both looking at me like they've never seen me before. Wow, it's been a while since we last had this conversation.

"Spirits are not welcome here," she says, by way of answer. "I'm impressed you got through the runes at the start of the drive. You must be very powerful."

I swallow, trying not to back down any farther, though along with panic, there's fear lingering inside me, probably from my confrontation with Viola. This woman is very much alive, but the crow's feet at the corners of her eyes and the lines around her mouth say she has seen some shit and she will not put up with any undead hijinks.

I say, "We're looking for the Leeds & Grenville Paranormal Society."

She laughs. Or maybe she chokes. Honestly, she looks like she has to be in her eighties. Maybe even older. She's got one hand on the doorknob and her knuckles are swollen with decades of arthritis. The other hand shakes slightly as she pulls the neck of her cardigan tighter around her throat.

"How did you find me?" she asks.

"Your address was on the website?" X says, sounding confused.

"What website?" She turns her suspicious gaze on him, and he and Jupiter also reflexively shrink back, which makes me feel a little better. Before they can answer though, she scoffs. "That internet thing my grandson made? Why would he put my address on it? I don't want people coming here."

"Do you want them going somewhere else?" X asks. He's got one hand buried in the golden retriever's fur, like if he has to make a break for it, the dog is coming with him. I don't know who this woman is, but dognapping feels ill-advised.

"Do you know about Viola?" I ask before she can threaten to call the police or hex us for trespassing or whatever it is she can do. Because if she's got runes on the driveway, she's not just an old widow living on the property she refuses to sell to unscrupulous land developers while she's shipped off to a retirement home.

Her gaze swings back to me, eyes narrowed. She takes a hesitant step onto the porch, still clutching her sweater to her throat. The dog lets out a wheezy bark and staggers toward her. He presses up against her side, and she rests a shaking hand on his back.

"Who are you exactly?" she asks.

"My name is Jupiter. This is X."

"Alexander," X puts in quickly. "My name is Alexander. Nice to meet you, ma'am."

"And that's Ember and Kelly," Jupiter finishes, pointing at us. "They're . . . uh . . ."

The woman nods, like she already knows the answer.

"You should probably come inside." She steps back. "The others will be here soon."

"Others? Which others?" X asks, but he doesn't waste any time walking right through the front door. The dog hobbles after him. Jupiter hesitates, looking back toward us.

"You'll have to . . . unlock the porch first," I say, knocking on the barrier. The light ripples. Kelly takes my hand, no doubt because they're not letting me get trapped a second time in as many days.

The woman sighs, weary, but she doesn't seem at all frightened. She licks her thumb and rubs it over a smudge on the doorframe. A rune, I realize too late, as she wipes it away.

The light ripples on its own this time, but when I reach forward again, nothing stops me. I glance over my shoulder at Kelly. They look tired, but we're going to get through this.

"Don't think I won't put it back up the second you're gone," she says, already disappearing inside.

Wordlessly, we walk up the porch and enter the house.

chapter
twenty

THE OLD WOMAN'S name is Beryl. The dog is Winston. Together, with a collective age of at least a hundred and fifty (if you combine their respective human and dog years), they walk us into a living room that can't have been painted or renovated in the twenty-first century. Flowery upholstered couch with no less than three crocheted blankets draped over the back. Nicotine-stained wallpaper. An assortment of dried-out potpourri, candles and artificial flowers in front of an old wood stove. I squint as we get closer to the candles. Familiar geometric designs have been carved into the wax, and while they aren't lit, even so, power I know well sizzles around them. When I touch them, something like static electricity zings through me.

"You're like Jupiter," I say.

Beryl glances at Jupiter and gives an indignant snort. "If I were, you'd have surprised me when you showed up on my porch. You think I'm new at this? I felt you coming when you turned off Highway 29."

In the protected confines of her old house, she moves less assertively than she did outside. Her shoulders are hunched, leaving a hump just beneath the collar. The room has tall windows that face the front of the house, and she goes from one to the next, pulling rust-coloured drapes shut.

"You shouldn't have come here," she says. "And whatever it is you think you're doing with Viola, it would be better for you to go back to wherever you came from." She glances at Kelly, her nose wrinkling like she smells something unpleasant. "You especially."

I nearly ask if she knows what Kelly is but bite it back because we can't overplay our hand.

"You know about Viola," I say instead. "You know she's a spectre."

Beryl grunts. "And if you know too, you also know you should keep as far away from her as you can."

This conversation feels like that meme with the three identical Spider-Mans all pointing at each other. I take a deep breath and skip over the back-and-forth.

"How do we stop her? We need to take her somewhere, and ideally without her turning us to dust in the process."

Beryl chuckles. It's a dry, rattling thing, coming from deep inside her chest, but eventually it evolves into a wet sucking sound. Winston grumbles, clearly offended. Jupiter makes a motion like she might offer a glass of water, or maybe to call 911, but Beryl only shakes her head and finally collects herself.

"I'm sorry," she says, though the words still come out with a phlegmy echo. "I'm ninety-seven years old and that is the funniest thing anyone has said to me since my husband died nearly thirty years ago."

"Ember can be very funny when she wants to," Kelly says. They've settled on the ugly pink and green flowered sofa, wrapping one of the blankets over their shoulders, and the circles under their eyes look like bruises. I'm so worried about it, I need a moment before I realize they've complimented me. In public, no less. Jesus Christ, they really are dying.

"That wasn't one of the times I was trying to be funny," I mutter. "We need to stop Viola."

"We already stopped her," Beryl says in irritation. "She's been trapped in that old house for longer than I've been alive."

"But she killed people," Jupiter says, hand going to her phone like she's going to read the Wikipedia page to Beryl.

"Until my grandparents locked her away in that attic." Despite her protestations that we aren't welcome, Beryl goes to the kitchen and gets the kettle going. We may not be welcome, but that doesn't mean she won't offer us a cup of tea.

"Woah," X says, sounding awestruck. "Grandma and Grandpa Badass."

"Watch your language, young man," Beryl says, setting out three teacups on her coffee table. She doesn't put one in front of me and Kelly, which is probably a snub of some sort, but I'm not in the mood for tea and a chat. "You wanted to know about the paranormal society. My grandparents started it in 1887. Not long after, when they realized what Viola was doing, they waited one night for her to go up to the attic at the old house, and they locked her in there."

"The barrier," I say, considering this arthritic old woman for a second time. I don't know a lot about the powers of humans like Jupiter and X, mostly because they don't either. But to put together something like that and keep it going for a hundred or more years? That's powerful. Probably more than either Jupiter or X are capable of. "That's you?"

"I hear there are a few others up there with her," she says, pouring hot water into a teapot. She sets it on the table before covering the whole thing in a crocheted cozy, then settles into one of the dusty rose barrel chairs by the fireplace. "I hope she enjoys the company."

"She's killing them," I say. "Consuming them to keep herself alive."

"They're already dead," Beryl says carelessly. I'm all for respecting your elders, but her lack of compassion would make a reaper proud and it has me sitting up straighter in my seat. Kelly puts a hand on my thigh, and my chest shakes with a gentle nudge on the link. "If they're thick enough to wander up there and get caught like flies on tape, then—"

"They're terrified. They—" I shake my head. I'm not here to launch a campaign for ghostly rights. We can debate the ethics of Beryl's little arrangement later. "We need you to take down the barrier."

She snorts. "Why would I do that?"

"Because we're taking Viola with us. Smith said—"

"Smith?" Beryl's amusement turns to indignation. "That old bastard. What did he promise you?"

We all shift nervously. Even Kelly leans forward with interest.

"You know Smith?" I ask. She grins. It seems miraculous that someone her age can even hear us, much less follow the conversation and drop surprising little truth bombs here and there. Maybe she's not human. A witch? Some other kind of ghost we still don't know the name of. We stopped on Wikipedia after S for Spectre. Who knows what's listed under T and U?

"The veil is thin sometimes between our world and the Other Side. Smith and I have had some lovely conversations. At my age, you don't sleep a lot, and Winston here isn't much of a talker." She reaches down to ruffle the dog's head, and when her fingers start working behind his ears, he groans in ecstasy. "Smith and I like to share old stories. Swap recipes. Everyone needs a little company."

Sounds cute. Maybe she's the one who gave him the recipe for jerk chicken. Also, the blankets on the back of her couch bear a not insignificant resemblance to the ones in that little tent Smith gave us for a nap. Is this how they get all those worldly supplies? Some sort of medium-to-shade bootlegging operation between dimensions?

A knock sounds at the door, making us all jump. Well, everyone except Beryl. Winston struggles to his feet, barking a wheezy greeting. Beryl doesn't bother going to open it, and a moment later, the door swings open, allowing entrance to three more people. Each of them looks like they were well into adult-hood during Pierre Trudeau's stint as Canada's Prime Minister, and possibly even remember a time before we adopted the Maple Leaf flag. Two men and another woman, laughing to each other as they enter, then the laughter dies as they realize Winston and Beryl have company.

"Bee?" the woman asks. "Who's this?" She's shorter than Beryl. Heavier. Her hair is more silver, and she's dressed in the uniform of women of a certain age—sensible leather shoes, shapeless pants too nice to be jeans but not fancy enough to be formal, and a printed blouse under a dusty rose fleece vest. A brooch shaped like a chickadee is pinned to her chest and she fiddles with it as she looks at us. There's zero hesitation as her gaze goes from Jupiter and X to me and Kelly, so I guess she's like Beryl.

"We were just getting to that," Beryl says dryly. "They showed up unexpectedly. Sounds like they've been having some adventures. Have a seat. I'll get more teacups."

The new woman's name is Lucille. The men are Ira and Ralph. Ira walks with a cane and wears suspenders to keep his pants hiked halfway up his torso. Ralph has the bluest eyes I've ever seen and kisses Jupiter on both cheeks when she introduces herself.

"You look like my granddaughter," he says. "She's a lesbian too."

Jupiter flushes and mumbles protests. X asks, "You're a lesbian?" with a confused frown. Ralph looks incredibly proud of his disclosure, no doubt pleased to be up to date on the slang the young people are using these days. Wait until Jupiter tries to explain pansexuality to him.

"Actually, I'm the lesbian," I say, stepping forward. Ralph's pride turns to bafflement, like he didn't know there could be two lesbians in the same room at the same time.

To prove the point, he says, "But you're dead."

Lucille puts a hand on his shoulder. "Come on, Ralphie. Help me open the tin in the kitchen so I can get us some cookies. Sounds like it's almost story time with these nice young people."

A few minutes later, with tea served to all the living people in the room and a plate of Danish butter cookies that make my mouth water—it's weird to be in a room where everyone can see me but I still can't eat the food; especially when I have a real affinity for Danish butter cookies since they were a staple in my grandmother's house while I was growing up. Beryl settles back into her pink chair and says, "This meeting of the Leeds & Grenville Paranormal Society has come to order."

"Does that mean we're members?" X asks, sounding excited. To make room for the other arrivals, he and Jupiter have squeezed themselves onto the sofa with me and Kelly. It's a tight fit, and Kelly's had to sling an arm around my shoulders to sit comfortably.

I look around the room and say, "You're the Paranormal Society? All of it?"

"Of course," Ira says with an indignant harrumph that only people over the age of eighty ever seem to be able to pull off convincingly. "The kids these days, with their internet and their reaction videos. They don't have time to be learning the real lore about the dead. Think they know everything already." He folds his arms over his chest, fending off an argument we're not going to bother with. Like Ralph and lesbians, I'd like to know what Ira thinks reaction videos are, but now isn't the time.

"We have to get Viola to the Other Side and bring her to Smith. Is that something you can help us do?"

They all get quiet, giving each other anxious glances. Winston whines, like even he's afraid of Viola. Ralph sucks air between his teeth and wrinkles his nose. Lucille fumbles with the bird pin on her vest.

"Assuming we did know," Beryl says. "Why would you want to take the risk of freeing her? What has Smith promised you?"

How much do we tell them? They clearly know more than

your average set of seniors, but that also makes us vulnerable. But without them, what are we going to do? Keep looking up spooky facts on Wikipedia and find a way to chisel through the barrier on our own?

I say, "Kelly's a reaper. And I'm haunting them. We're . . . connected, and it's causing some problems."

Lucille gasps softly. Beryl gets up and strides across the space, walking right up to us so she can put a palm to Kelly's forehead like she's checking for a fever. They jerk back, but they don't have anywhere to go, so soon enough the two of them are locked in a staring contest. Beryl studies them. Kelly holds still. I want to take their hand, but I have a feeling if anyone else touches Kelly right now, they might tear us all to pieces.

Finally, Beryl straightens and shuffles back to her chair.

"You've got yourself in quite the pickle, haven't you?" she asks. Winston sniffs at Kelly's knee, giving them a suspicious glance before shuffling back to his spot by Beryl's chair and flopping down with a heavy sigh and falls asleep. We should all be so lucky.

"Smith said Viola was the only one who could undo the haunting," I say, ignoring the instinct to defend our mistakes, which are undoubtedly numerous. We didn't know what was happening. We had to trust Smith because we had no other options. I'm aware that thinking Viola will help us is next-level naive, but what choice do I have? "The patch won't last much longer, and when it does . . ." I glance at Kelly. We've lost so much time. If this little senior Scooby Gang can't help us, it's probably game over.

"It's not like a haircut," Ralph says. "She's not going to take a little off the top and you're both free of each other."

"The logistics are a problem for later," I say with a conviction I can't feel. I saw the knot. In my wild escape from Viola's ballroom, I saw how deep our link goes. I have no idea how anyone could ever undo that. "How do we get her to the Other Side?" Also, I don't like the way Ralph said "free of each other." I want Kelly to stop seizing and dying. I don't want them out of my life . . . or afterlife. I give them another quick look. They're leaning back against the sofa, eyes half closed like they're fighting sleep. I put a hand in theirs and they start, inhaling sharply as they come back to wakefulness.

"Viola is powerful," Ira says. "There's a reason the society put the barrier up at Manor Rock, and it's a good thing she hasn't figured out how to tear it down. Do you think we can just call her up and invite her over for a chat?"

"You're the paranormal society," I say. "What is it exactly that you can do? Trapping her isn't a permeant solution. I'm offering to take her away from here so she can't hurt anyone else."

"We can help," Jupiter says, standing. She tries to look brave, but her fingers keep toying with the zipper on her jacket, whether she's doing it consciously or not. "Me and X. We're like you. The runes. I know how to make those."

Ralph snorts. "You're nothing like us. We've been at this since before you were born. Do you even think—"

"Kelly's our friend," Jupiter says. "We need to help them."

"And you think marching into my house without an invitation is the way to do that?" Beryl asks.

"That's the problem with young people these days," Ira says, crossing his arms over his chest. "So entitled, but they never want to learn what we have to teach them."

The psychics squabble. My head pounds. I glance down at Kelly and they've closed their eyes again. A trickle of blood oozes from their nose. They're so still it's like they're already gone.

X is begging everyone to take a breath. That is, until Ralph strides up to him. He's a full head shorter than X, but his stocky build is solid enough to butt up against X's chest and call him a "young palooka," whatever that means. That's all Jupiter needs to jump in and intervene, while Beryl and Lucille tell her not to get involved and Ira struggles to get out of his chair. Winston's trying to join the fray, squirming to get his geriatric joints working in unison so he can stand. He lets out a series of phlegmy barks to make sure everyone knows he has something to say.

There's a box of tissues on the side table by the couch. I take one so I can clean Kelly's face, but before I can reach them, their hand clasps around my wrist. The motion is so fast and sudden I don't have time to react. Kelly opens their eyes, and the pupils and irises are gone, leaving only colourless white. They're shaking, and the hair at their temples is going slick with perspiration. The corners of their mouth tremble with tension, and they're breathing hard.

"Guys," I say, trying to tear my gaze away and failing. "Everyone?"

The yelling around me gets louder. Ira has managed to join Ralph and is adding to the series of insults by calling Jupiter a "feral whippergong" while Lucille waves her hands and says something about respect, and Beryl keeps shouting at Winston to lie down before he hurts himself, which only gets her a wet gagging sound from the dog in reply as he hobbles into the fray.

"Hey!" I shout. Kelly's still holding on to my hand and a blast of power shoots from them to me, then outward to the room. The whole place gets quiet. Stone silent, in fact. I finally manage to look away from Kelly and everyone in the room has been frozen in place. It's a hilarious tableau, with the senior citizens bearing down on X and Jupiter, who are clearly torn between arguing back and not getting too close for fear of shattering ancient fragile bones. Even Winston is locked in position, lips puckered mid-howl.

"Talk to them," Kelly says, voice a rasp. "They're scared. Humans are always scared. But we can do this with their help."

I take a deep breath, centering myself like I used to before I turned on the camera to record a video or start broadcasting live. Dear Sparks, I know the world is big and overwhelming, but if we just work together, we can accomplish amazing things.

They're all still as statues, but those who can have at least directed their eyes toward me. The effect is both off-putting and hilarious. I let out the breath on a laugh.

"Sorry," I say, as Kelly lets go of my hand. "I needed your attention."

At the loss of contact, they all sag. Ira lurches forward, and X has to catch him. He grumbles, like he doesn't need the help, but also doesn't protest as X holds on to his elbow and leads him back to the armchair.

"This is a win-win," I say, collecting myself. "You get rid of the spectre haunting your town. We get what we want too. But we can't do it without your help. We need Viola. It doesn't look like you have anyone who is going to make sure the barrier holds twenty years from now. Wouldn't knowing that she can't hurt anybody else, either alive or dead, be a nice legacy for you all to leave?"

If only they knew what waits for them after death. Who cares about a legacy when you find that beyond the veil is nothing but waiting rooms and working groups.

The four members of the Leeds & Grenville Paranormal Society glance wordlessly at each other. Winston farts as he lies back on the carpet. But finally, Beryl clears her throat and settles in her chair once more.

"If we take down the barrier, how will you get her to go with you?"

Always with the questions I can't answer. When this is over, I'm going to need a massive vacation.

"We can slide," I say.

Jupiter gasps. "But wouldn't that—"

"We have the patch," I say. "If we work fast, we can get back to Smith and he and Viola can undo the link before it does more damage." I glance at Kelly. Their eyes are grey once more, but they're still shaking and their hand against my arm is clammy. Still, they nod once, confirming their support of my plan. We can do this. They know the risk, but it's the fastest way to get back to the Other Side.

"Instead of taking down the barrier, we could try a summoning," Lucile says, though she doesn't sound particularly sure about it. Her uncertainty gets worse when Beryl shoots her a glare, but Ralph cocks his head to one side like he's considering it. Or else he's trying to catch whatever is said next with whichever of his ears is the good one. Hard to say for sure.

The room gets quiet again, though a more living human quiet, instead of the supernatural petrification that just happened. Beryl purses her lips, and Ira blows his nose into a handkerchief, but there's a silent conversation happening. The exchange makes me wonder how long they've known each other. I can almost imagine them, much younger, discovering they each had some kind of ability that went beyond the usual human experience. Sixteen-year-old Beryl and Lucille learning to contact the dead in one of their bedrooms. Ira and Ralph doing their best to perform careless masculinity in their twenties, knowing that any hint they were unusual might bring the whole charade down. They may not know how to run a website, but they know a lot and I can't blame them for not wanting our arrival to spoil their peaceful twilight years.

As the silence stretches, X opens his mouth like he might say something. I'm too far away to stop him, but Jupiter shoots a hand out, slapping her palm over his lips. His expression turns hilariously surprised, but when she drops her hand back to her lap, he pinches his lips together and lowers his gaze again. She pats his knee. Kelly chuckles softly behind me. They're watching the two of them and something like dry amusement twitches the corners of their lips, but the ghostly smile vanishes the second they catch me spying.

Before I can say anything though, Beryl says, "All right. What's the worst that can happen? We've all lived longer than we had any right to. If you get us killed, I expect a limousine to take me right up to St. Peter's gates. Understand?"

What's the worst that can happen? Unfortunately for Beryl and her compatriots, the worst thing that could happen is that I might face this afterlifetime on my own. They've got their friendly little posse. Jupiter and X have each other. All I have is Kelly, and there's no way in hell—or HELL—I'm doing eternity by myself.

I smile at her sweetly, and her answering smile says she knows how very little sugar I've put into it.

"I'll call the limo driver and make sure he stocks the cooler with champagne so you can arrive in style."

She nods and extends one gnarled hand to shake.

"Young lady, you have yourself a deal."

TRAPPING A MALICIOUS SPECTRE NEEDS PREPARATION. Despite my earlier outburst, it's Beryl who takes charge as the night stretches onwards.

"I haven't done a summoning since the 1990s," she mutters as she rummages through a closet. "Lucille, do you remember if it's silk or cotton we used last time?" She emerges with five or six plastic shopping bags stuffed to overflowing with long strips of brightly coloured fabric, which she hands to X. "Do you know how to braid, son?"

X blinks like she's just asked if he can do advanced calculus. Jupiter takes the bags.

"I can show him," she says.

"It was two silk to one cotton," Lucille says. She's in the kitchen, standing over the stove as something green and lumpy bubbles in a large pot.

"Is that a potion?" X asks, sounding awed.

She chuckles. "Pea soup. If you want us playing with monsters like Viola, we need to eat."

"What can I do?" I ask.

"Go rest," Beryl says, without so much as a backward glance.

"Both of you. Can't have you dozing off once the fun starts. There's a spare room in the back."

"But I can help," I say. Pea soup. Cloth braids. None of this feels like it's going to be enough to catch Viola.

"That throbbing thing going on between the two of you will contaminate everything. Weaken the materials as we weave them together. Better for you to stay out of the way." She throws an uncomfortable glance towards Kelly, who is still lying on the sofa. "And he looks like he'll keel over faster than Ira if we ask you two to do anything more elaborate than sit tight."

"My knees are bad, but my hearing is fine," Ira grouches from the living room. He motions to Jupiter and X as they enter with their bags of cloth strips. "Give me those. We're going to need the big guns. A four-way round braid is better than three strips."

"I don't think I have enough silk for round braids, Ira," Beryl says. The bickering starts up again. Jupiter and X watch nervously. I think about intervening, but slowly the two of them get folded into the action, as Ira shows them the proper way to put together his famous round braids, while Beryl grumbles to Winston about how no one listens to her anymore. Maybe it'll be good for them. The Leeds & Grenville Paranormal Society, such as they are, would not inspire confidence under most circumstances. But they are like Jupiter and X. If they can stop arguing—and not drop dead of old age—for just a moment, they might even be able to teach them something. Set up the next generation, or whatever.

Speaking of not dropping dead . . .

"Come on," I say, holding my hand out to Kelly. "Time for another nap."

Being relegated to the sidelines is not comfortable for me. I ran my own show for such a long time while I was alive, and even in death, there was always another problem to solve or focus group to plan. I was in the weeds, getting shit done. Sort of. I at least got invited to the meetings. Being sent off for a rest isn't what I do. I don't like it.

Also, I don't like the way Beryl referred to the link as "throbbing." It's one of those words I've always had a visceral reaction to, the way some people don't like "moist" or "ooze." Mostly it goes back to my early twenties, when I thought I might be bi instead of a lesbian, and spent a semester mainlining historical romance novels, hoping I could convince myself I was also attracted to men. But the only ones I ever felt remotely interested in were fictional dukes with perfect teeth and improbably throbbing manhoods, and half the time I skipped over the sex scenes because eventually even a massive penis is still just a penis and I never really did get the fascination. In any case, nothing is throbbing between me and Kelly. It's a pulse at best, and Kelly's side of it is getting weaker and weaker.

"That's it," I say, helping them climb into Beryl's guest bed. It's a basic double with pink sheets and a quilt with more than a few moth-eaten holes in it. "Get some sleep. I'll wake you up in a little bit."

I'm not even sure they're still awake to hear me. But when I turn to go sit in the small peach chair by the dresser, Kelly reaches out and takes hold of my wrist, and even after everything, their grip is strong.

"I heard you screaming," they say.

Embarrassment creeps up the back of my neck at a conversation I had what feels like a lifetime ago with Jupiter. I'm a screamer. Kelly heard me and I wanted to die (again) of embarrassment. I didn't think they remembered any of it, not after everything.

"I wasn't screaming," I say.

"Not now." Their eyes are still closed, but their words are clear. They're awake and they know what they're saying, even if it doesn't make sense. "Before. At the house, when you were upstairs. I could hear you. I could feel your fear."

Oh. Not the kind of screaming I was thinking of. I sink to the bed, taking their hand in both of mine.

"I'm okay now," I say, trying hard not to think about those last few minutes at Viola's ball. The terror was real. I was going down, ready to give up with no one to save me.

Kelly looks at me. Their eyes have gone electric blue.

"No," they say, even more firmly than a moment ago. "I could feel it. Like it was mine. It was like I was inside you. Like I *was* you."

I blink, trying to understand what they're saying. Inside me? What even—

But then I remember the moment at Smith's after he'd put the patch on. I'd opened my eyes and found myself looking at myself. Was that it? Was I inside Kelly, looking back at myself? But how is that possible?

Gently, they creep back, making room for me, and I lie down, sliding under the covers so I'm next to them. Our hands are tangled together and Kelly waits patiently while I work through the implications. In the dark, as the spiders wrapped me up in their cocoon, I felt the link. Went looking for it, actually. And then I heard Kelly, telling me to hold on. It was like they were right behind me. So close I should have been able to feel them. More than that, even. Like we were standing in the same place. The exact same spot.

I look at our fingers, crisscrossing over each other. It's like the knot I saw, as I followed the link from that place of terror to the safety of Kelly's arms. We were connected. Tied. I close my eyes, picturing the knot, following it to Kelly, who is waiting for me.

I open my eyes and I'm looking at myself. Red hair pressed awkwardly where it's trapped between my cheek and the pillow.

"Woah. What's going on?" I ask. I mean . . . *I* ask. The other me. The one I'm looking at, as she lies there with the furrows between her brows getting deeper and deeper. "Kelly? Can you hear that?"

"Yes," they say, but the sound comes from inside me, like I'm listening to myself speaking. Not the me I'm looking at. Her lips don't move. The me that I am speaks. The one I hear talk every day. The one—

The link sputters. Okay, it throbs. Don't tell Beryl. It's overwhelming as it grabs me and shoves me, pushing me free. I gasp, and suddenly I'm myself again. Back in myself, I mean. Kelly's still watching me with crystal blue eyes, and when I speak, it's all as it usually would be.

"Is that what you felt?"

They nod. "I don't understand what we've done, but it's powerful. If it wasn't—" They wince, shifting like they're in pain. The link flutters. I tighten my grip on their hands.

"Hold on, okay?" I say, throat going tight. "You have to hold on. The others are getting ready. We'll have Viola in a few more hours. We'll go back to Smith and he'll fix this. He has to fix—" The last words get cut off on a sob. I can't lose them. Who'd have thought, a year later, I'd be crying over the reaper who didn't want anything to do with me? But I am, and I'm not sure I can stop. "I'm sorry," I say, though they've already said it's not my fault. Kelly leans back a little more and I snuggle into them, unwilling to let them get any farther away from me than absolutely necessary. They don't speak, but they do run a hand over my head and down my hair so they can settle me closer. I'm ashamed to need comfort right now when they're the one who's hurting, and the shame mixes with the never-ending reminders that I'm the one who made this happen. Kelly sighs, and I wipe my tears on their shirt, pushing my thoughts along the link. All I get in return are patience and calm. No blame or anger. Just Kelly. They are as old and immovable as rocks, but maybe that's what I've needed all along. In a dead life where nothing is certain and no one has answers, something as unchanging as Kelly may be the answer to it all.

We sleep for a bit. Or we lie silently. I poke mentally at the link from time to time, but Kelly's side of it is quiet. We don't talk about the other thing that happened during our little body swap adventure. Because hearing my own voice while watching my body like it belonged to someone else isn't all that happened. Because like Kelly said they'd felt my fear, I could feel them too. The pain. When I push from the outside, they may answer with calm reassurance. But inside, they're so sick and they don't know what to do about it besides wait for it to be over. I've been there. I know what that's like.

But this isn't the end for them. I'll make sure of it.

Sometime later, a soft tap on the door has me turning over. Jupiter appears, a small sliver of light shining behind her from the hallway.

"Hi. We're ready," she says. "You two okay?"

Kelly is already getting up before I can even answer. I follow after them, holding my chin up. We've got this.

The living room is quiet. Only Beryl, X, and Winston are waiting for us.

"Where are the others?" I ask.

"They went ahead. Had to make a detour. Ralph left his blood pressure medication at home." Beryl rolls her eyes. "I told him he should keep a few doses with him, just in case, but he never listens."

What did Kelly once say? A quack team. That's what we've got going here. We can do anything, as long as no one has a stroke in the process.

Beryl sees my misgivings and winks.

"And I didn't want us all to go in his car anyway. Ralph's the only one of us who can still drive. And I'm being generous here, because even after he had his cataracts done, he's had two collisions with a lamp post. He says he can drive in the dark or the snow but not both, but I don't see how the daylight helped him when he put his car in the ditch and had to walk two kilometres to my house last winter. I think he's paying someone off at the service office to keep renewing his license. But I'd rather do this with someone who won't get me killed." She gives us all a disdainful squint. "Or at least who won't get me killed in the car. I guess that's as much as I can ask for."

She squeezes into the SUV between me and Kelly. Winston gets loaded into the trunk but stands with his head over the seat, panting in my ear. Beryl wouldn't hear of him not coming along, and since you never know when a golden retriever is actually a golden retriever and when he's a pseudo-deity who might come in handy, we couldn't really argue.

Kelly's shivering beside her, and even the small distance between us feels dangerous. What if they have a seizure? We'll have blood pressure meds soon, but I don't think that will help.

"There's another way," Beryl says quietly, looking between us. "A more certain way."

"What do you mean?" I ask.

"I don't know what Smith said he could do for you, but if you want to stop the haunting, I can help you. It'll be easier, but—"

"But?" Kelly asks. They look like they can barely keep their eyes open to hear the answer.

"Well, you'd both be dead." Beryl's tone is flat. Factual. She's nearly a century old and death doesn't scare her anymore. "More dead, in your cases. You can choose to set the soul free. The one you share. If you both release it, then there's nothing left to haunt."

So easy. I've made that choice once before. You take stock of everything you've done in your lifetime—and now our afterlife-time—and decide that's good enough. That even though there's disappointment about the things you'll never get to see or do, it's not worth what it will take to get there.

If I was ready for oblivion once, I could be ready again. There's no guarantees with Viola and Smith. No guarantees for anything. Even if we stop the haunting this time, who's to say it won't happen again? Or that I'll start haunting someone else. I'll find myself spiritually bound to Minerva and be stuck following her from one meeting to another in perpetuity. I really would choose a final permanent death then. Maybe it's better to just get it over with now? Kelly would stop suffering, and I'd be free of Afterlife's dramatics finally.

"No."

The statement is Kelly's and comes with the weight of a boulder. They're so weak they look like they might poof out of existence at any moment, but the conviction in their eyes is clear. I glance towards the front seat to check if Jupiter and X are listening. I catch her throwing us a glance in the rearview mirror, while X scrolls on his phone, but she doesn't make any move to insert herself into the conversation.

"It's okay," I say softly, so only Kelly and Beryl can hear me. "I don't mind. If it's a sure thing, then—"

"No," Kelly says, just as firmly the second time, watching me around Beryl's slight body. "That's not the answer."

I bite my lip. Because sometimes it's the only answer. I chose MAID and set the date and time for my death. But even if you don't pick, sometimes you still don't get a choice.

Beryl nods and says, "I understand. It's the problem with hauntings. You always get saddled with the person you want to hurt the least . . . or love the most. That's why I let Winston haunt me. When he goes, I won't last long."

"Excuse me?" I whip my head around to stare down at the ancient dog. He looks up with cloudy eyes and a happy smile. All the fur around his eyes and muzzle are snow white. Beryl gives him a gentle scratch under his chin. "You're haunting your dog?"

"The other way around. After my husband died, I didn't want to be alone. Someone suggested I get a dog and a few years after Norman passed, I got Winston. He was exactly what I needed, but it became very clear only a few years in that it was a losing proposition. Dogs never live as long as we want them to." She digs her gnarled fingers behind his ears and he makes another ecstatic groaning sound. One of his back legs wiggles, like he'd scratch himself if he was sturdy enough to stand on just three paws. "It wasn't hard. A dog's love is so pure. I just let him in and that was it. We were linked. He'll be twenty-eight at Christmas. But we aren't going to last much longer than that."

I stare at them. The old woman and her even older companion. If we're counting in dog years, he's nearly a hundred and fifty, right? He looks up at her with such unquestioning devotion and adoration. No one's ever looked at me like that.

Wait . . . am I the dog or the old woman in this equation? If I'm slowly sucking the life out of Kelly, that makes me the dog, right?

Beryl sees the moment realization hits. Her smile is slow. She reminds me of Richard . . . or at least Richard when he's not being useless and annoying. The part of him that knows everything and is just waiting for the rest of us to figure it out.

"But that means . . ." I'm too afraid to voice it. I glance at Kelly. Their expression is only confusion. They haven't put the pieces together yet.

"Haunting is consensual. One of you has to want in, and the other has to allow it," Beryl says. "Winston didn't know what he was doing any more than you did. But I understood, and Kelly—"

Their eyes widen slightly. They know. Maybe they didn't do it as intentionally as Beryl did, but this wasn't all my doing either. I'm not a parasite. I was scared and confused and they offered me some safety. They let me in. Maybe they even knew what would happen, at least a little. Reapers know haunting exists. They're sketchy on the details, but if Kelly were really worried that hanging out with ghosts was so potentially damaging, it would have been easy for them to get rid of me. Drop me off at Afterlife and let me file appeal after appeal until they let me in and wiped my memory. Hell, they could have slid me to the top of the Himalayas or the bottom of the ocean and slid away again before I could stop them. I'd have found my way back to Toronto eventually—what else is there to do when you're dead but hone your extreme mountaineering skills?—but they could have just repeated the process over and over and kept themself safe. So they chose me. I'm so relieved I can't help the laugh that bubbles out of my chest. Something else bubbles inside it too. Kelly. With Beryl between us, we can't touch, but the silent pulse is enough. It ripples through me, leaving me feeling more confident than I have since I first found Kelly thrashing on the bed at home. The haunting isn't all my fault, and I have allies around me committed to fixing this mess. I glance at the rearview mirror again, and this time when my gaze meets Jupiter's, she smiles.

We can do this.

As we arrive at the old mansion once more, the line of cars parked on both sides of the road is even tighter than it was yesterday, but when Jupiter starts fretting about where to stop, Beryl simply says, "Keep going. We can park around back."

It only takes a wave of her old hand at the parking attendant for him to lift the orange cone away from the driveway, and we pull onto the property. No one stops us as Beryl gives us directions and we soon find ourselves on a wide gravel path that leads all the way around to the far side of the house. A tall square building bigger than our bungalow in Toronto is waiting. The open bay doors and cars parked inside say it's a garage, but the ornate roof and stonework would indicate it was probably a carriage house way back in the day.

Lucille, Ira and Ralph are waiting for us. Ira's produced a wheeling walker and is currently using it as a chair, while Lucille leans heavily against the car I last saw pulling out of Beryl's driveway, and Ralph is squinting at his cell phone.

"Took you long enough," Ira grumbles as we get out of the SUV.

"We were starting to worry you got lost," Lucille adds.

"Gosh dangit, how do I make it louder so I can hear this voicemail?" Ralph shakes his phone in frustration. "They said something about a warrant at the border for my arrest if I don't come pick up a package. What package?"

Lucille rolls her eyes and gently pulls the phone from Ralph's hand. "We've talked about this," she says. "It's a scam. Like that time you got that call from someone who said he was your grandson calling from jail?"

"You don't know," Ralph grumbles. "Marshall's had a tough go since my useless son left his wife. He could have been in real trouble." But he doesn't do anything to retrieve his phone.

Maybe we should have stuck with Wikipedia.

But Beryl's already walking toward the house, and Kelly's nose is bleeding again. No more time for research. We're going in and we're facing the monster that waits within this old house's walls. She doesn't know we're coming, and she won't be able to stop us until it's too late. Between the eight of us, we've got more than five thousand years of experience dealing with undead bullshit, and we're going to use every minute of it to stop Viola once and for all.

Whether it kills us or not.

chapter
twenty-two

BRENDA'S GUARDING the front door again, just like yesterday, but her serious expression brightens as she sees Beryl at the head of our little pack.

"I didn't know you were coming." She leans in and gives Beryl a peck on the cheek.

"We had some guests drop in. They're very interested in old houses." She throws us all a glance over her shoulder. Jupiter offers a nervous smile in return. X adds a jaunty salute.

Brenda's gaze narrows as she spots the others.

"Ralph. Ira. Nice to see you too," she says.

"Brenda," Lucille says with a sour smile that would make even Minerva flinch. The way her lips pucker at the end says she's about to tell Brenda to go suck lemons. Beryl must see it too because she hustles us inside before the octogenarian cat fight can get underway. A crowd of people have gathered in the large ballroom on the main floor. Rows and rows of chairs have been set up for the auction, and the dining room is full of paintings, vases and other relics from bygone eras ready to be sold to new owners. The grand staircase has been cordoned off, but once again, Beryl gets us through with a wave of her hand to the bespectacled man guarding the rope.

"What was that about?" I ask as we climb the stairs.

"What was what?" Beryl asks.

"With Brenda and Lucille?"

She and Winston are taking the stairs at a snail's pace, but I'm still worried she might topple over when she glances down at me with the same sour lemon expression Lucille had.

"Brenda's my sister," she says. "She and Lucille dated for a little while. It ended badly."

"It ended in 1982," Ira grouches from the back of our procession. X has taken the walker and is carrying it up the stairs, while Jupiter helps Ira make his way. This isn't good. Despite my initial confidence in the driveway, now I'm sure we're doomed. How are we going to stop someone like Viola when half our team can't even stand upright on their own?

It takes forever to climb up to the vacant third floor. By the time we do, the senior squad is all gasping and wheezing like they may not make the climb down. Kelly is also struggling, and I help them up the last few steps before guiding them to sit on a rickety wooden chair. They groan as they settle, and they have to close their eyes for a moment.

"Okay?" I ask, though I know the answer.

They clear their throat and wince, like even that much hurts.

Beryl is directing the others. X is standing on the walker's seat —god I hope he set the brakes first; the last thing we need is a head injury—and tying strips of white cloth from the rafters. Ralph and Ira move a heavy wooden door away from the wall and lay it in the centre of the room. How neither of them tear something or herniate a disk in the process is a small miracle. Lucille is rooting through the bags of what look to be different herbs and spices, which she sprinkles on the floor in a large circle around the door.

Jupiter is brushing Winston, who stares up at her with his tongue lolling to one side like she hung the moon.

"This is the best they could come up with for you to do?" I ask as I approach her.

She shrugs, murmuring sweet things to Winston. "Beryl said it was important." Her gaze when she glances up at me is worried. "This is going to work, right? Kelly . . . we're going to save Kelly. Right?"

I don't know what to tell her, other than I desperately want to believe that too. The others have surprised me. For their age and all their shuffling and mumbling, they do seem to know what they're doing now that we're here. It would be nice if they let the rest of us in on it.

Beryl lays down the long braids of cloth across the door. She smooths them flat over the floor until they reach the edges of the circle Lucille has set out. Jupiter nudges the mix of powders with her toe, being careful not to break the perimeter.

"What's in this?"

Beryl takes the clump of dog hair that Jupiter is holding and throws it over the door in tufts that settle over the wood and cloth.

"Ground bat claws, mostly," she says.

"It is?" X asks as he comes to stand beside Jupiter. He looks horrified, and I can't help but wonder if there's a humane way to collect the claws. I'd feel much better if no bats were harmed in the making of this séance . . . or summoning or whatever it is.

"No," Beryl says with a dry chuckle. "It's mostly sage, thyme, a little rosemary. And some indica."

"Weed?" X sounds like this is even more surprising than if it really had been bat claws.

"The devil's lettuce, son," Ira says, clapping a shaking hand on X's shoulder.

"I don't think Viola's going to be all too pleased that we've summoned her here," Beryl says. "We need something to calm her down."

And the solution is to hot box the top floor of a historic property? But no one else seems to think it's anything out of the ordinary as Beryl pulls a lighter from her pocket. She bends toward the floor, then must realize this is beyond the scope of her mobility, so she passes the lighter to Jupiter, who flicks the wheel and ignites the circle. It doesn't burst into flames so much as smoulder slowly. Instinctively, I hold my breath. We may need Viola to be cool and calm, but I need a clear head for what's about to happen. Then I remember I'm dead, so the odds of me getting stoned in this situation are low. Existentially torn to shreds? Much higher.

The Paranormal Society members step over the smouldering ring, and Beryl motions us to follow. When Kelly tries to rise, I shake my head. They can barely stand. What are they going to do against Viola? But Beryl says, "You should join us. As sick as you are, you're still a reaper. You've got more power in your little finger than most of us have at all."

Hard to believe, watching the way Kelly slowly staggers toward us. Reminds me of days spent shuffling up and down my condo hallway, hoping my bones wouldn't snap as I tried to pace off the nausea from the latest round of chemo. Everything hurt. Collapsing over the toilet to throw up was a relief because I didn't have to hold myself up anymore. Kelly even needs to take my hand to balance as they step over the smoking spices and weed. What are the people downstairs at the auction thinking? Has the odor of peanut butter, skunk, and roast turkey reached them yet? Is it making them question how much they really want this house and the things inside it?

Beryl clears her throat and I realize the others are all watching me, clearly waiting. I still have hold of Kelly's hand, and X is holding them on the other side, and the rest have also all linked hands. All I have to do is close the circle, twining my fingers with Lucille's. She gives me a kind smile.

"We'll be okay," she says softly. I return her smile, though it can't be very convincing. Feels like all my insides are quivering. Maybe Ira will lend me his walker in case my knees give out. I glance at Kelly. They don't smile, but they do squeeze my hand and despite everything their grip is firm. I nod tightly, mentally hyping myself up like an athlete before the big game. We can do this. A reaper, a lost soul, six mediums. That has to count for something, right?

"We're about to undertake a summoning," Beryl says, tone grave. "We'll be calling a spectre into our presence, and she won't be pleased to be here. Whatever you do, don't break the circle. The smoke will subdue her, but it's our job to keep her contained."

"You've done this before, right?" Jupiter asks, looking worried. "You said you had."

The circle gets quiet. Ralph coughs uncomfortably. Lucille finally says, "Yes. Once."

"Once?" Jupiter's worry turns to fear. "Did it go okay?"

"It will be fine," Beryl says firmly, which isn't an answer at all. Great. Just great. My fingers tighten around Kelly's so much they grunt softly and I have to consciously relax my grip. This is it. This is our best hope.

We're so screwed.

"Close your eyes," Beryl says. "Focus your intention on the centre of the circle. I'll bind her when she appears. At that point, whatever she says or does, don't let go."

An impossible wind swirls up around us, brushing over my ankles before pushing at my back. I tighten my hold on both Kelly and Lucille, while Beryl mutters low incantations in a language I don't recognize. Suddenly there's a feeling like a noose settling around our circle and cinching us tight. More than the wind, it pushes at my back, and the others around me take stumbling steps. Kelly pitches forward, dropping to their knees and I go to them, about to rip my hand from Lucille's, before she squeezes tight.

"Don't," she says, and all the kindness is gone from her. Her gaze is hard and purposeful. She tugs on our joined hands, pulling me back into place. Kelly is still on the ground, but they don't let go and slowly, they push back up to their feet, breathing hard with the effort.

"Viola," Beryl's voice rises over the blowing wind. The room is full of smoke, but somehow the ashy circle on the floor stays in place. "We call you to be bound. Hear us and come forward." The others echo her, asking for Viola's attention and presence. I hurry to mutter the same request. Not that Viola deserves so much politeness. She didn't show me nearly the same consideration when she tried to suck me off to the black nothingness.

A gasp comes from the other side of the circle. It's X, looking at the door lying on the floor. There's something there. A haze. The cloth that Lucille laid out shifts, twisting at the centre over the door, sort of like something is lying on top of it and trying to get comfortable. The haze coalesces into a shape that's human sized, if not exactly human shaped. The bottom half is too wide. It's Viola's skirts, I realize, as textures and colours solidify. Her massive ball gown spreads out over the floor, silk looking like rippling water on a pond. Slowly, as she takes a more and more solid form, the ends of the cloth braids rise up, carried by unseen hands and crisscrossing over her.

Viola's laugh is dark and sinister as she looks around the room.

"Hello, there. You called, my friends? Was there something you wanted?"

Beryl's chanting rises. The invisible rope around all of us tightens, pulling us a step closer to Viola, whose grin turns predatory as we approach.

"Don't be scared," she says. The door rises off the floor, hovering a foot or so above the ground. The braids twist and wrap until they're pulled tight into knots. It's a skill. Whatever it is Beryl and her friends are capable of, it's more than reading tea leaves and posting blog articles about haunted houses. Even Ira is standing up a little straighter, his mouth moving quietly over silent words. Ralph's gaze is sharp as he joins in the chanting. Lucille's lips are moving so fast I can't even tell what she's saying.

One of the braids slips. No, wait. It's not a braid. It's a snake. It slithers from between the ties, dangling to the floor, before making a slow turn beneath the door, like it's assessing the situation. Spiders follow, emerging from Viola's skirts and tumbling to the ground, skittering over the boards.

Jupiter makes a whimpering sound. Fear clutches at my guts. The spiders are coming faster, along with a few more snakes. They slither and dart, clearly testing an invisible perimeter.

Viola laughs again. "You didn't think I'd leave my friends behind, did you? When you've brought reinforcements."

A spider scurries over my shoe. I take an involuntary step back. Who can blame me, when last night the very same spiders were slowly suffocating me with their webs?

"Hold tight," Beryl says, gaze pointed in my direction. "Remember what I told you." Then she resumes her chant, voice growing louder. The wind is fully howling now too, and the house creaks under the strain.

Jupiter squeaks. A snake is coiling up her calf, tongue flicking out as it climbs higher. A dozen spiders follow, climbing over her torso. She shakes and ducks her head but doesn't let go. The spiders crawl down her arm, drawing long webs from her shoulder all the way down until they start spinning around the place where she and Beryl are holding hands. Jupiter whines, twisting to shake them off, but never letting go of Beryl or Lucille, not even when the spiders finish enveloping their hands and start working their way up Beryl's arm. The snake has made its way up Jupiter's torso and is winding around her neck. She coughs and gasps, her eyes going wide with terror.

"Babe!" X calls. The invisible rope around us tightens some more. All four society members appear to be shouting, but the wind is blowing so hard, I can barely hear them. I hear Viola, though. She cackles. The door she's bound to begins to turn, slowly at first, like a display case showing off its wares. Lucille's hand tightens around mine, but I can't tell if it's because of the spiders that are now wrapping webbing around her torso or because she didn't expect the spinning part. The door picks up speed, revolving like an off-kilter merry-go-round. Viola's laughter echoes above the chaos, even as the spinning sends more and more of her animal companions into the air. The others around me cry out and duck as they're bombarded with spiders that quickly set to work, wrapping us in thick lines of sticky silk. Fear threatens to drown me, but suddenly it's pushed away, leaving only warmth that pulses in my chest like waves on a sunny day at the beach.

Kelly's watching me. They're sweating, and not only is their nose bleeding, but there's a thick line of red trickling from their ear too. They give me a grim smile, and the warmth inside me grows. It's like every time Kelly takes my hand or puts a palm on my back. Reassurance. Trust. Caring, even. It's like—

No. The bond. They're pushing on the bond. Pushing the power I've slowly been taking all these months without permission, so that it's not just a steadying stream but an entire flood of it.

I shake my head, trying to yank my hand free, but Beryl was right. Even half dead as they are, Kelly is still the strongest among us.

Viola's carousel of horror is spinning so fast now I can't make out the details. It's just silk and terrible creatures that cascade down on us.

"Hold on," Beryl's voice strains over the cacophony. "Don't let her—"

The first of the bindings snaps. It's only simple cloth, but when it tears loose of the door, the sound is deafening and I duck as if to avoid a blast. The spinning slows, giving us a clear glimpse as one of Viola's claw-like hands springs free of her confinement, reaching for the next of the knots that ties her down.

Kelly pushes harder against me. There's a desperation to it, but I shake my head, pushing back. They can't give me this. Can't ask me to take it. We're not there yet. There's another way. There has to be.

Ralph drops to the floor, dragging Ira and X with him. They

don't lose hold of each other, but Ralph's gone pale, and his gaze is glassy. Ira's not looking great either.

Movement from my right has me looking the other way. Between Jupiter and Beryl's joined hands, Winston leaps through the air, moving with the strength and agility a dog his age—even one whose life has been supernaturally extended by a grieving but loving owner—shouldn't possess. He lands in the centre of the circle with an intimidating bark. His lips are curled back, showing gleaming white teeth, and with the next leap, he lunges for Viola, grabbing hold of the flowing material of her skirt and shaking his head with murderous fury.

"Touch the door," Beryl says, looking scared as her dog wages war with the furious spectre. "Bring your fists to the door to complete the ritual."

We wade forward, even as another of the bindings snaps. The floor is littered with snakes and spiders, leaving an unpleasant crunching feeling beneath my shoes. X and Ira drag Ralph between them, basically bracing him against their bodies. One by one, Viola's restraints are giving way, tearing under an unseen force. She's laughing again. Her face has sunken, the way it was when the ball first started. Whatever she gained by consuming the girl in the pink dress, it's gone now. She's back to being a monster.

And she's winning.

When the braid near her feet snaps, it sends Winston flying. Even I call out as the golden retriever hits the floor with a whimper. He's immediately covered up by a swirling mass of Viola's creatures. Tears stream down Beryl's cheeks at the sight, but she continues chanting as she slowly steps forward. We're only a few feet from Viola and the door. All we have to do is touch it. That's what she said.

We're too late.

The strap over Viola's chest snaps, and the ricochet is so loud it's physically painful. In a scene right out of a horror movie, Viola sits bolt upright, and a cascade of spiders, snakes and other squirming monstrosities tumble out from where she was lying only a second ago. It's like an eruption, and they spread over the floor in all directions, scurrying toward our feet.

"Hold the circle," Beryl says. "She can't leave if we hold the circle."

Viola turns her head slowly. Her eyes are hollowed sockets, and her teeth seem alarmingly large against shriveled lips. Her gaze settles on Beryl, seeming to register her as the leader of our intrusion, and with a silent flick of her wrist, she sends every single one of her crawling minions in Beryl's direction, swarming over her in a matter of seconds. They cover her legs, and despite all her strong control, even Beryl takes a frightened step back. It doesn't do any good. The snakes curl over her waist as the spiders begin their work of binding her beneath their webs.

Beside me, Kelly drops to the floor. The collapse is so sudden, I nearly lose their hand as they fall, and have to go down to one knee to hold on. They're gasping for breath, and the blood that has been flowing from their ears and nose now also has started dripping from their eyes. It's even more terrible than Viola's appearance because the implication is clear.

We're going to lose.

They push on the link again, and I grit my teeth, shaking my head. This can't be the answer. I won't let them go. The effort is enormous. Even in final death, Kelly is so powerful.

The spiders are at Beryl's throat. She's got her head tipped up like she's trying to stay above water, but I know what's next. She can't save herself. Not while she's holding the circle at the same time. And if she lets go, then none of us can be saved.

I glance at Jupiter and X. Jupiter is crying. X is the only one still standing on his side of the circle, and his perpetual happy dog expression is clouded with naked fear.

We're all going to die. First or second time, it doesn't matter. This is the end.

I open my mouth to apologize. To who, I'm not totally sure. All of them. Even the dog. They don't deserve this.

A snake coils over my ankle, its tongue flicking upward, like it's telling me what's about to happen.

With a ragged cry, Kelly pushes on the bond one last time, and the room plunges into darkness.

twenty-three

OH, hello there, death. It's been a while. Where are we going now?

"Ember."

I open my eyes and I'm staring at Kelly. They stand straight. Beautiful. Their hair is platinum white and braided over the top of their scalp again. A single diamond sparkles from their ear as they smile at me.

"Where are we?" I ask. I turn, but the world around me is so densely black it's like a sensory deprivation chamber. There's no depth. No shadows. Just darkness.

"You have to go back," they say. Even though they look healthy and strong again, the tension in their expression says we're not safe just yet. I feel along the link, and while I can still sense Kelly there, the whole thing is shorter. Blunted. Like coming to the end of a cul-de-sac.

"Go back? Go where?" I ask.

"To the house. To Viola." They hold out a hand and their palm and fingers are engulfed in a soft blue glow. "Take it. It's the only way you can save them."

I start to cry.

"No." I sniffle. "I'm not leaving you. I'm not letting you die."

"I'm not going anywhere," they say. "We're in the nothing. This isn't death. It's just a pause."

I wipe at my nose with my sleeve. Who knew that snot persisted, even after death?

"The nothing?" I ask, trying to understand. I blink, straining for even the faintest hint of light. Still nothing. Oh. "Like the *nothing* nothing?"

"The space between slides," Kelly says. They hold their hands up. "You said it existed, and I believe you. But if it really is the fraction as we slide from one place to another, then there's no time here. No real place. It's everywhere and nowhere. Leave me here and go help them. I'll be waiting."

Like they're ready to agree even before I say the words, my hands begin to glow too. I stuff them into my pockets, not ready to be betrayed just yet. Though Kelly's betrayal might be the worst of all.

"You can't give up," I say. "There's an answer. We can still beat Viola."

"Ember." They pull me close until we're nose to nose. "You know that's not true. They need both of us, but not separately. You can't help them if I'm dying next to you." Too late, I realize the warmth of their touch isn't just comfort. The glow spreads over me. Down my shoulders. Through my chest. The link pulses and fizzes, almost like it's a sentient thing that is pleased with this development. I struggle to free myself, but Kelly won't let go.

"But how will I get back? How will I find you?"

"I'm not going far," they say. "If I'm nowhere and everywhere, then I'm right beside you. All the time. When they're all safe and you know how to undo the haunting, I'll be right beside you."

I've heard this speech before. It sounds like a eulogy. Or the end of a movie where a dying loved one is offering the only comfort they have left to give. I might have even given this speech, once upon a time. Promised my sister's kids that even though they didn't get to see me anymore, I'd always be with them in their hearts. But I knew the truth. Maybe Kelly does too. I'll never see them again.

I'm really crying now. Fear and grief pour out of me, fighting back against the sacrifice Kelly is attempting to make for me. For our friends and even for people we only just met today. Because they may sound certain, but we don't know anything for sure. We don't understand the nothing. If they give me all their powers, isn't that effectively severing our link? Only the assumption that no time passes here means—

"Ember, you have to stop thinking and do this," they say. Each word is carved by their determined lips, even while I shake my head in silent protest. "Yes. It's not enough for us to be close to each other. We have to be together. Fully."

They kiss me.

It happens so fast I don't have time to prepare, and the collision of Kelly's mouth on mine is wet with my tears. I have the momentary thought that I didn't know they actually knew how to do this. Last time was so sudden and awkward it was hard to say if they were even responding or simply trying to understand what I was doing. But they do know. Their hands move from my shoulders to press around my back until I'm cradled in their arms. Kelly's lips are firm. Demanding. They taste faintly sweet, and their breath against my cheek is warm, before they go back to my mouth.

The link turns inward. Since my escape from Viola's ball, I've seen it as a cable with a terrible tangled knot in the middle, holding us to each other whether we want the connection or not. Now, though, it coils around itself, just like Kelly is coiled around me. It contracts, growing smaller, pulling us closer, even though we're already as close as we can physically get.

I moan, reaching for them without a conscious thought to do so. Now that we're here, now that we're doing this, it's all I want. Kelly. Jupiter was right. I love them. They're the ally I want by my side. Maybe the lover I want in my bed. But one thing is for sure: I can't leave them here.

The link between us is less than a foot long now. Just the coil of the perfect knot. I lean into it, pressing against it. Kelly makes a sound in the back of their throat. It's deep. Needy. Uncontrolled when everything about them has always been restrained. If we had anything to lean against, I would press them up against it, trapping them between my body and—

I gasp at the popping sensation between my ribs. Between one breath and the next, the kiss ends. I feel full. Too full. Like I'm carrying more than just myself now.

"I trust you," Kelly says in my ear, but they're gone. I can't see them anymore, no matter which way I turn and when I reach out my hands, they pass through endless black nothing.

"Kelly?" I call, hiccupping on a sob. They can't be gone. That couldn't have been goodbye, right? Not a kiss like that.

"Go," they say, still sounding like they're in my ear. And maybe they are. The weight against my breastbone is so much more than fear or desire pushing its way out. But I don't have time to examine it. Suddenly an invisible hand plants itself on my back, shoving me roughly forward. I stumble, trying to break my fall, only the floor never comes. Instead, once again in the space between one thought and the next, I'm back in the haunted attic. Lucille still has my hand, though there's not much of her left. She's covered from head to toe in spiderwebs. Somehow she manages to turn her head towards me. One eye remains uncovered, and it stares at me with milky cataract-laden horror.

The circle breaks. X and Beryl drop to the floor, dragged down by Ralph, who might be unconscious and is slowly being smothered by snakes. Jupiter has managed to scramble up on top of a wobbly chair and is reaching for the rafters, trying to keep her feet clear of the mass on the floor.

My chest pulses and on reflex I look to my other side, like Kelly will still be there. They aren't, of course, but even as disappointment crashes down on me, a warm sparkling sensation fills me. Are they laughing at me? Watching over my shoulder from the neverwhere or whatever and laughing at my sentimentality in the face of catastrophe?

Viola rises overhead, hovering like a supervillain at the end of the movie, marvelling at the destruction she has wrought. She's skeletal, but I watch in frozen terror as she reaches for Jupiter, who is still struggling to find a safe place. I've seen this part of the movie and I didn't like it.

Okay, Kelly. If you're watching, it's time to see if this thing really works.

I reach inside me, focusing until I find the link, which is now nestled in my chest like a glowing hearth ready to be blown back into a blaze. We've done this once already, though it was Kelly's decision, not mine. In Beryl's living room as the mediums argued and no one but me seemed to care that Kelly's survival was more important than their fear and resentments. The power went from Kelly to me, then out into the room. It seemed so fast and easy with Kelly touching me. Can I really do it on my own now?

Come on, Ember. You're not some feeble human. Act like it.

The thought might be mine. It might be Kelly's. It feels scratchy, like an overheard conversation in a busy room. Now's probably not the time to worry about it. I push my vision outward, picturing a tableau where everyone is stuck perfectly still, creating a moment in time but never moving that moment forward.

Kelly huffs. *So many theatrics. Just do it, Ember.*

If they're going to be the reaper on my shoulder the whole time, I'm not sure I want these shiny new powers.

I grit my teeth. Jupiter's grip slips on the rafter, leaving her dangling by one hand. The others are basically lost, completely covered under a blanket of webs that they'll never be able to tear through, even if they're still alive down there. With a push, I force my will out into the room. Everything frozen, nothing moving. Not even a breath taken, or a single hiss of a supernatural snake.

Yessss. Kelly's pride is so consuming I feel like I'm turning to goo and have to grit my teeth to keep from losing focus on the others around me, especially Viola.

Somewhere along the way, I've closed my eyes, and when I open them again, the room is still. Just like I pictured. Not a single flick of an eyelash or a breeze blowing silken cobweb strands. The people on the floor are motionless humps beneath the spiders' handiwork. Jupiter hangs, legs kicked out in different directions as she tries to regain her grip. And Viola hovers, the pointed toe of a leather boot dangling free of her many skirts.

For a second, I allow myself a little celebration, doing a few hops in a circle that ends in a fist bump to an unseen partner.

Focus, Ember.

Yeah, yeah. Grim reaper indeed. If you can't celebrate your successes, what's even the point of trying?

"What did you do?" The question comes on a raspy voice that makes me look first for a snake that has gained the gift of language. But every single one of Viola's pets is also stuck, frozen in place with their bodies twisted into S-curves, or with spindly little legs extended.

As it turns out, the question has come from Viola. Slowly, she drops to the floor. Unlike the others, she can move her head, if not the rest of her.

"What have you done?" I ask. "My friends. Tiffany. All the other women you've trapped here. Did you think it could go on forever?"

She settles on the floor more gently than I'd like. I'll have to work on the art of slamming your nemesis face-first into the floor-boards, but that's another task for another day. She struggles for a minute, but finally her knees give way and she drops to sitting with a graceless but gratifying thump.

"What are you?" she asks, sounding curious for the first time. I don't answer. Instead, I go about the room. I imagine my fingers are knives. Flaming ones. Maybe one of those lightsaber toast cutters you see on social media that both slice through the loaf of bread and toast it at the same time. I can practically hear Kelly roll their eyes at the mental picture, but if they didn't want a front row seat to my imagination, they should have come up with a better plan. The cobwebs that trap my friends are nothing against my saber fingers. I pull through them. Spiders burst in the heat and snakes are chopped in half with a sizzling popping sound. Viola screams like she's the one being sliced and diced. But she stays where she is, so I don't give her another glance until the others are uncovered. X is breathing. Ralph . . . it's hard to say. Eventually I even find Winston, though his chest is still and his tongue lolls onto the floor and he doesn't pull it back in when I nudge him.

Fuck, if the dog dies, I'm never forgiving Viola or anyone else who ever knew her.

Jupiter is still dangling from the rafters, and I don't have the physical strength to get her down on my own. I start looking for something soft to slide beneath her to break her landing whenever she finally falls, then start wondering if there's a way to unfreeze her while keeping Viola in place, then finally realize that I'm over-complicating this. When you've got high-octane reaper powers, gravity is irrelevant. I reach up and take hold of her ankle.

"Don't worry," I say to her frozen face. "I've got you."

Kelly and I should have worked out a system. Knock once for yes, twice for "this is a terrible idea." Too late now. I close my eyes and picture home.

The slide is so easy it's like blinking. One second, we're in the attic, the next we're standing in front of the TV at our little house in Etobicoke. It's exactly the way it should be. Empty mugs all over the coffee table. Discarded game controller on the couch. Lip Balm, who was sleeping on the windowsill in a sunbeam, notices our arrival and leaps to his feet, hissing and puffing up until his fur makes him look twice his usual size.

"Ember?" Jupiter gasps. "What happened? Where's Kelly?"

But we don't have time for answers. Jupiter is safe, but I don't know if the freezing works if I'm not there. I take her hand and picture the attic. The floors are littered with the corpses of creatures that tried to hurt us, and as we slide back into the fray, Viola is struggling against whatever part of my freezing has lingered. She hisses, sounding much like Lip Balm, when we reappear. The elapsed time has only been a split second. X has started slowly rising to his feet. Lucille is stirring.

"Look after them," I tell Jupiter, releasing her. She staggers, no doubt disoriented from the slide. She puts a hand against an exposed stud and shapes her lips like she's about to ask more questions. Later. When we're all back at the house, I will explain everything with Kelly by my side. For now, I have more important things to take care of.

Viola screams, raising a hand like she might slap me. I catch her wrist, holding tight. Her sunken eyes burn with fury. Good. Let her hate me. It'll distract her on our little inter-dimensional road trip.

A warm shiver flutters in my chest. Kelly, laughing with dark approval, maybe. I hope so. They may be everywhere and nowhere, but it helps to know they're still *here* more specifically.

I give Viola a grim smile. I may not be a reaper, but I can play the part.

"Let's go," I say as she struggles fruitlessly against me. Is this what Kelly always feels like? I could get used to it. No wonder their confidence and superiority are turned up to eleven. "There are some things you're going to do for me."

NAVIGATING to my house is easy. Navigating somewhere I haven't been before is harder. But I have a stop to make before I deliver Viola to Smith. And reapers do it all the time. More than once, back when they still worked at Afterlife, Kelly must have found themself dispatched to a village in the middle of nowhere they'd never been to before. So sliding must have some sort of built-in nav system.

WWKD? What would Kelly do?

You're overthinking this, Ember. Just point yourself in the direction you want to go, then go there.

Sure, sure. Easy for you who has had thousands of years of practice.

In the nothing space, with Viola still clawing at my hand like a pissed-off cat, I picture Tiffany and the others. Their voluminous skirts and their frightened expressions. I see the swirling cobwebs consuming them before they vanish into the dark for another year.

"No," Viola says, her struggles intensifying, even though she's wasted away even more than she had in the attic. There's so little left to her she reminds me of one of those mummies they pull out of bogs in Norway. Or is it Sweden? Anyway, one of those buried bodies where the skin has shriveled up but remained intact until they're basically a leather purse holding together a skeleton. That's what she looks like. Her little soul-eating party trick is clearly meant to keep her young and beautiful only if she enjoys a peaceful year of malice and relaxation. Because the more she fights me, the more withered she becomes. And clearly she's figured out where I'm taking her, because as I centre myself and get ready to slide, she sinks her teeth into my hand. Pain shoots up my arm, but a second later, something like lightning follows the opposite path, hurtling itself from my chest to my shoulder, then all the way to the point where she's trying to devour me, bones and all. She jerks back, wailing, and I have to brace to not lose hold of her.

"What the hell was that?" I can't help myself from asking. A sensation like a gentle squeeze on my shoulder then another just in front of my heart is the answer. Right. That's what Kelly would do. Zap the bitch and get on with it.

We slide. At the last second, a niggle of doubt pokes at my consciousness. We arrive in the dark. There's not even anything beneath me. We're falling and falling. Even Viola clutches at me, clearly having decided that her only chance at survival is to stick with me until we get our feet back underneath ourselves.

"You're going to get us both killed," she says somewhere close by. It's so dark I can't even see her. The only confirmation we're still tangled together is the feeling of her nails digging into my skin where she bit.

"We're already dead," I say, sounding so much like Kelly at their weariest I can't help the snort that follows the admonishment.

"There are worse things than human death," she says.

There are. Accidentally hurting those you care about. Taking choices away from innocent people. Using them for your own longevity, whether the action is intentional like Viola's or accidental like mine.

We're going to fix her bad choices first. Mine will be dealt with soon enough.

We slide out of our endless dive, and this time, when we arrive, we land safely on a solid surface. Still pretty dark, but dim light emanates from the walls and overhead, giving the space a similar vibe to peering through a storefront after hours. And like a closed store, the merchandise has been tucked away, waiting to be unwrapped for an interested customer. Both sides around us are lined with dim shapes partially hidden in shadow. If this were a horror movie, now would be the part where we run, because the mummified bodies are undoubtedly about to come to life and chase us down. But this isn't a horror movie, and Viola's shopping spree is also over.

Even she looks surprised at our arrival. She stares around her, mouth agape.

"What? How did you . . . No one has ever come to this place."

"No reaper has ever come looking, you mean." So much of Afterlife's systemic failure is not bothering to look beyond the narrowest of scopes. A century of heiresses dead and missing? Oh well, they must be wraiths. Ziggy's probably been reading them bedtime stories for years and we don't even know. Time to upgrade the filing software again. At no point would they ever admit spectres are real, much less a problem they actively need to investigate.

But even with Kelly tucked safely inside me, or wherever it is they are right this second, I'm still no reaper. I tried to change the system from within and got nowhere for months. It's time to ask the uncomfortable questions and stick my nose where it's not wanted.

"Let them go," I say.

She sneers. "Why would I do that? What do you think will happen to them? They were feeble enough for me to trap them in the first place. If you let them free, they'll wander the banks of the river until they're too rotted to be useful."

The sentiment is cruel, but she's right. Letting them go entirely will just create forty disoriented wraiths in small-town Ontario. And I'm not sure I can slide them all to the gates at Afterlife. Not all at once, and the longer this takes, the greater the risk Viola finds a way to escape and the more time I waste chasing her down. So instead, I let her go now. She takes a small step back, and her eyes narrow as her teeth shine in a terrifying line. I don't have time for theatrics. I flick my wrist, and her stumble ends so abruptly she has to pinwheel her arms to keep from collapsing again into her skirts.

"Stay," I tell her, like I'm talking to Winston. God, I hope he's okay. Even if we all make it out of this in one piece, if the dog doesn't come out alive, there will be no redeeming the story after the fact. Sure, I kept a millennia-old reaper from getting sucked dry and stopped a serial killer spectre who preyed on defenseless young women for more than a hundred years. But the golden retriever is now pushing up daisies in Beryl's front yard? Unforgivable.

Time to bring in reinforcements.

"Bang!" I say, pitching my voice loud enough that Viola flinches, though her feet don't unstick themself from the floor. Even a couple of the still forms, wound up in their spider silk wraps, look like they might shift, the way people do when they're fast asleep and trying hard to stay that way. Silence falls again when the word finishes echoing off the walls. When nothing follows, I do it again, a little louder. "Bang!"

"What? What do you want?" Bang finally slides in. "I was just on my way to a strategic planning—" Her eyes get wide behind her cat-eye glasses as she looks around us, then even bigger when she looks at me. "I mean . . . woah. What did I miss?" When she sees Viola, her lips pucker and her nose wrinkles. "Who are you?" She gasps. "Where's Kelly? What's going on?"

The ping-ponging of her attention makes me dizzy, and for a moment my focus flickers like a lightbulb in a hurricane. Viola sees her opportunity and lunges forward. Bang doesn't react fast enough and is knocked down, both of them crashing to the floor. Bang goes flying and one of the straps on the paint-splotched overalls she's wearing is torn. Viola hisses and screams. Freeze. I have to freeze everyone here even if I do the same to Bang. I'll figure out how to separate them after.

I don't get a chance. Before I can finish forming the thought, Viola gets blasted across the room, colliding with two of her mummified prisoners. They all topple to the ground. Viola whimpers. Her cheek has been slashed open, exposing the white bone beneath, and the eye above protrudes in its socket, like one more good knock and it will fall out entirely. She whimpers but doesn't get up, so whatever Bang just did, it clearly hurt. Good.

"What the truck is that?" Bang asks, brushing her knees as she gets to her feet.

"She's a spectre," I say. "A mean one."

Bang chuckles. "Spectres are myths. No one's ever—"

I freeze her to the spot. "We're not having this conversation anymore. None of us. She's a spectre, and these little human-shaped packages are her prisoners, but once they were real ghosts that you lost track of. Some of them have been dead for over a hundred years and none of you ever thought to go looking for them. So don't even begin to tell me what is and isn't—" I take a breath as something hard jabs at my ribs. From the inside. Kelly. My throat hurts. Was I shouting? Bang's eyes are wide, like they were when she first arrived. Her body jerks and I realize she's struggling to move her feet. I flick a finger and she stumbles forward. "Sorry. It's been a long day."

"I can see that," she says drily, still taking in the scene around her. When her gaze settles on me, her head tilts to one side. "Are you okay? You look a little . . ." Her mouth twists as she struggles for words. I can't imagine which one will fit . . . or what I look like. The last few days—if it's even been days; I'm quickly losing track of time—have been hellish. And that doesn't even take into account the reaper who is trapped in the nothing land, but also somehow watching everything unfold behind my eyes. Bang's eyes get even wider and now I'm going to have to worry about keeping them in their sockets too. "Kelly?" She gasps.

I close my eyes, like that's all I need to do to protect them. Embarrassed heat washes over me. Some of it is mine, some of it is probably Kelly's newfound shame at the prospect of being part of such a wibbly wobbly bag of emotion.

"What did you do?" Bang asks. Kelly kicks me in the metaphorical shins, prompting me to reply.

"I'll file an incident report later." I point at the bodies against the walls. "Take them all to Afterlife. They're ghosts, not wraiths."

"How long have they been here?" Bang asks. "You said a hundred years. If it's been a hundred years, then—"

"They're *not* wraiths," I say, stalking toward her. The head of Afterlife takes a gratifying step back.

"I can't just classify them as garden-variety ghosts," she stammers. "And we don't have coding for anything else. They would have died while Minerva was in charge. What am I—"

I jab a finger at her. "You stood up in front of Richard and volunteered to lead Afterlife. So lead. Throw out the whole goddamn coding system and start over. I don't care. Just get them out of here."

A new pair of glasses materializes on her face, just in time for her to nervously push them back up the bridge of her nose. She glances uneasily at Viola, who is still lying motionless on the ground.

"What about her? I guess Ziggy could—"

But I shake my head. Viola's not going to get anything so nice as a locked cell in the depths of HELL. When this is all over, I'll make sure the siren in that dark river drags her down so deep she'll never swim to the surface again. I'll trap her in the most monotonous part of HECK where she plays bingo forever and ever but the caller never calls a single one of the numbers on her sheet and her dabber always runs dry. There are lots of places I could send someone like Viola, and none of them will be pleasant.

"We've got stuff to do. If she's still around after, I'll call you." I go to grab hold of Viola to slide to our next destination, then have a thought. "But if any of the members of the Leeds and Grenville Paranormal Society show up at Afterlife for intake, make sure you let Beryl bring her dog, okay?"

"Dog? We don't take—"

"You'll take this one," I say, and there's an echoing pulse of approval from Kelly. They've never been what I would call an animal lover. They've tolerated living with Carrot Stick and Lip Balm with the same weary resignation they live with humans, but I don't think they'd even notice if the cat disappeared tomorrow. Somehow, though, they understand what Winston means to Beryl. Maybe we're finally starting to squeeze some humanity into them after all.

Bang takes a nervous step back, holding her palms out like she's worried she's about to get smoted. Smited? Smitten? You'd really think, after all this time among the non-living, I'd know how to properly conjugate that verb, but I don't. And anyway, smiting Bang defeats the whole purpose of her being here, what with Viola's captives still all wrapped up. And at the end of the day, reapers frustrate me, but I do like Bang. Her heart's in a good place; she's just so deeply entrenched in the Afterlife way of doing things she can't see a way out of the tunnel.

Speaking of tunnels . . .

I grab hold of Viola's ankle. She groans. I don't bother asking if she's okay. I kind of hope she isn't. Smith didn't specify she had to come back in one piece. If she shows up at the Other Side a little worse for wear, that's no skin off my nose.

I don't bother saying goodbye to Bang before I slide away, taking Kelly and Viola with me. Time to go back to the Other Side.

WE LAND ON THE HILLSIDE, the one that slopes down toward the dark river. I tumble downward, quite literally bouncing head over heels. Every impact reverberates through me as rock and body slam together over and over. Instinct has me curling around myself, like I need to protect Kelly. Can they even feel this? The worst that they'll probably get is a bad case of motion sickness.

I come to a halt along the gravelly shoreline with a groan. My cheek basically stops the skid. Maybe my teeth. When I sit up, I have to spit something black and gooey onto the stones to keep from choking on it.

"I knew we shouldn't have let you drive," a dry voice says in my head. Here on the Other Side, Kelly's voice is clearer. More like we're having a conversation, less like I'm picking up a far-off radio signal.

"No one likes a backseat reaper, Kelly," I say. Viola is sprawled on the ground beside me. Her heavy skirts are torn and stained from our barrel roll down the hillside. But when she faces me, the withered crone is gone. She's back to the healthy young woman she was after she consumed the girl in the pink dress. The woman in the portrait.

And she's pissed.

"What have you done?" she hisses, pushing up to her knees. Her face may be young, but her hands are gnarled claws and she digs at the ground like a pissed-off bull. "What did you do?" Her gaze is wicked but lopsided, with her one eye still protruding unnervingly in its socket. If she still had blood pressure, I wouldn't have to raise it much more to get the little sucker to come squirting out of there like a peeled grape.

"You came back!" a childlike voice calls from behind us. I turn, and Sareesha is running down the hill. She has no trouble keeping her footing as she sets off a tiny avalanche of stones from her run.

"No," I shout, waving her off. "Get away. It's dangerous. Find Smith. Tell him—" But I don't get to finish my warning before I'm knocked down from behind as Viola tackles me, hissing and shrieking.

"Smith?" she asks as she turns me over to face her. "Smith? You brought me back to that? To him?" She claws at me, tearing at my clothes and my hands and arms as I fight her off. She is furious. Whoever Smith is to her, she's not happy to be here.

"You couldn't stay there," I say. "You were hurting those women. You'd trapped them."

"Like Smith tried to trap me here? Like the reapers trap ghosts at Afterlife? Why do they get to decide what happens?" She puts a hand to my throat, and I have just enough time to think that strangling the dead is a useless thing to do before a long snake slithers from beneath her sleeve and coils itself around my throat. Strangulation might not be effective on someone like me, but a magical undead snake appears to have other skills. It only needs a few revolutions before its head meets its tail. Then it squeezes. The pressure is crushing. I gasp. Viola is still on top of me, pinning my arms to my sides with her knees while more of her slithery subjects emerge, twining themselves around me.

"Your friends thought they could summon me," she says, voice dripping with malice. "They thought some simple cloth and a few runes would be enough to bind me. I'm so much more powerful than mere mortals."

The snakes pull tight, sending pain shooting through me. I can practically feel every single one of my bones snapping like dried twigs and I scream.

"Ember?" Kelly's voice is loud inside me. "Ember, what's wrong?"

Kelly. I'd almost forgotten they were there. Who cares about the reaper using you as a viewfinder from another half dimension when you're being crushed in this one?

"Get out," I say. The words are more gasp than actual syllables. "Get out of there. Now."

In a few short minutes, I'm going to be dead. *Really* dead. Like the girl in the pink dress, I'll be nothing more than a heap of clothes and maybe a mound of dust that will eventually get washed into the dark river.

Viola's brows knit in confusion and she lifts her lip disdainfully, clearly thinking I'm talking to her when in fact I'm telling Kelly to let me go. Untangle the link if they can, but at the very least, stop this out-of-body thing they're doing, because who knows what that will mean for them when I have no body left for them to hang out in?

"So weak," Viola sneers. "There's hardly any fight in you at all, is there?"

There's fight, but the pain from the snakes is excruciating, making it impossible to think clearly enough to mount a defense. So no, maybe I don't have much fight in me after all.

But I have a reaper, and that's the next best thing.

One second, Kelly's fearful voice is asking me what's wrong, and the next they're there. Here. Wherever. They rise up out of me like a monster in a horror movie, putting their hand around Viola's throat the way she did to me. But Kelly's grasp is strong. They don't need snake sidekicks. They can do it all by themselves.

"Let go of her," they say on a growl as they force Viola back. "Release Ember, now."

But Viola only laughs. "You? A reaper? What do you care about her? When have reapers ever cared about humans?"

They glance back at me. For once, they might actually look better than I do, which is to say they still look like shit, but they're not getting their eyeballs squeezed out of their head, so there's that.

"She's my friend," they say softly when our eyes meet. It should hurt. If I really held any hope of Kelly falling in love with me, their words should be a disappointment. But they aren't. It's enough. Being Kelly's friend is enough. The link pulses in my chest, a soft moment of relief before Viola's snakes tighten even further, choking off any warm feelings I might have had with a scream.

"Then you can watch your friend die," Viola says. She takes hold of Kelly's wrist like she might wrestle their hand away from her throat, but at the contact she stills. Even the snakes seem to back off a little. Her eyes go wide and her sneer turns into the predator's smile I saw in the ballroom. Whatever fucked-up history she has with Smith, I can see where their paths might have aligned for a while.

"Well," Viola says, slowly, curling the word over her tongue. "What have we here? A haunting." Her vipers slide to me. "No wonder you're so hard to destroy. But hard is not impossible." Her grip tightens on Kelly, and her talon-like fingernails dig into their skin. Kelly gasps, and to my shock, the pain radiates over me, turning the connection in my chest white hot and searing. I struggle to escape it, but the snakes hold me tight while blood oozes from Kelly's arm.

"Haunting is very strong," she says, almost conversationally, as Kelly struggles against her. Whatever little rejuvenating burst they might have brought with them from the nothing is gone now. They're pale and the ear closest to me is bleeding, even though

Viola's been nowhere near it. When they throw another worried glance in my direction, their nose is bleeding too. "Smith and I haunted each other for a while. He said we would be together forever. But it was clear that he wouldn't be enough for me. Every haunting burns out one of the participants eventually. So I took what I could from him, left him as a shade, and went looking for more." She twists Kelly's arm, wrenching it painfully far. They cry out, and the sound has me desperately writhing to be free of the snakes once more. I've never heard them make a noise like that. Pain. Fear. Even as they've been fading away on me these last few days, they've been almost frustratingly stoic. But now, as Viola continues to mercilessly twist, sending Kelly to their knees, their agony is clear. I can feel it inside of me, and it's almost enough to send me into a different kind of darkness. The one where there truly is nothing. No awareness. No pain. No way to help my friend.

Viola is still taunting Kelly. "I'm sure you've noticed it's easier to carry the souls of the ones you haunt inside one of you, rather than letting them exist separately. I've been carrying the souls of haunted damsels ever since I left this place and it's served me well. But I think"—she smiles again, and even her teeth seem to almost have grown pointed and fang-like—"that claiming your two souls at once will be enough to sustain me for another century or more. And since you've been kind enough to free me from that dusty old attic, well . . ."

With no more warning, she slams her hand into Kelly's chest. All the way in. The force of it knocks them to the ground and she goes with them until her arm is buried to her elbow inside them. Kelly arches and convulses, and so do I. I can feel her. Inside me, Inside Kelly. She roots around like I once did on a lonely night when I was sure there were a few more chips crushed into the corner of the bag. But she's not feeling for snacks. She's looking for something more.

When she touches the link, I gasp. My vision fades, and when it clears again, I'm looking right up at her leering face. I'm in Kelly. Watching like it's happening to me.

"The thing about joining your souls," she says, "is that all it takes is one good tug." She pulls. I scream. Kelly does too. Viola's expression darkens even further. "Oh, I like a challenge. You two are stronger than I gave you credit for."

I force myself back out into my own awareness. I can't help Kelly from inside them. They're too weak. The only way for me to save us both is to escape the snakes while Viola's attention is elsewhere and save us both from the outside.

"Viola! Stop!" Smith's voice comes from far away, probably the top of the hillside. Maybe Sareesha really did go get him after all. But we don't have time to find out.

I struggle once more against the reptiles wrapped around me. They hiss a warning for me to hold still. They're waiting for orders from their mistress. The searing pain in my chest says her attention is still on ripping both me and Kelly out of ourselves and into her. Tough shit, lady. I'm nobody's fountain of youth.

The snakes don't give. No amount of me rolling and shifting loosens them. Rocks tumble down on my head as Smith gets closer, but he's still too far away to do anything but plead with Viola to stop.

I close my eyes and stop fighting. Focus on the pain. Follow it down until I find the thrumming knot that ties me and Kelly together. There's a third part now. Something long and glowing a sickly green. It's wound itself around the knot like a vine slowly strangling a tree. If I can just get Kelly away from here . . . if I can just get their power, even for a moment, I can freeze the snakes. Maybe even burst through them and force Viola to fight us on two fronts.

I grab hold of the link and pull. Kelly feels so far away. So sluggish and slow to respond.

"Please," I say, hoping they can hear me from here. "Hold on. Just a little longer. I need you to hold it together and help."

The green tendrils get brighter, glowing like a neon sign. Somewhere—but I can still hear her here—Viola laughs.

"You really are still just another silly human girl, aren't you?" she asks. "What do you think you can do now that I have a hold on you? How can you escape? What do you know about any of this? You probably didn't even know the haunting was happening, did you?"

She wants me to feel small. Inadequate. Viola is a bully who preys upon fear and weakness. But I stopped fearing death a while ago. The only thing she can take from me is Kelly, and I will fight until the link is nothing but threads and torn pieces to keep that from happening.

"Stop! Wait!" Smith is closer now. Maybe he's already reached the bottom of the hill. Maybe he's already ripping snakes off me or pulling Viola away from Kelly. But the green menace wrapped around the part of me that I have learned to love more than anything else—the part that connects me to Kelly—is being overcome by her tendrils, so there's no time for me to see if help has arrived. Instead, I gather the knot up in my arms. I pull it close to my chest. The green burns through my clothes and stings my arm.

"This isn't yours," I say. "It's ours. We chose each other. We are a team. You don't get to be a part of that."

Then I pull. Hard. I take it all. Kelly. Me. Viola's tendrils hold tight for a moment, like a ball of roots refusing to leave the ground, but I put every ounce of my metaphysical weight and every second of my intention behind my action. I dig my heels in and yank, ripping and tearing, until she finally gives way with a shriek. The release flings me backward sending me spinning and tumbling though everything and nothing. It's like the worst slide I've ever done. Desperately, I clutch the knot to me. I can't let go of it. Maybe we'll never be able to undo the haunting, but that doesn't mean I'm just going to fling Kelly into the ether either.

Suddenly I'm back in my body. Still wrapped in a mass of snakes. My insides feel like they've just gone through a blender, then repackaged back inside me, with maybe a few extras that weren't there before. I'm an overstuffed transcendental sausage.

"Viola. Viola." Smith is somewhere off to my left. All his smooth control from our previous meeting is gone. He sounds panicked now.

The pain is gone. I can't feel any of it—mine or Kelly's.

I can't feel them at all.

"Kelly? Kelly?" I say as I writhe against my bonds, sounding not unlike Smith. I thrash, and suddenly the snakes give way, letting go all at once and practically disintegrating, until they're nothing more than husks on the ground around me.

"Are you okay?" Sareesha asks. She's standing nearby, wringing her hands nervously. "I called Smith."

I should thank her, but I'm already scrambling, climbing desperately over the rocks. Viola is slumped over Kelly, and neither of them are moving.

"No. No, please no." Smith is already there, saying the words out loud that are echoing over and over in my head. He pulls Viola up and away, and she goes with him like she's made of paper. No resistance, no response.

But all I can see is Kelly.

They're lying on the ground. Mouth agape. Silver-grey eyes fixed on a point overhead. Their shirt is soaked with red-black blood, and the gaping wound in their chest is almost too gruesome to look at.

"Kelly. Kelly!" But they don't move. They don't blink. They're as still as death, and that's saying something because I've seen death and it can be very active when it wants to.

"What did you do?" Smith's voice is anguished. He's only a few feet away, cradling Viola's still form in a position not unlike Renaissance-style sculptures I once saw in an art history textbook. Viola's gaze is vacant, and her head and arms are limp. Whoever and whatever spectres are, there's no consciousness left in her.

"Is she—" I start to ask, before Smith swings his gaze to me. His features are contorted in misery.

"What have you done? What did you do to her?"

Why does it sound like an accusation? She's the one who attacked us. Who was hurting people. I move so that I'm protectively crouched between the two of them—though I'm not sure Viola's a cause for concern anymore—and Kelly's still form.

"You asked me to bring her here," I say. "You didn't say she'd try to kill us in the process."

"So you killed her instead?" Smith caresses her face like he can't see the monster she is. Did he not know what she was doing back in the living world? Tears pour over his cheeks. "Where is it? Where did it go?"

"Where is what?" I ask.

"Her soul!" He spits it at me with tortured sorrow. "*My* soul. She took it when she left. I just wanted it back. I've waited all this time and—"

A gasp comes behind me. Kelly jerks back into being, then immediately spews an entire mouthful of blood.

"Kelly?" I turn my back on Smith and his grief. "Kelly, Kelly, look at me."

Their eyes roll for a moment. I take their hands and the touch makes Kelly start like they didn't know I was there.

"Ember?" My name on their lips is wet and gurgled. I turn them on their side, supporting their head. The position is not entirely unlike the one Smith and Viola still hold, other than the fact that she still hasn't woken up. "What happened?"

"I don't know." I'm crying again, and this time I don't think it's going to stop. Because the blood pouring out of Kelly's chest won't stop either. It forms a glossy pool around us, soaking into my knees. I reach inside myself, looking for the knot. It's there, but Kelly's half feels so flimsy that if I pull on it, I'm afraid it might disintegrate just like the snakes did. And Viola's influence is still there, poisoning us both. She's haunting us now, whether she meant to or not.

"The haunting," I say, forcing myself to look away from Kelly long enough to catch Smith's attention. "You said to bring you Viola and you'd help us undo it."

But he only shakes his head, lifting Viola as he rises. He turns his back to us, walking straight towards the river.

"Wait!" I call out, rushing after him, though every step I take from Kelly is agony. "The haunting. You promised to help us if we held up our end of the deal."

He has her cradled to his chest like a child, and his gaze swells with regret when it meets mine.

"I can't. Not like this, when I'm still a shade," he says, shifting her gently in his arms. "You were supposed to bring her here and she would give it back. It's been so long. She doesn't need my soul anymore. Not when she has the others."

Sour bile rises in my throat. We were right not to trust him. He knew what she was doing. Kelly and I both knew he was leaving out certain details when he sent us after her, but I never suspected he knew the monster she had become. Beryl must have told him during one of their crafting bees or late-night chats. I don't feel any more sympathy at his obvious grief than he does for all the women whose afterlives she took.

Smith stands, staggering with Viola in his arms while his feet sink in the sand. A song comes over the air, mournful and plaintive.

"We'll be together. I promise," he says softly, kissing her cheek. "I waited for you. We'll be together. Wherever the river takes us, it will be together this time."

He's not speaking to me anymore. I might as well not even be here. Still, I crawl after him, reaching for the back of his shirt as he steps into the river.

Love makes us selfish, doesn't it?

Yeah, jackass. So selfish you're willing to leave me and Kelly on the shores of this weird-ass river in the middle of who the fuck knows, with no one but Cerise's forgotten childhood to troubleshoot while Kelly bleeds out on the—

"Ember." My name sounds inside me, but the voice is unmistakeably Kelly's. When I turn, Sareesha is kneeling by them, smoothing their hair away from their forehead. Their whole chin is stained with blood and they're shivering so hard rocks periodically grind together where their feet kick at the ground.

"Shh," I say, rushing back to them. I glance at the river once. Smith is more than a third of the way to the middle and he's up to his chest. He's holding Viola out like he's teaching her how to swim. Then in a blink, they're gone. Panic tries to choke me. They're gone. My one chance to save Kelly, and it just slipped beneath the surface.

"Where did he go?" Sareesha asks, voice tinged with uncomplicated fear. But I don't have it in me to comfort her. She isn't my priority.

"Shh. It's okay." I lie down alongside Kelly, putting my head to their shoulder, like we were in Beryl's guest room not that long ago. I listen for any sign my closeness is painful, but if anything, once we're touching, Kelly's half of the link feels a little stronger, if only for a moment.

Sareesha pats Kelly's cheek, then mine.

"It was nice to see you again," she says. Then without another word, she skips away down the shore. Just as well. I'm happy she's happy, but I don't want her to see what happens next. Children—even immortal ones—shouldn't have to witness death.

"Should we go home?" I ask, though as soon as I say the words, I know it's not possible. We can't slide out of here. Kelly was barely surviving the sliding before all this started. Doing it now would almost certainly kill them, or possibly even blow them all to bits in transit. They'd wind up like stardust on the hillside, and I'd never find all their pieces after.

"It's all right," they say, voice rough. "I didn't want to go back there. Humans are uncomfortable in homes where someone's died. I wouldn't want to do that to Jupiter."

The consideration makes me angry because it's so out of character. My disdainful, disinterested reaper—the one who would never worry about something as pedestrian as how others would feel once they were gone—isn't here anymore. I've already lost them. But even now that we're out of options, I can't stop myself from wanting to fight.

"We can find a cure," I say desperately. "There's time. We can go to the nothing place. You can stay there. I'm sorry I made you come back. I was scared I wouldn't be able to fight Viola on my own. You should have stayed there where you were safe." My words are coming from the same place of despair they always do when people are faced with death. It's not rational. That's what happens with grief. It's never a straight line and I'm back to bargaining.

Kelly closes their eyes. They wrap an arm around me, like I'm the one who needs comfort. We're probably both covered in blood. How are they even bleeding? It's not like they have a heart. But the anatomy of the dead is irrelevant. I'm losing them.

"I don't remember my first death." Their voice, with its odd accent, rumbles beneath my cheek. I wipe away tears. "I'm glad I'm not alone for this one."

"I'm sorry," I say again. What am I apologizing for? I may be haunting them, but I didn't do it on purpose. Did I ask the cancer to apologize to me?

They squeeze me tighter. "We did this to ourselves. It's fine. It solves a problem, anyway."

"What's that?"

"Me. My existence. I'm a reaper who doesn't reap. I have no purpose. I can't spend the rest of eternity doing nothing."

Why not? They've been pretty happy so far with video games, thinking pizza, and being annoyed when I suggest they go outside for some fresh air. What they're describing is basically eternal adolescence. I know a lot of burnt-out twenty somethings who would love to revert back to a life of zero responsibilities and endless takeout orders.

But eternity really is a long time. Kelly's already lived—or existed—fifty times longer than a well-preserved granny at the retirement home. It's like trying to understand the difference between a thousand grains of rice and a million. Or a million and a billion. Maybe there really is an end to everything, even living forever.

We lie like that for a while. Kelly's breathing takes on a raspy quality. The link between us is still there, invisibly pulsing, but the rhythm grows erratic. Viola is still there too, malignant and angry, but she's stopped forcing her way in. Now she's more like a scar. Not sentient in any way. So I push along the tenuous place where Kelly and I are still joined, like that might help, but Kelly bats at my hand.

"Stop that," they say.

"What am I supposed to do?" Now my voice is raspy, though it's not from disease, only sadness.

"Just stay," they say, wrapping their arm around me even tighter. "It won't be much longer."

I twist, looking up. Their face is stained in blood. Their eyes are fully white. Every breath looks painful. I want to kiss them. One last time. We won't get the big love story. Not everyone does. I'm just glad I got to know them.

"Can I ask you a question?"

The corner of their mouth quirks up. "If you must."

"What is Kelly really short for?"

The quirk turns into a genuine smile.

"I don't remember," they say.

"What?" I can't help myself when I swat at their shoulder. "What is it really?"

They shake their head, wincing with the motion. "It's been a long time. There were nicknames. Jokes. But I don't—" They start coughing. "To you, I'll always be Kelly."

They cough some more. Their lips shine red. I'm not sure they'll stop this time. This isn't how I want to remember them.

"I'll be right back," I say, pushing up to an elbow. Kelly grabs hold of my wrist before I can stand.

"Wait."

"I won't go far. Just need to clean you up a bit."

I walk to the edge of the river. No sign of Smith or Viola. One of my sleeves has been ripped. Where? Can't say. Might have been Viola. Or our headlong rush down the rocky hill. Either way, the job's already started, so I finish it and pull the sleeve free. I drop it in the water, soaking it. I'll clean Kelly's face and we'll say our goodbyes. The best thing I can give them is a good death.

My face reflects in the water, rippling slowly as it eddies and flows. It's the first time I've seen my reflection. It's not the same as seeing myself through Kelly's eyes. My features are reversed. My skin is streaked reddish-black. My eyes are endlessly sad. I'm going to regret this for the rest of my afterlife, however long that will be.

Kelly's still lying in the sand. A dying reaper who can't even slide anymore. All because of something I did, whether I meant to or not. The haunting is my fault, and it's deeply unfair that I'm the one who's going to survive because of it. This was never how it was supposed to be. I said my goodbyes, closed my eyes in the hospital, and waited for the end, whether that was a black void or a cozy spot on my personal cloud. Instead, I got so much more. Adventure. A chance to understand how much bigger the world is than anyone alive might have ever imagined. Who else had that opportunity? I even got Kelly, an all-powerful reaper who somehow decided to hitch their wagon to mine through this undead rollercoaster.

So it's probably time for me to go. Outliving Kelly feels impossible. I've been here on borrowed days and weeks since the start. If things had gone the way they were supposed to, I'd be a blank ball of energy with no memory of who I ever was. Kelly, whether they wanted to be dragged into my orbit or not, gave me an overtime period I never deserved.

I glance over my shoulder. They're resting. It would be easy to tell myself they're okay. That I'm rushing. The moment for drastic measures isn't here yet. But I had those arguments with my doctors and my parents back in the hospital. Better to cut it short by an hour or a day than wait too long and not be able to make the call at all.

Beryl said there was another way . . .

My hands shake a little as I clean up Kelly's face. They don't seem to notice. Their eyes are closed, and their brow pinches like they're in pain. They don't speak as I wipe their lips. I take their hand, pressing the knuckles to my mouth; they smile, but it's a faraway expression, like they're dreaming or reliving a happy memory.

I nudge the link, tugging at it. Kelly's frown deepens.

"What are you doing?" they ask.

"Get in, reaper. We're going swimming." I hold out my arms, like I used to do before we would slide.

They snort, opening their eyes just a bit. "I'm very powerful, but it's probably time to admit I can't swim."

"Doesn't matter." Now is not the time for jokes. I pull harder on the link, pulling what's left of them inside me where I can keep them safe. The Kelly lying on the beach grimaces. But what are they going to do? There's no fight left in them.

Kelly's side of the link is so fragile. I gather it towards me, cradling them close in my relatively undamaged soul. I'm careful not to touch Viola's remains, like if I squeeze her too tight, she might burst and spread like an infection. It's weird to think that I can wield any part of this. Manipulate it. Makes me feel like a wizard. I just hope I'm strong enough to save us both.

"Wait. Ember. Stop." Kelly's eyes are fully open now. Their face is etched with worry and pain.

I kiss them, brushing my lips and nose against their temple.

"Please trust me," I say. "Let me take you with me. Beryl said this would work and I want to try."

Their body is cold beneath mine. Finally, they nod. I fold the link inside myself. They give a long sigh and close their eyes. Then there's nothing left. The Kelly on the beach is just an empty vessel. All that really remains of them is tucked safely inside me. I brush their hair from their forehead one last time, then slowly get to my feet.

"I love you," I say softly. Maybe they can hear me. I push what I hope feels like warm comfort down the link, then walk back to the shoreline. The water laps over the toes of my shoes.

My time is up. Beryl said we both had to give up the soul. I assumed she meant we had to release it at the same time, but this should work fine too. One and three quarters of a soul, impossibly tied together, and gone a little mouldy on the outside from Viola's interference. Better to let it wash away to parts unknown.

I'm up to my knees when the singing starts. The siren. Just another entry on the list of endless weirdness in my life after death. I'm sorry I won't get to say goodbye to Jupiter and X. I close my eyes, wading in deeper. I wait for the song to take hold, like it did the first time in the tunnel. But it doesn't. My mind remains clear, still reciting the litany of regrets and goodbyes. I open one eye. The tentacles are rising, disturbing the surface of the water. But she doesn't reach for me. Doesn't grab like she did the first time. She's waiting. Letting me do this in my own time.

"We're ready," I say, taking a few more steps until the water is up to my waist. Something inside me shudders. Kelly, maybe. Or some remaining part of Viola's consciousness, protesting. She didn't get a say in this. Too bad. Our souls are not a democracy.

When the siren reaches for me this time, she's gentle. She winds a tentacle around my middle, then pulls me slowly farther out into the river. I float on my back, staring up at the eerie twinkling cavern overhead.

"Okay," I say, turning my attention inward. I'm still in my body but once again feel like I'm looking through someone else's eyes. There's no panic when the siren pulls us under. It really is like my death all over again. I've made this choice. Last time, I didn't want to be sick anymore. This time, I don't want to be here without Kelly.

"Ember?" Their voice is inside me too, from the glowing ball of the link. Blue, with shades of Viola's green. I reach for them, wanting to tell them everything will be okay. My shoulder bumps against something for a moment. I assume it's a tentacle, but when I turn my head, even in the water, I can clearly make out Kelly beside me. My Kelly, healthy and beautiful once more. They float, looking confused and relieved. Their eyes are clear blue, and their white hair floats above their head like wild tendrils of seaweed. But when they smile, it's a confident, strong expression. They're better. In here, they're already healed.

Another tentacle pushes through the water. It comes up to my hands, prodding at my fingers, almost like it's asking for permission. The soul ball is bright in my arms. I look at Kelly, then at it. This is the right choice. The very end. Let the siren take us.

I open my arms and our souls float free. The siren takes them, manipulating it with the tips of two tentacles. She's surprisingly dexterous, which is a ridiculous thought to have, but at this point, I shouldn't be surprised by anything.

I don't have much longer to consider, though, before she takes the top of the tangled mass and tears. The souls come apart—knot and all—like she's ripping a piece of cloth in half. Just as quickly, Kelly is pulled away from me, hurtling through the water until they're out of sight. I don't even have time to reach for them before I'm being sucked away too. Like deep down at the bottom of this flowing river, someone has pulled the stopper out of the drain. The current becomes a vortex, swirling around itself in tight circles. Pressure starts in my chest. Maybe I really am drowning. A bright blue and green light floats in front of me, keeping pace as I tumble and churn. I reach for it, but just as my fingers touch its bright edges, it glows so brightly I have to close my eyes. Something has latched on to my breastbone and ripped an opening in my chest. The pain becomes even brighter. Hotter. The dark behind my eyelids goes vivid white. My mouth opens on a scream that no one will ever hear underwater. Distantly, there's a flutter of terror. It's an echo of what I'm feeling. Kelly. They're in pain, just like I am.

I open my eyes again and they're there, floating in front of me, glowing with the same intense light that turns them blue around the edges. They're changing, shifting, like I've seen them do so many times. The wound in their chest is still there, but it's closing up as the glow encapsulates them, covering the terrible opening with new skin. Kelly smiles fondly. A final goodbye. The expression says I'm foolish. Silly human. Reapers don't do long goodbyes.

When the wound closes over fully, it takes all the light with it. I feel inside myself, and the link is silent. Kelly is truly gone. Their absence is heavy, like the breath between lightning and thunder.

But I'm still here, so what does that mean?

Then the thunder comes, and the percussive boom is so loud it sends me spinning off through the dark water once more, only this time I'm alone.

twenty-six

DEAR SPARKS, the nice thing about being dead is you don't have to breathe, and yet as I get carried away in the black current, I gasp for air I don't need, then gasp again when I hit something hard and solid. I slide down a smooth surface like a cartoon coyote crashing back to earth. There's even a squeak like a damp cloth on glass before I finally slump to the ground. All of me hurts. Every joint, every muscle. But most of all my chest. I touch my sternum, expecting shredded flesh and shattered bone, but the skin there is smooth, just like it was for Kelly. Yet despite being healed, the pain that flares beneath my touch feels like it will never stop.

How many times am I going to have to die before it finally sticks?

"You have to watch the landing," a sly voice says behind me. Slowly, I turn around, keeping to my hands and knees on the ground, because I'm pretty sure any attempt to stand up will only result in my crashing back down in a heap.

I'm in a white room. It's got the look and feel of a hospital waiting room in desperate need of renovation. Peeling linoleum floors. Vinyl chairs lining the wall. The corners of the room are turning grey in a way that no amount of dusting will ever save. Back at the beginning, if I'd died in the hospital and woken up here, I'd have questioned nothing. Welcome to heaven's waiting room. A reaper will be with you shortly.

Now I question everything, including the only other person here.

Sitting in one of the chairs is Beryl. She's still in her purple sweater and stained gardening pants. Winston pants lazily at her feet, and his tail thumps on the floor when he catches me looking. They both look utterly serene.

"Are we dead?" I ask. My throat feels impossibly dry, like I didn't just get hurled out of a river that I would never have been able to drain no matter how much I drank.

Beryl snorts. "No more than you were before." She puts a hand to Winston's head, ruffling his fur. He looks up at her with blind adoration. "But Winston and I thought it was time for new scenery. That last little summoning didn't quite go according to plan."

Shit. The dog really did die.

"I'm sorry," I say, scuttling towards them. Winston happily licks my face as I approach. "We never meant for anyone to get hurt. We only wanted—"

"It's fine," she says, waving my apology away like it's been offered because I forgot to pick up milk on the way home and not because I got her and her dog killed. "We had a good run. More years than we deserved. And there wasn't enough left for us both to make it after our little stand-off with that creature. I wouldn't have wanted to come back without Winston, and he wouldn't have survived without me. This way, we get to be together here." She looks around the empty waiting room. "Wherever here is, exactly."

Who knows? Yet another room in Afterlife I've never seen before. If we're even in Afterlife. Could be another failed startup meant to challenge Afterlife's monopoly. Abandoned office space with a sun-bleached For Lease sign in the window.

"You could be waiting here a long time," I say.

Beryl shrugs. "What's time when you're dead?"

Nothing. It means nothing.

Slowly, I push myself to standing. I sway for a moment when I get there, but finally the room stops spinning.

"I have to find Kelly," I say. If I'm still—not alive, exactly—around, then they must be too, right? I can't feel them, so does that mean they have their soul back? Did the siren pull us apart like string cheese and give them back their half? I need to know.

There's a door on the far side of the room. The knob wobbles as I take hold. Someone needs to file a ticket with maintenance to come tighten some screws. But it still twists and the door swings open.

"Oh, I wouldn't—" Beryl says, but she doesn't bother to finish the warning as I grab hold of the doorframe to keep myself from pitching out into the giant space beyond. It's another black nothing. But unlike the others, it's not empty. If anything, it's practically full to bursting. Like a zero-gravity storage room, or one of those phone games where you have to sort through a pile of random objects until you find the two matching beachballs or the teddy bears with identical red ribbons around their necks. Here, these things float lazily on invisible currents, bobbing and circling. I look up and down, and the space goes on and on. A confused-looking baby doll in a pink dress floats by, so close I can nearly touch it. If she has a twin, I don't see her.

"Is there any other way out of here?" I ask, though there isn't another door anywhere else.

"Not as far as I can tell." Beryl's back to sitting in one of the hard chairs. "I was thinking of sitting around here for a few years to see if anyone else pops by."

That's great for her, but I can't stay.

Beryl groans. "I know that look. You need answers, don't you?"

I barely know what the questions are, but Kelly has to be out there somewhere and I have to find them. I don't answer Beryl, but she nods like I have, rising once more as she rummages around in her pockets.

"Here," she says. "Take this with you." She holds out her hand and I expect her to be offering me a hard candy and maybe the lint it's been stuck to for the last decade or so. Instead she offers me a glowing purple ball. It's almost the same colour as her sweater.

"What is it?" I ask. It burns invitingly. I kind of want to slip it under my shirt and cuddle with it.

"Something for the road." She drops it into my hand and the glow subsides. It's a pendant. An irregular purple stone about the size of a marble hung on a thin chain. "To offset the straggler you've picked up. You're looking worse for wear. A three-way haunting can often make strange things happen, so you need a little protection. Winston and I don't need it anymore."

At the word "straggler," something inside me flutters like a bird trying to escape against a closed window. Viola, I think. Whatever part of her I still have, she's not happy to be here, and her struggles only intensify as I slip the chain over my head. But as soon as it settles around my neck, she goes silent.

"You had this the whole time?" I ask. "Why didn't you give it to us before?"

"I told you." She glances down at the dog. "We were using it. It's multifunctional. If you're haunting someone, it slows the progress. If you find yourself in possession of a malicious soul fragment, it keeps her under lock and key so you can go about your day."

I have to bite back a million curses and accusations. Beryl did attempt to help us, at least, but even she never told us the whole truth. "Where did you find it?"

She winks. "Brenda found it at one of her auctions. The jewelry never sells well. She didn't know it did more than sparkle, of course, but she liked the colour. The world is full of little trinkets that everyone assumes are just rocks."

I feel like I should apologize again. Only she genuinely doesn't seem upset about how the summoning shook out. But I wish she'd made it. Winston too, but mostly Beryl. She should have spent time with Jupiter and X. They'd have loved learning what she knows, and she'd probably love the company.

"You're going to be okay?" I ask, looking again around the blank empty room.

She chuckles. "I'm very patient. And who knows? Maybe the next time I open that door, it'll lead me somewhere else. I'll find a nice spot on the beach where Winston can chase the seagulls while I work on my tan. Can't get skin cancer when you're already dead."

Sounds like she should meet Richard. They might get along. Though I don't know how he'll feel about Winston after spending so many years as a cat.

I open the door a second time. The world's weirdest zero-G toy store awaits me. Actually, there's more than toys. Along with the dolls and action figures, I see a spatula, a little charcoal grill, and an inflatable alligator like people use to float around in the pool. Maybe I should grab it and give it to Beryl. But as I stretch to see how far away it really is, the floor falls away from me and—yup, yet again—I'm tumbling through empty space.

This time, the drop is fast and wind blows at my face as I plummet. Skydiving was never something I wanted to do while I was alive, and if it was anything like this, I'm glad I waited until I was dead. As I fall, Beryl's pendant lifts from inside my shirt, the stone pointing upwards. The chain catches on my earlobe, which is the only thing that keeps it from slipping off my head before I can catch it. I keep it clutched around my throat. Not like I need my hands to hold on to anything. I'm freefalling through limitless space. The floating household items are way above me now, but as far as I can tell, there's nothing below me but more endlessness.

Now would be a really good time to slide back to the nothing again. But when I close my eyes and picture the cosmic blender sensation of sliding, all that follows is the rushing wind in my ears.

Nothing. Like actual nothing. Just more falling over and over. Looks like my access to reaper powers is gone. Hopefully Kelly has them all again.

Beneath me, the light shifts. Instead of empty black, a white circle forms. As I drop, it gets bigger and bigger. The white resolves into colours. Blue. Green. It's like I'm looking down on the world from way up high. The blues and greens pick up streaks of white. It's water, rolling over waves. A bird with black and white wings soars through the centre of the circle before disappearing on the other side. Am I looking through an opening? If so, what am I looking at? Some world-coloured theme park, maybe, or a new pilot project of Minerva's. Let the people think they're still at home so they don't ask more questions.

It's getting closer. Water. Waves. A beach to the left. And suddenly . . . I squint as I slip through whatever hole is at the bottom of the toy chamber and the sun nearly blinds me. I drop through the sky with no way to slow myself. The water is coming up fast. I wince and close my eyes. Isn't falling into water from really high up supposed to be painful? I think I read once about a cliff diver who broke his neck. And I've fallen from higher than a cliff. But also, I'm dead, so . . .

Yup. The impact of hitting the water's surface hurts like a sonofabitch. It forces the air from my lungs. I gasp, taking in a huge lungful of water, and my whole body protests. Panic and pain, my old friends. Also, holy shit, the water is freezing. The siren's river was only a few degrees below body temperature . . . or whatever temperature I exist at now. This water, though—along with my lungs screaming for air, my joints and muscles contract, desperately preserving any warmth they can. It's a familiar but unfamiliar sensation. Something I used to know but haven't felt in a while.

Finally, I break the surface. I gasp and choke, gagging on swampy-tasting water expelled from my lungs. I splash, trying to orient myself. The sun is still so bright it gives me a headache, and the weight of my clothes filling with water makes it hard to keep my head in breathing territory. I go under. Kicking doesn't seem to help. My sleeves billow in the water. The heavy knit of my sweater weighs me down further. Is this what's next? An endless fall through a bottomless lake?

An arm catches me around my middle, and a second later I'm back above the water . . . or my head is, anyway. Once again, I cough. It's so violent it feels like my organs are about to turn inside out.

"Hang on," a voice says. Presumably it belongs to the same person as the arm. They're a strong swimmer. All I can see above me is sky and birds and that oh-so-bright sun.

"Where am I?" I ask. My voice sounds weird.

Finally, we reach shallower water. My feet touch the bottom and it's rocky and uneven, even more than the bottom of the dark river. I scramble to the shore, shivering. The beach is just as rocky and the stones dig painfully into my palms as I scramble through them and slip on rotten-smelling weeds. Finally, my exhausted body gives up, and I drop to the ground, breathing hard. A stone digs into my sternum, but when I shift away from it, it turns out it's the purple stone from Beryl, still dangling from my neck.

"Are you all right?" A soft hand settles on my back. I forgot about my rescuer.

"Yes. Yes, I think so." I struggle to get turned around so I can see them and thank whoever it is properly. But when I do finally face them, the thanks get caught in my throat.

Kelly? It must be. How many times have we been in this situation? How many times have they dragged me away from danger?

But it's not them. Or is it? I blink, shading my eyes from the sun so I can see more clearly. It looks like Kelly . . . in the same way someone might if they were Kelly's sibling, or maybe a cousin. Their eyes are a familiar shade of blue, but not as brilliant as they were the last time I saw them. Their lips are pinched in concern that could easily be mistaken for disdain. But their eyes are rounder than I'm used to and the skin just beneath them sags ever so slightly, like they need more sleep than they get. Same androgynous appearance, though the angles aren't as sharp. Cheekbones, jaw, even the collarbones that peek out of the collar of their partially unzipped hoodie aren't as prominent as Kelly's usually are.

"Ember? Is that you?" Their voice is different too. Still accented, but smoother. Higher. Like it's coming from a slightly different-sized chest.

My chest. I put a hand to it, feeling inside for the link, but it's still gone. If this really is Kelly, we aren't connected anymore. That's some small comfort, at least?

I pull my hair over my shoulder to wring it out and freeze. Even wet, my hair is always distinctly red. Or it should be. Dark copper, especially in sunlight. But the dripping strands between my fingers are so dark they're nearly black. No matter which way I twist them, they don't reflect any more colour.

Also, my hands are wrong. I start shaking as I let go of my hair. The skin is still the same colour, but the size is wrong. The fingers are too long. The nailbeds are too short and the nails are weirdly rounded at the top. I flip them over and the mole on the inside of my wrist is gone too.

"Ember?" the not-quite-Kelly asks again.

"I . . . I think so. I mean yes. Yes, it's me." I glance down the front of my sopping shirt. The breasts inside are bigger than mine were too. Noticeably so. "Sort of me." I look up and they're watching me. "Kelly?"

They nod, wiping a hand over their face. I expect the gesture to result in a slight shift, until they're back to looking the way they normally do. But they stay as they are. Familiar, but different enough to make me uneasy.

"Where are we?" I ask.

"I don't know. I was only in the water for a few seconds before you fell in. It's . . . it looks different but . . ." Their voice slows and dies to nothing as they look out toward the lake. The day is actually really nice now that the imminent fear of drowning has passed. Warm. Sunny. A boat zips across the horizon.

Oh. I see why Kelly ran out of words.

Across the water, beyond a familiar lakeshore and the planes taking off from the downtown island airport, is the CN Tower—Toronto's signature landmark.

We're home.

"Is that . . . is that it? Did we make it?" I clutch the hard weight of Beryl's stone under my shirt. I put my other hand to Kelly's chest. They're warming slowly after our swim, and the rhythm of their heart is unhurried. Their breathing is uneven, but slowly it steadies. I can't help myself when I fold against them, pressing my cheek to their shoulder and close my eyes.

"Yes," they say. "We made it. Somehow."

When their arms wrap around me, I could cry. I inhale deeply, burying my nose into their shirt. They smell like lake water—Lake Ontario has a particular odour that cannot be missed—but beneath, there's a scent of something warm. Like cinnamon and—

I jerk back. My heart rattles in alarm.

"What? What is it?" The voice is still wrong, but the strong grip of Kelly's hands around my wrists is unmistakable. As is the familiar smell of lake and the wet stones beneath me.

I whirl, looking around. We're on a beach several metres beneath a wooded path. A man is walking a dog. He's giving us nervous glances, and when he sees us watching him, he says, "Hey, are you okay?"

I gape.

"You can see me?"

Kelly puts a protective arm around me, pulling me a few steps back.

"Fine," they say. "Just a late night with a few regrets."

The man frowns, but the dog barks at something out of sight and pulls on the leash, and they both hurry on.

"Kelly," I say. I grope behind me until I find their hand, then tug them along, stumbling over the rocks and climbing up the bank until we're on the path above. The man and dog are greeting another man and a pair of huskies. A woman jogs past them, then gives us a polite smile as she passes us too.

"What is going on?" I ask. My breath is coming fast now too, keeping time with my heartbeat.

Wait. My heartbeat?

My knees give out as my hand goes to my chest once more. My heart slams against my palm, telling me that we are in danger and that I need to get away.

My heart, which hasn't actually beat in over a year, despite the endless threats and catastrophes that have faced me since the moment I died.

"Ember." Kelly's beside me, looking like they can't decide if they should be worried or annoyed with my dramatics. The expression is so completely them that it eliminates any lingering doubts that they're actually a Kelly-shaped stranger. A delirious giggle escapes from my chest.

The men with the dogs are hurrying back.

"Seriously," the first says. "If you're not okay, I can call an ambulance. It's no big deal. My sister is a nurse and she says—"

I wave him away as I try to control my laughter, but their twin expressions of concern, coupled with a wet dog nose shoved in my face as one of their furry companions checks on me, just makes me laugh harder.

"Really," Kelly says, though the strain in their eyes is clear. "We're fine."

The two give us a few more cautious glances over their shoulders before coaxing their dogs along, until they finally disappear around a curve in the path.

"Now," Kelly says when we're alone again. They're bent over me, staring down. "Tell me what's happening."

Without any warning, I lurch to my feet and throw myself at

them. They grunt in surprise when my lips meet theirs, but the shock only lasts a few seconds before they relax. Their lips brush over mine in response, and when my tongue presses against their mouth, they open for me. It's perfect. Joyful. They taste like chocolate and sunlight and—

I release them, taking in deep breaths of the humid morning air. Toronto in the warmer months. The sun is bright, the people are venturing out, and also, one of my knees is bleeding, probably scraped on the rocks as we crawled out of the lake. And now that I'm not looking directly into the sun, one of Kelly's cheeks is scratched too, along with the back of one of their hands.

I take it in mine, twining our fingers together. My hands don't look like mine, just like their face isn't quite right either. But one thing is becoming increasingly clear, from the way I can taste and smell things I haven't sensed in ages, to the way average people can see me as they go about their mornings.

"Kelly," I say slowly, trying and failing to contain my mounting joy at being back somewhere I know and understand.

"Yes?" they say slowly. They don't look nearly as excited as I feel. I tighten my hold on them, brushing my fingers over their wrist, and the frantic thump of their pulse beneath my touch is undeniable. Reapers don't do that.

"I think . . ." I clear my throat. A year ago, I died. It was a permanent solution. Or so I thought. "I think we're home."

They snort. "Yes, Ember. That's obvious."

I squeeze their hand willing them to be patient as I figure out what to say. We're home and—

"Kelly, I think we're alive."

about the author

Alli lives in Toronto with her very patient husband and a growing pack of rescue pets. She tries to split her time between writing, community theatre stage management, and traveling anywhere that has good wine. Tragically, this leaves no time to clean the house.

lgbtq+ fantasy by alli temple

Afterlife Incorporated

Only Mostly Dead

Hate To Haunt You

Vacation From Hell (coming in 2026)

The Pirate & Her Princess

Uncharted

Unbroken

Unleashed

lgbtq+ romances by allison temple

Out & About

Work-Love Balance

Honeymoon Sweet

The Seacroft Series

Top Shelf

Cold Pressed

Hot Potato

Shared Series

My Not-So-Super Blind Date (part of Subparheroes)

Under Her Roof (part of Accidentally Undercover)

Puppuccino (part of Bold Brew)

Standalone

Destination Bedding

The Neighbourly Thing

Up North

Boyfriend With Benefits

The Pick Up